# HER WHOLE HEART

## ROWENA SPARK

LIME TIGER ENTERPRISES

# COPYRIGHT

**HER WHOLE HEART**
**By Rowena Spark**

NATIONAL LIBRARY OF AUSTRALIA
A catalogue record of this book is available from: www.trove.nla.gov.au

**ISBN (print): 978-0-6489089–1-3**

**ISBN (eBook) : 978-0-6489089-0-6**

**Editor: SHAZ**

**Cover Design: Clove Creative**

**Cover Images: Shutterstock & Nick Fox**

**Interior design: Project Heart Publishing**

**Print typesetting and eBook productions: Vellum**

# CHAPTER 1

## ALEX

*A*lex cast a serene glance over the vast paddocks of green rye as her old John Deere rumbled beneath her. They were looking lush and thick, ready to be put back into rotation for the cows to graze. They could use a bit of rain though, she mused, glancing up into the clear blue sky, but she was grateful that the weather was holding out while she re-fenced the south paddock.

After years of being satisfied with his stretch of grass, the bull had suddenly carried out his urge to see if the grass was, indeed, greener on the other side. He'd stripped the wires and torn out quite a few of the old rotten posts on his way to freedom. If Alex had a good run, the new posts would be in by Wednesday, and the wiring would be completed by Friday.

It was all hers, as far as the gentle hills and valleys stretched. It shouldn't have been. It was the dream she had shared with her brother, Ryan. They were supposed to run the whole cattle operation together, remodel the house for them both, and their eventual families would live and work the farm like the generations of Arlingtons before them. The fertile soils of Australia's southern mountain ranges ran deep through her veins.

Her tractor, Old John, clattered its way through the gate and into the south paddock. Alex hummed a tune, her spirits as crisp and bright as the morning. They were headed for a great Spring, and the cattle would be more likely to give birth to a few twin calves, bringing in that little bit extra she was hoping for this year to get out of the red finally. She chewed on her lip. *As long as she played nice with Edward.*

The stock horse mare, Horace, ambled slowly beside her, and Alex grinned. Most farmers had cattle dogs as companions, who doubled as help to round up cattle, but Alex was never a dog person. Horace did everything a dog could do, and she could also be used to pull, cart and ride. She didn't have her own paddock at the farm. It wasn't necessary. Horace was never far away, and tended to prefer sleeping in the woodshed beside the house than in the barn. She was Alex 's best friend. She and Ryan had picked Horace up as a yearling from a farm a few towns over who were at their wits end trying to get rid of their apparently troublesome horse. They virtually gave her away, offering to load her up immediately into the float and deliver her before Alex and Ryan found out and changed their minds.

Old John shattered the serenity by dropping revs. Alex pumped the accelerator, but the machine clattered and slowed, finishing its dramatic show with great plumes of smoke from the stack.

"No no no no no" Alex chanted as she flicked the key and clambered to the ground. "Oh no, no, no, Old John. Don't do this now, you old bastard." She clutched the front tyre, dropping to her knees and craning her head under the green body to where the engine sat. Finding nothing obviously leaking or broken, she sighed in defeat.

"Why couldn't you have held out just one more season?" She rubbed her hand in exasperation across her forehead. Flopping on her stomach in the long grass, Alex pulled out her phone.

*I am Alexandria Arlington, sixth generation farmer, a woman of steel with the land in my veins. I am not afraid of anything.*

"Jimmy? Yeah, Old John just died again." She rolled her eyes at the response with a blade of grass between her teeth.

"I know, Jimmy, but I *did* pay it off. All of it. We're square now. Look, I got enough if Old John's done a head, and if it's something else I'll re-evaluate it with you, okay?" She reasoned sweetly.

A satisfied expression washed over her.

"Yes, Jimmy, thank you. Yes. Tell him to follow Horace with the van into the south paddock. The tracks are good."

Alex flicked her wrist and noted the time. 10am. The day was creeping away, and in an hour the mechanic would arrive. She pulled a lead rope from the tractor and called out to Horace. Alex had modified the rope to hold a clip on each end, which she attached now to Horace's halter to fashion makeshift reins. Alex swung herself up smoothly onto the bare back and gave the horse a pat on the neck.

"Let's go see Brandy while we wait" She said. Horace broke into a gallop, taking Alex to the homestead with a clatter of hooves.

The homestead was a dilapidated beauty. It was stunning once, before the white paint had cracked and peeled, and the weather rotted half the structural beams. The bluestone walls stood firm under the decaying verandah which was propped up with makeshift supports of eucalyptus branches near the doorway. The rest of the decking held layers of dust that suggested nobody had walked the perimeter for years. The English garden, once a tranquil space of blossom and order, held overgrown rosebushes, struggling weeping cherries and an abundance of weeds. Horace bounced to a halt, heading over to an old marble water feature for a drink as soon as Alex slid from her back.

"Brandy?" Alex 's voice filled the rooms.

"Mummy!" A squeal burst from the centre of the house, and a toddler tore through the hall, leaping into her mother's arms. Alex caught her and lifted her into her chest, snuggling the child tight to her. Chubby arms pulled tight around the back of Alex 's neck as she covered her daughter in kisses.

"Oh, I missed you, Little Button!"

"You're back early. We didn't expect you for another few hours. What happened?" Sabrina Arlington leaned against the door frame, her slim figure wrapped in a thick navy dressing gown. Her white hair was cut into a short bob, highlighting the same delicate structure of her face that her daughter shared.

Alex forced a light tone at her Mother.

"Old John's sick. The mechanic'll be here in a half hour or so, so I figured I'd sneak a cuddle before he gets here." She poked the soft skin on her daughter's belly and was rewarded by a giggle. Brandy's dark hair fell in gentle waves around the olive complexion of her face. So very different from Alex's own honey brown tresses. Brandy's startling grey eyes gazed adoringly at her mother, and Alex felt the familiar tug of her heart. Her daughter's eyes were the same as her father's; silver oceans of beautiful emotion swirling and bare. When Alex closed her eyes, she saw his face, tattooed on her heart.

"I love you the size of the world, baby girl." She whispered into Brandy's neck.

"Love you bigger, Mum." Her sweet voice purred. Then she squirmed until she was deposited on the ground.

"Can we afford it, Lex?" Sabrina inquired gently. Alex sighed and dropped onto the couch, stretching her denim-clad legs out in front of her. She avoided her mother's gaze, intently focused on the toddler climbing onto the couch beside her.

"I can spare enough for a couple of days. It shouldn't need more than that. Jimmy's okay about it."

Sabrina took a few shaky steps towards her.

"You look better, Mum. Good day?" Alex asked, hoping Sabrina would drop it.

"Yeah, feeling better. I'll make up sandwiches for you then. Send Horace to pick them up when you're hungry. You'd better go back and wait for the mechanic."

"Yeah. Thanks Mum. And thanks for watching Squirt for me." She covered Brandy's face in kisses again.

"I'm not Squirt, I'm Mummy's Princess!" Brandy's face screwed up in annoyance.

Alex giggled. "You are. You're Princess Squirt."

Brandy's attempt at rolling her eyes caused a chuckle to bubble from her mother.

"I wish Ryan was here. He could have fixed it." Sabrina murmured. Alex saw the pain crash over her mother's expression and her own heart caught in her throat.

"I know, Ma. Me too. More than anything." Alex turned to the large photo on the hallway stand, kissed two fingers and placed it over the picture.

"Miss you, Ry." She said. It was the last photo they'd taken together. Ryan, with their Father's dark hair, dwarfed Alex, who barely reached his shoulders. He was a beautiful man, muscles sculptured from farm work, a grin plastered on his face as he gazed down adoringly at his little sister. His arm was around her shoulder, and hers held Brandy against her hip. Sabrina had taken the photo a year ago almost to the day, before the weeds had crept into the garden. Alex pulled air into her lungs. It was hers, now, the farm, and she would push through and succeed at any cost. She blew a kiss to her daughter and stepped outside into the sunshine. Horace clopped slowly to her.

"Ready, Horace?" Horace planted her feet and shook her whole body, dust clouding from her coat.

"Yeah, me neither." Alex mounted and let her horse find her own way back.

She looked over Old John while she waited, while talking to Horace. The mare nosed her shoulder occasionally in reply, and followed the woman closely.

"I'll tighten up these hoses while I'm waiting. I might as well be productive, hey?" She asked her horse. Horace snorted. She pulled the tool kit from the tractor and set about checking hoses.

She looked up when Horace jerked her head and snorted softly.

"Okay, girl, go get the mechanic. Bring him to me." The large bay trotted off, ears pricked forward. She checked her watch. He was late. Making a mental note to deduct the lost time from her bill, she finished checking the hydraulics and slipped underneath to unwind the hay band wrapped around the axle. Twisted around and amongst the twine was a thick strand of wire. She untangled it with hands thickened from years of labour. It seemed to take forever, and she grunted and cursed aloud as she coaxed the wire free. Horace reached down and nibbled her shirt, telling her they had company. Alex twisted her head around to see, and grunted. While she couldn't see his face, his body was toned and muscled. And he was standing there, obviously trying to find a human in amongst the tractor. She sighed in frustration. Jimmy had sent a new guy out. The other mechanics were trained to arrive already swinging their spanners, but this one obviously needed to be hounded to get him going. She leaned over and offered him the end of the wire.

"Well, are those muscles painted on or can you actually use them?" She asked.

Without a sound, the mechanic gripped the end and yanked. The wire flicked free and sprung away, catching Alex on the cheek.

"Damn!" She cursed in surprise.

"Are you okay?" A deep voice rumbled in concern. Her brow furrowed as her nerve endings sizzled at his tone.

"Yeah. Just surprised me is all. I know better than to be so close to wire. My fault" She dismissed. She felt the slow tickle of blood sliding down her cheek, and she smeared it away. It wasn't deep, and Old John needed more attention than a scratch on her face did.

Alex shuffled from under the tractor and shaded the sun from her eyes, squinting up at the visitor. She couldn't help the gasp that escaped her at the hard granite face that glared back at her.

# CHAPTER 2

## JAY

*J*ay glanced at his schedule apprehensively. It was his only appointment booked until three that afternoon, but with Jimmy managing the morning mayhem, Jay was fifteen minutes behind the allotted time. With every second, his carefully choreographed existence burned away at the edges.

Jimmy wedged the phone between cheek and shoulder as he jotted an address with one hand and flagged down a mechanic with the other. He moved quickly despite his advancing age, his keen eyes darting around the workshop missing nothing.

"I know we were supposed to have a meeting, Jay, but I'm snowed under. Monday's are usually quiet, but today is a shit storm." Jimmy explained as he filled in job cards and shoved them at his employees as they zipped past.

"Fertile Soils have two trucks they need fixed to get orders out before the rain, the excavator at Harrow's farm needs work done to finish digging out the new dam on the edge of town, and we have four, that's *four* cattle trucks out of action, with the market on Wednesday. I need another six guys today." Jimmy rubbed his palm over his balding head as he watched his team of tradesmen efficiently snap up some overalls and leap into vans. The vans were fitted with all the tools needed to work remotely, the best investment Jimmy had made. Thanks to Jay.

"Well, I don't have to ask if the vans are working out for you then." Jay grinned and lifted an eyebrow at the last van leaving the workshop. Jimmy offered a tired smile and sighed.

"Okay, we might as well do this now." He glanced at the large clock above the smoko room door.

"I have an hour, and then it looks like I'm on the tools again today."

Jimmy led Jay into the office, a tiny, dark room with carpet black from grease and layered with dust from diesel soot. Jimmy dropped into a swivel chair, stuffing leaking from the tears in the cushions, and gestured for Jay to sit. Jay dragged a plastic seat over to the desk, draping his arm over the back as he sprawled.

"Yeah, the vans have been a godsend, thanks. They have increased productivity by…well, you saw them go. And the boys are taking care of them. The vans started out completely stocked, and very little has gone missing. I think the few tools lost are due to the vans being personally allocated to each mechanic. They get shitty when they lose a socket or a spanner here or there, and I can replace them. No thefts, just from the fellas losing them on the job. That also boosts profits."

"That's great news. What is the feedback you're getting about the company itself?" Jay pressed. The company was his father's baby. It was the first workshop he'd opened after he finished his apprenticeship, and built it on a foundation of excellent workmanship and strong work ethics. He insisted every employee was an extension of the company name and produced work of the highest quality. Since his father was now beginning to back away from the company, priming his son to take over, Jay was able to make changes that had so far been successfully implemented, starting with Jimmy's shop. There were eighteen businesses in all, spread over a few towns in the state, and Jay was keen to introduce the vans to each of them, too, depending on how it lifted the bottom line.

"It's all very positive. Actually, Brennan's workshop is starting to struggle a bit, now we are able to pump out more work. Most customers don't give evaluation at all, but they are passing on our details to friends, which is the best feedback of all in my opinion."

Jay creased his forehead appreciatively.

"That's fantastic. Dad will be delighted. Where are the financials at?" Jimmy dumped a manilla folder in front of him, and Jay shuffled through it, his eyes widening. He scrawled notes into the pages of his planner to report on later. Finally, he flipped the folder closed and looked at Jimmy.

"Right now, Jimmy, I'll give you absolutely anything you need. These figures are excellent." Jimmy cut him off with a finger as the phone rang.

"Joseph's Diesel Repairs, Jimmy speaking" He answered. He listened for a moment and his eyes rolled.

"Of course it died. It's been dying for years, and I'm never sure we'll get paid for it...." Jay could see Jimmy was dealing with a trouble client, when his stare captured Jay. A slow grin emerged, an evil glint directed at him.

"Okay, Alex, I'll send someone out. I'll get a van ready and they'll be there in about an hour." He disconnected the call on a chuckle.

"How long has it been since you were on the tools, Jay?" Jimmy grinned, his coffee stained teeth bared at his boss.

"Christ, Jimmy! You should know that any gesture of kindness on my part was just for show!" He laughed.

"I'm holding you to it, Jay!" He stated firmly. "And be prepared to work like a dog. Alex Arlington will make you bleed!" He laughed, and handed a scribbled job card to Jay. Jay copied the information into his diary.

"There's spare overalls in the lockers that should fit, and thankfully you don't show up in those useless suits anymore, because by the end of the day, that heap of John Deere is going to destroy you, and whatever you're wearing!"

Jay groaned. He should have known better than to give Jimmy an inch, but the man had turned the small town workshop to gold, and Jay was pleased he could help out here and there. Jimmy was creeping up to retirement age and Jay didn't know anyone who could step into his shoes and be as efficient.

Jay followed him from the office, and at the lockers, Jimmy grabbed orange overalls and pushed them into Jay's chest.

"I'll get the van ready. Its the first one we had, so be gentle on the gears, but it'll do the trick. I threw in some lunch for you, too. We don't want the boss man to starve out there."

A shiver of excitement ran through Jay as he slipped on the overalls. It had been a few years, but he imagined he would remember everything once he saw an engine again. He'd enjoyed the feeling of accomplishment derived from breathing life into a dead machine, watching the farmer's relieved smile when he knew he could plant his crops, or spray his paddocks.

Staring in the mirror smeared with grease, he grinned stupidly at his reflection. There was something honest about oil spattered overalls.

* * *

"Okay Jimmy, what's the go with Arlington's tractor" A background on the machine always helped. The old man sighed.

"It's an ancient John Deere that's done so many head gaskets, I'm amazed it's not been scrapped, but Alex adamantly refuses to replace it. I think it's an issue with the coin. It's probably done another head, from what I could gather, so just have a look. If you like, just give it a once over and see if you can delay the work for a couple of days if you don't want to do it. I just wanted someone to turn up. It's good for the company image."

"Sure thing, Jimmy. I'll see what I can do." Jay turned to walk away, then hesitated.

"How will I know where to find it?"

Jimmy snorted into his hand, and gave Jay a strange stare.

"Believe me, you'll find it!" He shook his head and disappeared into the office to answer another call.

Jay punched the address into his phone. The farm was an hour away, meaning he'd arrive a little late, but hopefully the farmer wouldn't notice. His palm pressed against his pocket unconsciously, and his shoulders relaxed when his fingers detected the tiny object inside. Feeling the familiar lump grounded him. His eyes flicked in pleasure from the road to the paddocks that verged the road. Grass was rippling in waves with the wind. For a farmer, the length indicated wealth. It meant that less hay and silage would need to be fed out and they could save it for the winter months when the growth was slow. Jay missed it. He'd grown up on a farm, but when the workshop took off, his father had moved the family closer, buying a smaller parcel of land a few towns over. Jay had been upset when they'd left the farm, struggling to adjust to the confines of a suburban fenced in yard, wrestling with little legs that ached to run through paddocks. That same youthful exuberance roused and yawned when his gaze hungrily absorbed the perfect little country town.

The pub in the main street was rickety and thrown together with wood and tin. It had character. And history. The main street was still wide from the days of horse and cart, with a thin strip of asphalt running like a stranger through the centre. Ancient oak trees interrupted the towering eucalyptus until the edge of town where the oak stopped and the fences began. Occasionally he'd pass the vivid yellow of canola fields. Here and there a farmer would lift a hand in greeting when they saw his van. It warmed his heart to know his father's company was so well liked. It meant more than the substantial profits.

As he approached the address, he crossed a grass edged meandering creek weaving around the foothills and cutting under a wooden bridge. He spotted the frayed rope of an old tree swing on the side. He could imagine the local kids congregating there on the hot days, spreading out in the shade and cooling off with a swim. This would have been a wonderful place to bring Lightning, his old pony. The gentle sloping bank would allow them both to walk straight in and splash through the crystal shallows. It reminded him of the summer days that stretched on forever in the mind of a younger Jay where the most pressing issue was having to be home before dark, riding home from the creek with a reluctance that made them late more often than not. They'd walk through the kitchen door with dry hair and soaking shorts for their justified lecture. If it were too cool for a swim, he and his brother Daniel would spend the days climbing the thick staircase of hay bales stacked in the shed, or flattening the long grass along the tree belts playing war games and catching cicadas. Their fun was limited only by their imaginations, and the soil on their farm was rich with inspiration. After lunch was his favourite part of the day. He and Daniel were allowed to ride double on Lightning to meet up with the other kids from town. They would buy icy poles with the money they'd pilfered from their mother's purse and sit around with the other kids before ambling towards home in the cooler afternoon stinking of pony and sweat.

He indicated right down a long overgrown driveway, easing the old van through the potholes. Pulling up in the circular driveway, he understood Jimmy's comment about the lack of money. The house was neglected and shabby. With the verandah on the verge of collapse, he hoped without conviction that there was another home-stead further into the farm in better shape where the farmer actually lived. He scanned the paddocks unsuccessfully for any sign of a tractor.

Jay turned off the ignition and opened the door. He was about to step out when the door pushed back on him. He looked up, startled, as he stared into the muzzle of a horse pressed against the window. Jay glanced around. There was no sign of the farmer, or anyone for that matter. When he cautiously opened the door again, he reached for the halter, but the mare backed out of reach, tossing her head.

Before Jay could move, the horse darted forward, nudging him back behind the wheel. He collapsed into the bucket seat and managed to pull his feet in quickly before the horse nosed the door closed again. Jay stared incredulously as the mare trotted towards the laneway on his right before swinging her head back to look at him.

"You've got to be kidding me." He muttered in disbelief. He started the van again and the horse jerked her head up and down as if she approved, trotting further down the lane.

"Okay, you weird thing, I'm following!" He whispered. She kept up her steady trot, glancing occasionally over her shoulder as if to ensure he followed. Before long, the stack and roof of an old tractor came into sight. "Well, I'll be damned!" Jay followed the horse into the paddock where he pulled up behind the tractor.

Blundstones poked out from underneath the ancient pile of scrap metal, moving and wiggling as the rest of the body wrestled with something. As he approached, the sound of soft cursing erupted randomly through the nonsensical conversation of the farmer.

A woman! Not what Jay expected. He wondered if she'd heard him arrive, when a length of wire was poked out.

"Well, are those muscles painted on or can you actually use them?" She demanded from beneath the tractor. The silver in her voice made his blood sing. Jay grinned at his body's embarrassing response as he suppressed the spontaneous flare of desire. The farmer was probably an older, weathered woman, a far cry from where Jay's interest lay.

He grasped the wire and gave it a hard tug. The wire coiled free easier than expected.

She cursed in pain.

"Are you okay?" His voice tight with concern. If this financially destitute farmer recognised him, it would be the perfect opportunity for a lawsuit. He didn't think of that when he agreed to help Jimmy.

"Yeah. Just surprised me is all. I know better than to be so close to wire. My fault" She dismissed, still muffled by the tractor above her. Jay sighed in relief. Tough old thing, by the sound of it.

He watched as the boots shuffled and grew long shapely legs, delicious curved hips and a tiny waist. Jay shook his head. He was getting aroused by an old farmer. He'd never mention *this* to his brother. Firm, full breasts emerged next, youthful and perky. He held his breath as the rest of her appeared, bent towards the ground to duck under the chassis, the messy honey brown bun piled high on her head.

Recognition slammed him in his gut even before she lifted her face to him. Before she looked at him, he knew her warm, chocolate brown eyes would be framed with long eyelashes and naturally arched eyebrows. He knew her full lips would taunt him from between her exotic, high cheekbones. He knew she tasted of vanilla and honey. He knew that every delicious contour of her body was carved from perfection by a horde of angels. He knew because he still saw her in his dreams, the creamy skin taut and arched beneath him, branded in his memory, every single night. He knew because he'd spent three years searching the state for her. And here she was, only two towns away from him this whole time, and clearly unperturbed by his absence from her life. He stumbled over a wall of emotions. He filled his empty lungs on oxygen heavy with fear, clenched his jaw and waited. Would she even remember him? His heart squeezed and his fists clenched. He forced his expression clear of emotion, but his eyes narrowed on her as she finally met his gaze. She gasped, and his heart sang.

She remembered him.

He watched as a firestorm of different emotions crashed across her beautiful face. Joy? She was happy to see him? His heart warmed. A pale wave of fear finally settled in. Fear?. He didn't know what to do with that unexpected response, so instead he remained silent while she carefully got to her feet. She devoured him with her eyes, pulling her bottom lip between her teeth as she did. He fought an irresistible desire to throw his arms around her and rain three years worth of kisses on her mouth.

"Hello?" She muttered warily, appearing much like a frightened kitten. He'd have to tread carefully until he worked out what was going on. He wasn't sure why he hesitated, or why he'd swallowed his courage, but his words fell without notice.

"Hi, Alex? Jimmy sent me. I'm Jay." Obvious relief chased away a grimace of anguish. Interesting. She drew a shaky breath, sagging against the wheel of the tractor.

"Yeah, uh, its Alexandria, actually, but most people call me Alex." She wouldn't meet his eyes. Jay filled his lungs slowly, trying to remain calm. Lexi. He'd called her Lexi. He'd found her.

"The wire cut your face. You're bleeding." He moved towards her, and she instantly stepped back. He dropped his hand to his side.

"It's nothing. I'm fine. I don't need help." She mumbled. He looked at the blood, smeared into the dirt and grease on her face. He swallowed. He'd never seen anything more beautiful than she was at that moment. He fought the urge to press her against the tractor and taste her lips, to remind himself of that sweet ambrosia that destroyed him that night. He flexed his restraint and gritted his teeth.

"So, lets have a look at the old girl."

"He!" She corrected. Jay frowned.

"Old John. I call him Old John."

His mouth twitched.

Jay examined the machine. When he gave his verdict, Lexi's face fell.

"An engine rebuild? Damn". She chewed her lip.

"I can get started on it now if you like, but there's a week or so of work in this. Ideally, we'd have it in a shed in case it rains." And there he was, committing to fixing a tractor when he had other commitments already scheduled through the week.

"Can it be done faster if I help?" She pleaded. He tasted her offer. The seed of an idea sprouted in his mind.

"If money's an issue, we can come to an arrangement that suits both of us if you're willing."

She wrapped her arms around herself and eyed Jay suspiciously.

"Like what?" She asked warily. *Jesus.* Something was going on with her. He'd been reading body language for years. It helped him gain foothold in difficult meetings when he could sense tension and alleviate any concerns. Hers was screaming at him that something wasn't even close to right. He watched her carefully, scrutinising every reaction as he lay his offer down.

# CHAPTER 3

## ALEX

She barely held herself together. She couldn't believe he was here, standing before her, and he couldn't even remember her. He was even more handsome than she recalled. He was tall and wide with firm brawn hidden beneath his overalls. The body of a god. But his face was incredible too. Dark hair thick and just long enough to catch fingers in. Thick lips that promised. She remembered how they pressed hot and hungry against her body. Her mouth dried as she reacquainted herself with chiselled edges of his jaw, the strong arched eyebrows. And his eyes. Treasure caches of silver dipped in desire. They pulled her into their depths and drowned her. His every cell was etched into her thoughts and she was a mere stranger to him. The thought gutted her.

Humiliation swirled inside her recalling how she searched for him afterwards. She'd thought it meant something. She closed her eyes for a moment and it played out in her mind. She'd approached the counter of that hotel, The White Hawk, and had asked if anybody by the name of Jay, unknown surname, had checked in. The man behind the desk pointed behind her, and her world caved in as she turned. He stood, oozing sex appeal in the tailored blue suit with his profile to her. She'd taken a step towards him. Perhaps two. And then her entire world broke apart. The agony tore through her heart, spearing her belly.

So what did he want now? Another night of fun that he wouldn't remember in exchange for work? She just couldn't. She wouldn't survive it. It was three years since she'd seen him, touched him, given her heart to him, and it was as raw as the day it occurred. She'd lost so much since then. She was beaten and worn already. She had to protect her heart.

He stared at her. No. He stared *through* her, eyes as cold and empty as space, beautiful hard jaw twitching. Then in his deep, rumbling voice he disarmed her.

"I'm looking at buying a farm. Like this one, but I don't know the first thing about running it. I was hoping you could show me how to fence, to care for a herd, tell me what I'd need to run it."

Alex snorted. How cruel was he to mock her.

"Does this look like a successful farm to you? I can barely keep up with the work, let alone make the time to explain to someone how to do what needs to be done." She wanted him to leave her so she could pull together the last shreds of her heart on her own.

She'd started to choke on the pain, and turned away to hide the tears that threatened.

"You do all this on your own?" His unexpectedly harsh tone pushed her over, and she turned her back on him, swiping the tears away.

"No. My awesome team of elves and fairies keep this place in tip top condition." She snapped sarcastically. She drew a trembling breath. She was crumbling, and she refused to do it in front of him.

"Look, you probably should just leave. I'll pay you for your time and let you go. Tell Jimmy….thanks."

Alex felt Horace's hot breath at her shoulder, pressing her muzzle softly against her cheek. Alex sought the familiar comfort of her tenderness. The mare always seemed to understand when her company was needed. She grasped a handful of mane, swung herself gracefully onto her back and touched her heels to the mare. Horace bunched under her, carrying her away from Jay with long strides, away from the broken tractor, away from all her problems.

Horace slowed to an amble as they reached the stream. Alex slipped off and hugged her friend. This was the place she allowed herself to fall apart, to leave the hopelessness, heartbreak and despair among the roots of the gnarled peppercorn so she could paint on her smile and face another day. She'd given many days to the peppercorn over the last year, since Ryan passed. Ryan. She opened her heart and spilled her grief. Her brother was dead. Her father was dead. Three years ago her life had been a picture of perfection. The house was filled with the love and laughter of the four of them, Max, Sabrina, Ryan and Alex. The farm was thriving, the seasons great. Then Max went out to the north paddock and never came home. Ryan found him curled peacefully amongst the pastures he loved with his hand on his chest. When Alex discovered she was pregnant, it was a shock. She'd always been safe and used protection, but it failed. And she was in her second trimester when she found out. She hadn't had any symptoms at all. A perfect pregnancy, the doctors happily informed her. But it was like they cursed her, and the second and third trimester passed with violent nausea, aches and scares. Ryan doubled his efforts and cared for her as well as the farm.

Sabrina was living in an aged care facility in the next town at that time. She'd been unwell for years, but she'd been diagnosed with brittle bones and with Alex incapacitated and Ryan farming, they couldn't care for her, too. Sabrina enjoyed the social aspect of the facility, so that alleviated much of their guilt.

Brandy was born, and Sabrina and Ryan had been at her side. It was perfect. But the tiny human she'd created took much of her time, and her brother continued to pick up her slack on the land. Ryan was fantastic with his niece. He stepped into the role of uncle with delight. Brandy worshipped him. She would only smile for him. For a year they were perfectly happy.

Then Ryan headed into town one day. The cop said it was fatigue. He'd stretched his hours too thin between Alex and the farm and simply went to sleep at the wheel. Her world crashed again. Brandy went with her mum into the paddocks after that, on the tractor, into the herds for months until she was almost trampled one day. That was when Sabrina decided she was needed to care for her grand-daughter, and Alex reluctantly withdrew her from care and brought her back home. Sabrina never once complained, but Alex knew she missed her friends.

Alex chewed her lip and frowned. Now Old John was dead and she didn't have the money on hand to fix him. And after all these years, Jay appeared straight from her nightmares and back into her life. She'd spent the last three years trying to erase him from her memory and her heart only to have him walk into her world and rip open her scars.

She balled her fists at her side, threw her head back and roared her frustration. She knew she couldn't control the weeds, mend the fences, or feed out hay to her cattle without a tractor. She felt ill to her stomach. She'd have to take Jay up on his deal. And with Jay around she'd have to be so very careful. Keep him away from the house. She could make it work though. Ask him to meet her out in the paddocks, away from her mother and daughter. He could learn on the job, and hopefully she would be able to get on top of some of the work. With the paddock full of young calves still on the cows, he would be useful to help get them through the yards for tagging and drenching.

Alex's biggest fear was that once Jay learned about Brandy, he would take her away. Alex knew what he saw. What everyone saw. A woman living in a dilapidated home on an unkempt farm looking after a sick old woman and a toddler on her own. Even Alex knew that it wasn't the ideal situation to raise a child. But she was trying.

It was easier when her father was alive. He'd run the farm on a stiff schedule and no paddock missed out on maintenance. Her father died on a perfectly normal day in Spring. She'd had breakfast with him; bacon and eggs, she recalled with a tilt of her lips; The breakfast of champions. They'd discussed an upcoming rodeo, and that once he'd finished ploughing along the creek, he'd be free for the week and they'd all go. Alex had hugged him. She remembered the familiar tickle of his dark beard on her head as she squeezed him tight. He knew how much she loved watching the bulls. Then he hadn't come in for dinner.

When she lost Ryan, the hard work required to run the farm tripled. Too late she grasped the amount of work he was contributing. Her mother once suggested she find herself a cowboy to settle down with who could help out with the farm, but she just wasn't ready, or remotely capable of stomaching another man's touch. And she knew because she'd tried. She went on one date after Jay, but as soon as he'd slid his hand over hers, her skin recoiled in disgust. It wasn't that he was unattractive, in fact, the young policeman was incredibly handsome. But the connection she'd felt with Jay just wasn't there, and he certainly wouldn't be the sort to get his hands dirty either. When she'd cut their evening short, he began to pursue her, despite her constant refusal. No matter what she did to dissuade his advances, Edward wouldn't let her be.

Leaning against the rough ridges of the peppercorn, Alex took a few moments to inhale the crisp scent of fresh grass. She felt the air clean her lungs while the sky filled with the chatter and whistle of birds as they foraged for food among the dense foliage in the fenced-off tree belts. They sounded like sweet freedom and brave purpose. Her sweeping gaze paused on the shimmer of water in the creek as it curled and crawled over a graveyard of fallen branches, and thought about the generations of Arlingtons who stood once where she was now. She rubbed the tear stains from her cheeks, preparing to face Jay. She'd never backed down before and she wouldn't start now. Like everything else, she'd face Jay with courage and just push through another day. But she'd sear this moment into her mind, because if Jay ever met his daughter, her entire world would be destroyed.

# CHAPTER 4

## JAY

*H*e wasn't sure how long he stared after her, hoping she'd look back at him. He couldn't believe she was managing the entire farm on her own. He'd known she was a woman of grit and determination, but he also knew damn well you needed three seasoned farmers to keep on top of a property of this size.

The fire and earth in her spirit amazed him. And she wanted him gone. She didn't need him beyond the repair of her tractor. He wasn't relevant in her life. It was obvious he had been nothing more than a bit of fun for the night, a notch on her bedpost. It took him by surprise at how deeply the pain of that penetrated.

"Hey, Jimmy. It needs a rebuild. She can't afford it. I'm heading back soon." He stared at the phone long after the screen went black. He'd finally found her and now he was planning to walk away, this time knowing that what they had was all in his imagination. He wanted her, but she clearly didn't feel the same. His heart hollowed out as he consciously ran his fingers over a small lump in his pocket. Like a splinter embedded beneath his skin it prickled, reminding him that at one time, she was everything to him.

Jay began gathering his tools when the sound of a quad bike reached his ears. The almost reluctant purr of the slowly advancing motor struck him as odd. Farmers generally roar around on them at top speed. An older, grey haired woman came slowly into view, peering into the grass, slowing down for the ruts. She pulled up on the other side of Old John, making no effort to get off.

"Hi. I was just looking for Lexi. She didn't call for her lunch so I thought something might have happened."

Jay looked up from his tools. He watched as panic crashed through her eyes.

"What are *you* doing here?" The woman gasped.

Jay frowned at the odd reception.

"I'm the mechanic Jimmy sent to fix the tractor." The woman gawked at him openly. She searched his face frantically. It made him uneasy.

"Do I know you?" Jay asked, bringing her attention to the fact she was staring. The woman started at the question and dropped her scrutiny. She cleared her throat.

"No. Sorry. We don't get many visitors here. I didn't mean to be rude. I'm Sabrina, Alex's mum. And you are?"

"Jay. Nice to meet you, Sabrina. Lex…er…Alex just left on the horse. I think she had to check on some paddocks." That wasn't entirely true, but there was nothing he could say to explain what had happened.

Sabrina's eyes narrowed.

"What did you say to her?" Her voice dripped like acid. Jay raised his eyebrows. This had to be the strangest day he'd ever had. The woman looked, had she been armed, as if she would be pointing it directly at him, finger on a hair trigger.

Jay lifted his hands in surrender.

"I didn't say shit to her, Sab..." His words were cut off as a tiny body emerged, squirming out from behind Sabrina. Jay had been so engrossed with thoughts of Lexi and the strange conversation with Sabrina that he'd failed to notice the set of chubby legs tucked behind the woman on the quad.

The toddler defiantly stepped up to him, tiny fists buried in her waist.

"Mummy says shit is a bad word!" Her grey eyes scolded Jay.

Jay's legs buckled beneath him, and he tried to conceal it by falling into a crouch. Alex had a daughter? She had to be hers. The girl had her mum's delicate features, the same confidence. Her hair was darker, though, and her eyes weren't the deep brown of her mothers. Her darker complexion must have come from her father. His heart lurched. She had a family with a man, and forgot all about Jay. He swallowed a burning lump.

"I'm sorry, little lady. It is a bad word, and I shouldn't have said it." Her little face lit up in delight at his humble apology, and she giggled. So much like her mother's laugh. He was caught off guard by this miniature human Alex had created.

"I'm Jay. And who might you be?" Her tiny mouth opened to respond.

"Baby! Come here now. We have to go." Sabrina snapped, and the little angel ran obediently back, scrambling onto the quad.

Sabrina glared at him.

"I think you had better leave, now." She dismissed him and turned the quad bike carefully, slowly creeping back to the house. The little girl grinned and waved as they went.

Jay blew out a breath and rubbed the back of his neck. His lungs, his heart, his mind, they all throbbed and hurt. From the moment he pulled into the driveway his emotions short-circuited, and the many layers of mystery grew and thickened like walls around her.

A daughter. Fiery and brave like her mother. But where was her father? Who would leave a woman like Alex, and a gorgeous little girl, to live in a derelict house? Any self-respecting man would make every effort to ensure the safety and comfort of his family. Instead, the farm had plunged into disrepair, and Sabrina was left to care for her granddaughter. There was something decidedly off about the situation. A flicker of curiosity warmed then caught fire in his stomach, feeding that niggling doubt that he couldn't explain. Sabrina's cold reception settled over him like a net, trapping his thoughts in whatever was going on that she wasn't saying. Jay felt that whatever was being hidden from him and the rest of the world was somehow his responsibility to uncover. Or perhaps it was just his overwhelming desire to understand why she left him; a ruined man pining for her.

He glanced in the direction Alex left. She was nowhere to be seen. He fished his phone from his overalls.

"Hey, Jimmy. I'm going to need the van for a couple of weeks. I've decided I'm getting a start on this rebuild." He smiled as the response rose a few pitches.

"Yes, I think I am *definitely* out of my mind."

Jay mentally scanned his work diary, knowing it to be full of appointments tomorrow. Busy. Just the way he liked it. Until suddenly, in this moment, his schedule seemed so trivial, so unimportant. Veering off his routine made his stomach roll a little. He'd filled the times with appointments so he could watch his life pass in fifteen minute intervals and know he'd made it through another day. But now? He pictured an empty diary page and mentally filled it with a big black question mark.

A little thread of anticipation danced on the edge of his guilt. He wasn't entirely certain why he'd pretended not to know her, but the expression of anguish she wore suggested she wasn't entirely immune to him. Maybe, just maybe, she felt the connection that crackled between them, too. He could hope. But if not, he needed the morbid details of how she'd moved on to help him heal. After so long he had to see this through. Get closure.

He worked with a frown, puzzling over the day's events. He glanced at his Rolex. Only an hour and a half since he landed at ground zero. He found his muscles were beginning to ache and burn from the physical demands of labouring. It was different to maintaining them in the gym. He huffed a laugh. Alex was right, they felt like they were painted on. He straightened his back to relieve some tightness from hunching over the engine block when realisation struck him with a grin. If Alex's man was no longer around, perhaps there would be room in her life for him. But the child? He'd always wanted a family, but he'd pictured himself surrounded by his own children, not someone else's kids. She was adorable, though. Sassy and bold.

Not a very warm reception from Sabrina, though. Jay was positive the woman recognised him, but he'd never seen her in his life, and she was in a hurry to get the little girl away from him. Shaking his head to clear the mounting confusion, he rolled up his sleeves under the sunshine and picked up a spanner.

Jay glanced up warily at a noise. Today was full of surprises, and he had no idea what to expect next. Alex had dismounted and was walking guardedly towards him, the horse clopping close behind her. She was back. His heart leapt. He noted puffy eyes and dirt smeared on her face. She'd been crying. What had caused her tears? He fought the urge to take her in his arms and fight off her sadness. Instead he forced a neutral expression.

Her shoulders slumped in defeat, she spoke softly. "You're still here?"

"Yep." He braced himself for battle. He wasn't going to go unless she had him physically removed.

"Why?"

"I need to get this tractor fixed so you can start showing me how to run a farm." He set his chin and kept working the spanners.

He tuned into her, and caught her shaky breath.

"Why are you doing this for me?" She looked caged. He leaned back and gave her the full force of his stare. A little lie wouldn't hurt, surely.

"I'm not. The other farmers have shiny new fences, and don't need any more done. Because there was no way I could learn how to eradicate weeds in a spotless paddock. I don't want a brand new farm, Alex. I want something with character, something I can work and watch the fruits of my labour. You are the only one who can help me, so I'm fixing this so you will have to agree."

He focused on the engine, and held his breath. He tried to remain impassive, hoping with his entire soul that she would relent. Allow him to spend time with her and unravel some of her mysteries. He wasn't sure what he'd do if she still wanted him gone, but he was stubborn enough to risk returning until the old tractor was running. That was something he needed to do for her for a reason he couldn't quite fathom. The silence stretched. He snuck a peek at her. She pinched her brow, mulling over his proposal. She pulled her lip between her teeth in that painfully beautiful way that made his breath hiss and pulse race.

"What?" She asked.

"What, what?" he parried.

"You made a noise. What was that?" The confusion on her face was gorgeous. Her expressions were a canvas of everything she felt, on display for the world to see. He wanted to tell her he'd searched for her in that moment, snatch her up in an embrace and tell her he would make everything okay for her if she would just let him into her life. But the fear and suspicion lingering around her like a poisonous cloud held him in check. He cleared his heart from his throat.

"Just adjusting my grip, that's all." He dismissed.

An uncomfortable silence ensued and Jay focused all his attention on behaving like he wasn't wound up tight with his effort to not reach out and touch her.

"Okay." She said quietly.

"Okay what?" Jay fired back.

"Okay, I'll show you what you need to learn if you help me resurrect Old John."

He threw her a wide grin, and his body warmed when he saw her eyes ignite. He remembered her admitting that his smile was the best foreplay. The spark was still there.

# CHAPTER 5

## ALEX

This was a very bad idea. Having him so close had her body humming in excitement, while her heart was bleeding.

She watched as his muscles flexed and twitched in that hypnotic way that fired up her pulse. And then he'd smiled and she'd nearly come undone. She almost opened herself to him, then, demanding to know why he had slept with her and then discarded her without a thought, why he let her believe they had something special only to make her irrelevant when the sun rose. Force him to look at the scars he left on her heart, then ensuring she could never erase him from her mind by giving her a child with eyes like his. Her heart flared for him all over again every time she looked at her daughter.

She noticed that there was no band on his wedding finger. Most mechanics didn't wear them, she recalled, after she'd asked Rick, her last mechanic, why his band was missing. He told her if they were caught on something, they could crush or slice a finger off. She couldn't even detect an indentation on Jay's finger. Perhaps he was satisfying himself with several women instead of tying himself to just one. Imagining him as a player stung only marginally less than knowing he'd found a woman he wanted to settle down with.

While his attention was focused on Old John's insides, she took her fill of him. He sat perched on the edge of the engine bay, his long muscled legs finding purchase around the block. He was bent forward and his overalls were pulled tight enough to watch the muscles on his back work. Alex closed her eyes on the memory of how they felt beneath her fingers, satin slick with sweat, the wild heat in his burning gaze that became the centre of her world. The hungry look that made her believe she was everything to him. Bullshit.

And now she'd agreed to let him into her life again.

Dammit.

"So what's the deal with the horse?" The gravelly timbre of his voice interrupted her thoughts.

The ghost of a smile played on her lips.

"She's pretty special, isn't she? I like to think she's a human trapped in a horse's body. I couldn't keep up with the work as much as I do without her. She's transport, companion, cattle dog and carer for all of us." She tensed at her accidental reference to Sabrina and Brandy, but he didn't appear to detect it.

"Why 'Horace'?" He asked through his teeth as he wrestled with a rusted bolt.

"We never knew what to call her. We'd never named a horse before. We'd called her 'horse' for so long, that we thought if we gave her another name she wouldn't understand. 'Horace' sounds enough like 'horse' to work in both cases."

"We?" Did she imagine that his tone seemed to tighten? She couldn't help the pain in her voice when she explained.

"Ryan and I." She pictured him with his arms around Horace's neck, laughing at the name they'd decided on. She looked over at the stock horse grazing happily on the patch of clover she'd discovered in the lane way. It made her aware that she'd missed lunch, and her mother would worry.

"Horace, lunchtime." Horace swung her head up and trotted leisurely towards the homestead.

"And why isn't this 'Ryan' helping you out on the farm?" There was definitely an edge to his inquiry.

"He, uh….passed away last year." Tears threatened and she forced them back.

"I'm sorry" He muttered.

She gave herself a mental shake. Jay's arrival had turned her mind to chaos and she needed to pull herself together. If she didn't, she might slip up and expose her secrets. She filled her lungs and focused on why Jay would just appear out of the blue after so long.

"Have you been working long with Jimmy? You haven't been out here before." She asked. Her urge to uncover his web of lies getting the better of her.

"No, I only dropped in today to visit him, actually, and he roped me into getting dirty." He gave her a lopsided grin that heated her blood.

"You're not a local, then?" She pressed.

"Nope." He was giving her nothing to work with. She sighed and surveyed his work. The fuel tank had already been removed and was stowed away near the back wheel. There were hoses unclipped and bolts scattered throughout the engine bay. She grunted under her breath. At least he worked fast.

"What else needs to be done?" She asked, lifting up on her toes and peering in.

"I have another hour or so before I get the head off, then I have to pull the pistons. The casings on this are going to be fun." He shot a frown at her. "He hasn't had a rebuild before?"

"No. He's done a few heads, but this is new. What can I do to help?"

He dropped another rusted bolt into a tray and straightened his back, flicking his wrist to check the time. She zeroed in on the expensive watch.

"Nothing at the moment. But after a quick bite you can drain the sump for me if you like?" He teased.

"Okay."

His eyebrows shot up, but before he could respond she interrupted. "And how does a simple mechanic manage to afford a Rolex, Jay? Especially one that he's blase about rubbing grease into?"

"It was a gift from my father, actually. And I forgot to take it off. I wasn't supposed to be working today, remember?" He climbed out of the engine bay, peeling down the overalls to his waist when he reached the ground. Alex turned away, but watched from the corner of her eye. A blue t-shirt pulled tight against his torso, highlighting the contours of his abs, and taunting her with the exposed flesh of his biceps. She continued watching in silence as he soaped up and rinsed off with the water in his van. A trickle of sudded water splashed on his chest. Alex licked her lips as she watched it travel towards his navel with torturing languor. He dried his hands on the inside of his overalls and looked at her. She hurriedly tore her gaze away. When she turned back to him, he wore a smug expression and she knew he'd caught her staring. Irritation made her grind her teeth.

"Ah, here's my lunch, too." She muttered in relief as the calm and rhythmic thud of Horace's unshod shoes shifted her attention. In the awkwardness that followed, she was grateful for the distraction of fetching her lunch from Horace. She unclipped the cloth bag that was fastened around the horse's neck, pulling out a ham and cheese sandwich. She fished out a lump of sugar she knew she would find, rewarding Horace for her help.

"Tell me about the farm." He invited as he pulled out a brown paper bag, opening it warily. She quirked an eyebrow at him when he chuckled at its contents. He reached in and produced an oversized pink cupcake decorated with edible glitter and a pink icing rose.

"When Jimmy packs your lunch…." He shook his head. Alex laughed at the sight of his flushed face and a giant pink cupcake in his hand. His expression suddenly became something dark and intense as he studied her, and she choked her mirth into silence. She licked her lips uncertainly. He watched her intently as she studied him openly, his back leaning on the front wheel of his van, his long muscled legs stretched out in front of him in the flattened grass. She shifted her weight as she sought a comfortable perch. Finally deciding, she sank gracefully to sit cross-legged a metre from him. The further away the better, as far as she was concerned.

"The farm?" She deflected. "What is there to know? For over a hundred years the Arlingtons have called this patch of dirt home. It started out as a dairy, then my great grandfather made the change to beef when the milk prices started plummeting. He sold off a slab of the farm to keep afloat. I'm sticking with the beef. They are more forgiving of less than pristine pastures, and it's not so intensive as milking. The farm doesn't fall apart if I get sick and need a day off with a beef herd. I run Simmental here. Simply because I think they're pretty, and I'm the one who has to look at them day in, day out, after all. You know what I mean? There's an added buzz when you look over your herd and see more than just black or red cows. The patches of white are beautifully individual." She mused, tilting her head.

"That's such a girly thing to say." He teased.

She felt her lips curl in amusement. "Yeah. I guess it is. What are you planning on running on your farm? Beef or milkers?"

"Definitely beef. Especially in the beginning. And probably ongoing, too. I like to wake up slowly in the mornings." Her sandwich suddenly lost flavour. Likes to sleep in? At seven in the morning she'd reached for him, and the bed was already empty. He must have been in a real hurry to leave.

"Then keep away from dairy!" She heard herself snapping.

Jay appraised her for a moment. "Okay…I'll keep that in mind."

Guilt crept in. The guy had no idea who she was, and she was acting like a scorned lover. Which she was, really. She didn't need to bite his head off, though. Having him around was going to test her tolerance. She needed to ensure the conversation was restricted to farm management.

"Will you hire staff to work it with you, or will you just get a smaller farm you can expand down the track? I know a few farm hands who would be happy for some part time work if you can afford it."

He stopped chewing and locked his eyes on her.

"I'm hoping my wife might want to work the farm with me." She felt herself visibly blanch, and she let the hand holding her sandwich drop into her lap. He was married? Her stomach clenched, threatening to expel its contents.

# CHAPTER 6

## JAY

"*A*re you okay?" Jay scrambled to his feet and dropped to his knees before her. He regretted saying that the moment the words fell from his lips. He wasn't thinking. Or, truthfully speaking, he was imagining Alex and he running a farm together. He cursed himself silently. If she thought he was married, his chances of winning her over would be destroyed.

"Yes." Alex croaked. "Just got something stuck in my throat." He watched her closely as she regained her composure. He saw through her lie immediately, and hope stirred inside that perhaps she was upset at the thought he was married. He wondered if enjoying her distress made him a horrible person.

"I'm not married, Alex. I just like the idea of having that kind of lifestyle with a wife who would love it like I do." He was rewarded by a strange glimmer that graced her expression.

"I'm sure that's none of my business, Jay." She glared at him. Jay's heart glowed. He loved the way her spark ignited the animal in him. His gaze simmered on her until she began fidgeting in discomfort.

"Why did you get into farming?" he asked. He knew she loved it. She'd told him three years before. He asked because he wanted to hear her voice, feel her tones make him tingle in all the right places. He wanted her to relax. And gradually it began to work. Her entire body leaned and twisted in delight as she animatedly expressed her love of the land and described the utter contentment of collapsing into bed exhausted after a big day. He pictured her, lips slack in sleep with her hair in a halo across her pillow. How she looked the morning she disappeared from his life.

He told her about the farm of his own childhood. The tales of mischief he and Daniel, his little brother, got into. How angry their father was when they'd tried smoking and managed to set the hay shed on fire. He shivered as her laughter caressed his ears.

By the time he was ready to call it a day, she was sprawled out in the long grass with arms stretched out above her head and a goofy smile on her face. Strands of her honey locks had pulled free and fell about her face. Jay's grey eyes devoured her. She'd closed her eyes and it reminded him of how she looked exactly like that, beneath him. He had to touch her. He had waited so long to find her that it would be criminal not to. He couldn't hesitate a second longer. He dropped to his knees in the grass beside her before he was even aware he'd moved. Her eyes shot open. She froze, and he heard her pull a breath. He swallowed thickly. She glanced at him with a burning stare that deepened and enticed him closer, but when he leaned in, she blinked it away, replacing it with trepidation.

He just couldn't afford to scare her away. Not now. So instead he reached out an oily finger and smudged it on her cheek. She squealed in mock horror, leaping up and out of his reach, easy laughter rattling between them. She bent and scooped up some waste oil and stalked towards him, her cheeks rounded with sinister intent.

She launched at him, catching Jay off guard with her speed before rebounding in shuddering victory. An oily smear painted Jay from his lip to his chest, and Lexi doubled over as he stood stiff and stunned. Jay chuckled as he lifted the hem of his shirt to wipe his mouth clean, and saw her lips part at the show of skin.

Then as suddenly as it appeared, her light dulled as her attention shifted behind him. He turned to see the shimmer of metal from a car creeping up the driveway.

"Uh, I gotta go. Thanks for today." She dismissed him, agitation stiffening her posture. Horace's ears were shooting back and forth. The horse was as uneasy as Alex was. She dragged her hand clean on her jeans.

"Expecting someone?" He prodded carefully for information.

"I'll, ah, see you tomorrow." He stood, helpless, as Alex grabbed Horace's mane and swung gracefully onto her back, the horse appearing as reluctant as her rider to greet the visitor.

His forehead wrinkled. More layers of mystery.

* * *

Stowing Jimmy's tools away, Jay's van slowly approached the homestead. A police car was pulled up close to the house. Jay dropped to a crawl when he spotted the cop. He was standing so close to her he could be forgiven for assuming familiarity, but it was obvious that she wasn't enjoying his proximity. She had her back pressed against the bluestone like she was trying to sink through it and her arms were wrapped around her waist protectively. Her head was bent so low that her chin was resting on her chest.

The cop reached out and pushed a loose strand of hair behind her ear and Jay heard the steering wheel creak in protest as his grip threatened to break it. She was obviously uncomfortable, her flinch at his touch had Jay barely resisting the urge to grab the cop away from Lexi. But he had no right.

"Christ!" His clenched fist connected with the inside of the door instead and he forced the rage back into his belly, rolling slowly away from her. His eyes locked on the mirror until she was out of view.

"Jay! Where the hell were you today? You don't bother showing up for lunch, and you don't think to call and let us know? Daniel and I were stuck with your client for hours making excuses. They were not impressed at all! Your father is furious, Jay. This was going to land him another three branches, and he spent months organising it!"

Jay grinned stupidly as the stunning blonde ranted angrily. She didn't notice, continuing on with her tirade.

"For Christ's sake, Jay. We thought something had happened to you. Daniel called Jimmy who said you were on site fixing a tractor! Fixing a tractor?! What the hell is going on, Jay? You've never even been late once, and suddenly you're a no-show and back on the tools? This had better be good!" The woman stopped pacing and thinned her pretty lips.

"I found her." He whispered. It felt good to say it out loud. It made it real somehow. Her exasperation crashed.

"Oh, Jay! Sweet Jesus!" She took in his goofy grin and grabbed him in a tight embrace, her anger forgotten.

"Where's Daniel?" He inquired. He needed his little brother. He swiped his fingers through his hair as he scanned the bar.

"He's on damage control outside. I'll call him in while you get us a couple of rounds. Oh my God, Jay. I'm so happy for you." She leaned across the space and planted a delighted kiss on his lips before spinning away to fetch Daniel. "But you're still in trouble!"

* * *

"You're shitting me! She's actually real? Like as in, flesh and blood? I thought it was just some bullshit excuse for you to become a reformed monk!" Daniel leaned in, taunting his brother. Jay refused to take the bait. He couldn't shift the feeling of euphoria.

"She's more stunning than I remember her. She runs Arlington Farm on her own. It's getting on top of her, but she's got this energy, this spirit of fire and the determination of the earth that never gives up. I just know she'll keep going and not let it beat her. And she's got this weird horse who thinks she's a person." He knew he was babbling, but he couldn't help it.

"And? Was it love at first sight? For the second time, I mean." Tilly's fingertips bit into Daniel's arm as she impatiently waited for details.

Jay frowned at that. He wasn't sure what was going on. He wrapped a hand around the back of his neck and let out a breath.

"It's complicated. There's something going on that doesn't make sense. She's terrified of something. I have to be careful until I know what's happening with her. She's got a kid now…."

"A kid, Jay? Shit. Is she…?" Daniel didn't meet his eyes.

"Married? No. There's no ring, and she mentioned that the farm used to belong to her and a guy, Ryan. But then she said he'd died."

"Wow, a kid, though. How does that make you feel?" Jay smirked at Tilly. Always the psychologist.

"I'm not sure, actually. You know I always wanted kids, but that's a lot of baggage right there. The kid's adorable and feisty. Much like her mum. The thing is, I'm struggling with the fact that she went on to build a life with someone else. I mean, I've been looking for her all this time, and she just… I don't know… moved on like it meant nothing to her."

Tilly nodded solemnly. "It's a lot to take in. Take some time to process that one. You need to decide how that's likely to impact a potential relationship." She frowned, and tapped a fingertip on her glass for a moment.

"How did she react to you?"

"That's another weird thing. I knew something was off straight away, so I introduced myself as if I didn't know her. She looked real hurt for a second, and then relieved. Relieved? I don't understand at all. I kind of had this image in my mind of her leaping into my arms and us riding off into the sunset."

"Jay, women are weird creatures". Daniel grinned and flinched as Tilly shoved his arm in mock anger. "They make no sense whatsoever."

"So what now, Jay?" Tilly tilted her head at him.

He rubbed his chin thoughtfully. He needed help on this one.

"Well, I was hoping you two can hold fort for me for a bit. I'm also suddenly on the lookout for some real estate…"

"Holy shit! Where is my brother who even has bathroom breaks scheduled a week in advance? And who replaced him with Mr Brash and Spontaneous here?" Daniel jibed.

Tilly flicked Daniel's chest.

"Don't mind Daniel, he's an imbecile. Of course we'll help out."

# CHAPTER 7

## ALEX

She sagged against the wall of the house watching the plume of dust retreat down the driveway. She always felt like a shower after Edward Lawson dropped in.

What a day. It had begun so beautiful and serene and turned into something worse than a nightmare. She rubbed her throbbing temple. Damn. Like clockwork, an Edward-induced migraine followed, and she could feel it was going to be a nasty one. She walked slowly inside, releasing the tension in her muscles. As she passed the hall stand, she habitually kissed her fingers and pressed it to Ryan's picture. On days like this, she missed him so much it hurt. He'd have known what to do.

Sabrina was waiting on the couch.

"Well? Care to tell me about him?" Her voice carried a threatening undertone.

"There's nothing to say, Mum. Edward…"

"Don't pretend I'm stupid, Alex! I'm not talking about that parasite and you know it!" She snapped. "The second I saw his eyes I could tell who he was!"

"When did you see him, Mum?" Alex grabbed her mother's wrists frantically, catching her stare.

Sabrina lifted her chin defiantly.

"You didn't send Horace for lunch so I went to find you. I thought something had happened to you."

"You left Brandy alone?" Alex rubbed her face in frustration.

"No, Lex. I didn't leave her alone." Sabrina whispered. Alex clutched her stomach and gagged as the gravity registered.

"Oh, Christ! What happened?" Her lungs wouldn't work and she sank down beside her mother. Sabrina looped a comforting arm around her daughter's waist.

"He didn't know, Lex. Its okay. I saw him leave, too, so you don't have to concern yourself."

Alex groaned inwardly. She couldn't bring herself to explain her new arrangement with him to her mum.

"Where's Brandy?"

"You know she doesn't like that douche. She ran to her room and hid when he arrived. Ah, speak of the devil." They both grinned as Brandy appeared with a red feather boa draped unevenly around her neck and a plastic tiara balanced on her dark hair.

"Oh my, its Princess Brandy!" Alex clasped her chest. The toddler giggled and attempted to curtsey.

"We are meant to curtsey to *you* if you're a Princess, Little Button." Alex laughed. She appraised her daughter with adoration. She was an angel of joy, the one light in her dark fight for happiness. She was in awe that this precious, glowing gem came from her body. She created perfection. Shuddering, she reminisced to when she discovered she was pregnant. Had she found out earlier she wouldn't have hesitated to terminate. Alex figured the undetected pregnancy was the Universe's way of ensuring this precious soul came into the world.

"But you are the Queen. Queen's don't curtsey at Princesses!" She frowned at her Mother.

"Oh, does that make Nana the King then?" She indulged her daughter.

"No, silly. Jay is King!" Sabrina and Alex gasped as Brandy skipped off down the hall.

"Mum. What just happened?" Alex's stomach was ice.

During the night Alex's migraine morphed into a demon of pain. The ticking of the kitchen clock grated against her raw skull. Her brain was expanding with every heartbeat and the burning in her eyes made rest impossible.

"Mummy, Nana's sick."

Alex opened her eyes a slit. The blurry toddler looked frightened, dragging her blue bunny rug behind her.

She opened her mouth to console her, but the movement brought on nausea, and she barely made it to the bucket beside her.

"You're sick, too, Mummy." She whispered. She stood for a while before closing the door softly. Alex couldn't breathe without pain. There was no way she'd be able to get up.

* * *

"Shhhh, Mummy's head hurts" The deep rumble stabbed her skull. Then she felt a warm palm press painfully on her forehead. She winced, and emptied her stomach again.

"Try and swallow this." Low vocals, like satin on velvet lifted her gently and slid a tablet past her lips. Cool water flooded her mouth and she swallowed weakly. Her brain was too fuzzy to register anything but the need to lay down.

* * *

In her dream, Jay's silver heat bored into her. She felt his body completely covering hers in a delicious warm blanket. His lips, red and puffy from passion, dipped to her neck, and she groaned as flames spread through her veins. When she leaned into him, he pulled back, his dark hair tousled in sexy spikes.

"Tell me," He said in his sexy drawl, "Do you want honey or jam?"

"What?" She blinked in confusion.

"Okay" He chuckled. "Peanut butter it is."

She blinked awake. The calamity in her head had softened remarkably into a dull roar, and although queasy, Alex no longer felt the urge to vomit. She sat up carefully. The world spun, then righted itself. Alex glanced down at the bedside table, popped the two tablets left for her and took a long gulp of the water. After a few lungfuls of air, she staggered towards the sound of her daughter giggling in the kitchen.

When she reached the doorway she froze. Brandy sat cross-legged on the table top with toast in her fists. She was deep in her bizarre brand of conversation with the man who sat at the table facing her, his own toast poking out of his mouth. His legs were clad in tight denim, and he was missing his shirt. Alex knew that body. Remembered the silky texture of his flesh, the hard corners and contours of his muscles. Her body ached.

Her daughter, the light in her life, was having breakfast with her father. And neither of them knew. He laughed at her nonsense and talked back to her as if they were old friends. Alex's heart thumped painfully in her throat. It was her deepest desire unfolding before her eyes. Her fantasy family. If only it were possible. Brandy needed her father, Alex realised. She needed to know him, and understand that part of her that she hadn't connected to anybody yet. And she clearly thought the world of Jay. She'd already bonded with him, over breakfast and nonsense. But what was good for Brandy would rip her away from Alex. It could never be. Edward's image pierced her skull.

Brandy missing out on her father brought tears to her eyes. Wanting the impossible family scene with this man, this perfect, beautiful man who didn't remember her, made them overflow.

"Lexi?" His voice was tight with concern and her heart twisted traitorously as she registered his term of endearment.

He was suddenly wrapped all around her, his bare chest pressed against her cheek, his strong arms securing her to his body. To feel the thump of his heart again and the heat of his flesh was exquisite torture. The weight of the broken tractor, seeing Jay again, and Edward's visit, combined with finding Jay planted in her home like a hot dream overwhelmed her. Alex sobbed. She heaved her heart out, fuelled by his alluring scent, the heady masculinity triggering a tsunami of sensations and emotions she couldn't control. Her tears soaked his chest, but he didn't let her go. Not even when her grief eased into soft hiccoughs.

"Everything's okay, sweetheart. It's all okay." She could feel his words rumble in his chest, and she was aware of her palm resting against him, the heat of his skin sending sparks through her veins. Reluctantly, she pulled away. The loss of contact caused her to wince.

"I'm so sorry, Jay. I couldn't…." reality slammed into her. "Mum?" She bit out frantically.

"Its okay, Lexi. She's unwell. She's sleeping, but she's on the mend." Alex frowned.

"What happened?" She felt bewildered, like she stepped out of her life and missed a couple of chapters.

"I'll get you a drink and some toast, and I'll tell you."

She sat drained and weak at the table. He placed a glass in front of her, something to replace electrolytes she'd lost to nausea. She sipped it as she followed his movements around her kitchen. He opened the crockery cupboard and retrieved a plate. He snatched the butter from the fridge by feel alone, then grabbed the honey from the table. He moved about like he lived here. She swallowed against her constricting heart.

"How long have you been here?" She asked slowly.

"Two days." He watched her cautiously. The muscles in his jaw twitched. Alex fought a ball of dread down from her throat. He wasn't supposed to ever enter her home. Or meet Brandy. She dropped her head into her hands as he explained.

"Sabrina wasn't well, either. I couldn't leave Sass here to fend for herself."

She lifted her head and tilted it. "Sass?"

"Sass. You know, Miss Sassy." Did he sound a little sheepish? She let him talk, allowing herself to be soothed by his timbre, until the familiar pinch of unease settled over her.

"Mum ran out of medicine last month, Jay, how is…"

"We got her prescription filled yesterday." Alex 's stomach curled.

"We?"

"Sass and I. I couldn't well leave her home with both of you inca-pacitated. Anyway, she helped show me which chemist to go to." He shrugged it off.

"Hey, Princess, come and finish your breakfast. Oh, damn, sorry Lex, I should keep my voice down."

It wasn't the volume that made her wince. It was the familiar nick-name that erased the years of silence, coupled with the display of domestic bliss in her kitchen. It caused her to crave things. Wonderful things. Things Edward would never allow her to have with Jay..

"Just…put a shirt on, will you?!" She snapped. His naked chest was playing havoc with her heart. He gave her a lopsided grin and her pulse exploded. She clenched her teeth against it.

"Good to see you're feeling better."

Jay sent her off to have a shower after he was satisfied she was well enough. She emerged feeling much better, and more energised. Brandy was dancing around her mother, delighted to have her back.

"And then we went to town, and Jay got me an ice cream with *sprinkles*! I got to choose the flavour and everything!" Alex laughed at her daughter's excitement.

"What flavour did you choose, Little Button?" She asked, tickling laughter out of her.

"Green!" She squeaked. Alex pulled her daughter against her tightly.

"I missed you while I was sick. I'll have to give you extra snuggles to make up for the ones I missed."

"No you don't. Jay gave me your snuggles already." Alex closed her eyes on that picture.

"Can Jay play with me forever, Mum?" Her sparkling grey eyes made Alex's heart lurch.

"No, sweetness. He has his own life, and work. He's here to help for a bit. That's all."

"Can he make the peeseman go away?" Her sweet voice begged innocently.

"Oh, Little Button, you don't like him, do you?" Alex pressed her nose into the girl's silken hair.

"No, Mummy, he makes you sad, then he makes you sick." She whispered.

"You get that, huh? I'll tell you a secret? Mummy doesn't like him either.".

# CHAPTER 8

## JAY

*J*ay struggled with the guilt of enjoying the fact that Lexi and Sabrina were ill. Now that they were on the mend, he mentally counted the hours until Lexi would eventually ask him to leave.

Rustling up meals for Brandy and caring for the women filled a hole inside that he wasn't aware he had. Brandy was an utter delight with her untarnished, optimistic chatter. She was strong minded like Lexi, stubborn and spirited, and those traits bloomed in the child who was a miniature of the woman who bore her. He couldn't help but adore her. The fact that she belonged to another man seemed to have lost importance between the giggles and hugs.

His decision to plant himself in Lexi's life was overshadowed by the pictures around the house. There were very few of Lexi as a child, but it seemed that on every wall hung images of the same three faces. Brandy, Lexi, and a man. The man was classically handsome, with neat dark wavy hair. His smile seemed to be his natural expression. One of those people who were always happy.

That everybody liked. Of course he was. He had Lexi. And in every picture he was staring adoringly at her and Brandy. Jay's chest constricted at every glance. They were framed reminders of the love between Lexi and a man who wasn't him. His stomach rolled. He might have passed away, but his presence was still firmly planted in every one of their days. Jay was prepared to deal with an ex, but he wasn't sure how to vanquish a ghost.

But he'd seen how Lexi reacted to him. How her pupils dilated when she caught him sitting topless at the kitchen table. He'd felt the erratic beat of her heart against his chest when he held her. He'd finally been able to touch her. Finally. And she felt so good, so *right* in his arms. He was almost grateful to pull his shirt on, hoping to cover the obvious bulge pressing against the zipper on his jeans.

He opened the curtains in Sabrina's room, the light flooding in.

"What if I wanted to sleep?" She snapped. Jay felt himself grin. That's where Lexi got her sting from.

"Sabrina, you can't stay in bed forever. I know you're feeling better, and its a lovely day out there. I think you need to get out into it." Jay scolded her. She glared at him and her eyes narrowed.

"Why are you doing this? You're here two minutes and you're playing nurse and babysitter." She scrutinised him with her unwavering stare. Jay leaned back against the wall, instantly speechless, unsure how to best respond when he hadn't even considered it himself. He didn't think. He just followed his heart and did what he wanted to do. For Lexi. The entire situation was odd, but deciding to step up like he had was almost creepy to someone looking in. He opened his mouth, but couldn't offer a satisfactory explanation, so he closed it again. Sabrina zeroed in on his uncertainty. His fear.

"You don't understand what's happening here, Jay. Everything is so messy. You shouldn't be here inside our home. You shouldn't talk to Brandy. You shouldn't be here at all."

Confusion blended with frustration. He knew there were things happening he wasn't privy to, but this was a clear warning.

"What's going on, Sabrina?" he pleaded. She shook her head and looked away.

"I'm grateful, Jay. I really am. I don't know how we would have managed with both of us ill at the same time. You are a good man. But it's not my story to tell. She won't tell you, either, so don't bother asking."

"What can I do?" His brow furrowed at her refusal to elaborate. She fixed him with a sad gaze. Tears shone in her eyes.

"Jay, you need to leave. Not just today. You need to go and never come back." Jay huffed out his shock.

"Jay?" Brandy's sweet voice flowed down the hall and into his ears, and her tiny figure rushed after it. There was more he needed to discuss with Sabrina, but not with Brandy there. She grinned as her eyes lit on him, and leapt into his arms. With a grin, Jay caught her and swung her up in the air. He dropped his eyes to Sabrina's face, pinched with pain against her pillow, eyes fixed on them.

"Hey squirt, what's happening?" His throat felt thick with emotion.

"Just want a hug, Jay." He snuggled into her warmth.

He couldn't meet Sabrina's eyes again, so he carried Brandy to the kitchen where Lexi was finishing the dishes.

"Let me help." He slid Brandy to the floor and snatched up a dish cloth as she disappeared into her room. As he stepped close to Lexi,

Jay's nostrils were saturated by the delectable scent that was pure Lexi. He quivered with the flashback it invoked. *That same erotic aroma of vanilla wrapped around him, filling his lungs, flooding his heart. Her lips dropping open in ecstasy as he moved inside her, her creamy skin flushed with lust beneath him.*

His pulse clattered.

Lexi must have sensed it, too, because she looked up at him, pools of melted chocolate fixed on him, her breaths sharp and erratic. He growled his hunger at her and unable to resist a second longer, dropped the dish cloth, catching her face in his palms, his long fingers stroking the sensitive skin below her ears. With an urgency beyond reason, he crashed his mouth to hers, surrounded by the electric jolts of their connection.

He kissed her with abandon, relishing her taste, completely submerged in the sensation of her soft warm lips beneath his. This was his Lexi, in his arms. Where she belonged. She'd been out of reach for so long that his need for her was ferocious, and he shuddered as she opened to him. He deepened the kiss, euphorically aware of her fingers curling around his neck and stabbing into his hair. He pulled her body into his, craving her heat, needing to feel all of her against all of him. He swallowed her soft groans as she surrendered so perfectly. He delighted in her chest heaving against his, her nipples hardened and stroked him through her top with every gasp of air she took. The zipper on his jeans strained in agony and he pressed it against her. He needed her more than he needed his next breath. He slid one hand around the back of her head, the other reacquainting itself with the contours and edges of her body. His excitement was palpable. His breath rasped and shuddered and a fire within his body raged as he gently pressed her against the kitchen cupboards.

He felt a strangled cry erupt from her chest and she broke the kiss suddenly. Like a predator Jay stepped towards her again, hungrily fixed on her mouth. He felt her palms press against his chest, forcing distance between them. He searched her eyes quizzically, darkened to black with desire and burning with lust. He watched the pulse in her neck jumping against her skin.

"Don't…please." Her tone dripped with agony. She wrapped her arms around her stomach and stepped away.

"Why?" He demanded, his voice deeper with his own pain, jabbing his fingers through his hair. She belonged to him. She felt it, and she'd wanted him, too. Why would she fight it?

She closed her eyes on a shuddering breath.

"I ….can't….I won't…you. Uh, just go, Jay." She kept her eyes closed. He stared at her, willing her eyes to fall on him again. He needed to see the truth in them. Instead, she remained as she was, shoulders dropped, breath still rasping in her chest.

His neck bobbed on a swallow. He brought a finger to his lips, still tingling from her touch. He knew that if he reached out to her now, she'd respond to him. She couldn't resist the connection between them for long. His body, his heart, his soul screamed at him to claim her, but she looked so fragile in that moment, and he knew that if she submitted to their passion now, something important would break inside her, forever damaging something that was still growing.

He took a long look at her before he strode out the kitchen door, across the verandah and into his van. As he peeled out onto the road, he pulled onto the shoulder and ripped on the handbrake. Only then did he allow himself to roar in frustration.

* * *

"What did you find?" Jay handed Daniel a beer and sipped his own.

"So, Arlington Farm was subdivided sixty odd years ago and sold off to fund the transition from dairy to beef when the milk prices slumped. The divided lot is around 500 odd acres with a creek running through the centre. Its external fences are sound, but some of the internal ones need replacing. Good, fertile soils with a good fertiliser history." Daniel's eyes sparkled as he revealed the outcome of his research.

"That's great, Daniel, but how's that important? I asked you to help me buy a farm, not tell me the history of Lexi's farm" He didn't intend to sound ungrateful, but he was still nursing his damaged heart from earlier.

Daniel leaned in closer. "Well, I thought it fitting for you to know the history of the farm you now own." His smile widened.

Jay's eyes rounded. "No way! How did you do that?" Jay straightened on the stool.

His brother smirked. "Well, it seems you generously overpaid a farmer who was already considering retirement. You paid him enough that he was happy to leave all the farm equipment there for you. Quick settlement, too. It settles next month."

He raised his glass at Jay, a smug smile lodged firmly in place.

The waitress appeared at their table. Her bleached blonde hair bobbing around her shoulders, her slim body on display in a short skirt and low cut figure hugging top. She dipped her cleavage level to Jay's line of sight. Jay tilted his head to her heavily painted face.

"Can I get you anything, boys? Something a little stronger...on the house?" She asked huskily, eyes locked on Jay's. He blinked at her in confusion and shook his head, gesturing to the full glass in his hand. Her lips pressed into thin lines as she spun away from them, leaving Daniel in fits of laughter.

"Oh, Jay, you seriously have no idea, do you?"

"About what?" Jay furrowed his brows at his brother.

"The waitress was flirting with you, you idiot!" Jay raised an eyebrow at his brother, shaking his head.

"Jesus, Jay, are you sure you're not a monk? When was the last time you got laid?" He snapped a glare at Daniel.

"You know perfectly well, Daniel." Jay warned. Three years ago.

"I kissed her." Daniel's jaw fell.

"And?"

"And she kissed me back. For a moment, anyway."

"Don't leave me hanging!" Daniel groaned.

Jay explained the last two days with Lexi and Brandy, Sabrina's warning and Lexi's refusal to entertain the lust between them.

"I don't understand, Daniel. She wouldn't look at me. Just told me to leave, when it was obvious she wanted me as much as I wanted her." Jay rapped his knuckles softly on the table in uncertainty.

"Do you think she's playing you?" Daniel's query burned. After the night Lexi had disappeared from his world without a backwards glance, he'd searched for her in every bar and cafe in the state with no luck. Now he'd found her, she'd kept him at arms length for no obvious reason. Until today, when she responded to him with the same hunger he'd felt. And she still pushed him away. Jay dropped his shoulders.

"I don't know. I feel like I don't even know her. I want to... but she won't let me in."

"What are you going to do, then?" Daniel's words hung like a noose above him.

Jay swirled a sip of beer around his mouth as he tested his options. He swallowed. "I think I'm going to fix that tractor like I promised."

# CHAPTER 9

## ALEX

*S*he sank to the floor as his footsteps faded away. Her body throbbed with disappointment. She had to fight it with everything she had to stop him, but she wanted him. She wanted to be consumed by him, let him detonate all her nerve endings as he flooded her senses. She wanted to see stars with him again.

But she knew that if she let him in again, she wouldn't recover when it finished. She'd give herself to him just to have her heart ripped out again, but there weren't enough pieces of her heart left to break. He was toying with her, and he'd leave her.

*She ran her palm over the ridges of his chest, the bunching and flexing strength beneath his skin so potently masculine. So perfect. And he was all hers. She continued her hungry exploration. His firm round buttocks, the dip of his spine, the flex of his shoulders and biceps as they shifted his weight over her. That exquisite craving as he pressed against her entrance...*

Alex pressed her knuckle against her lips to stifle a scream of frustration. Only when her pulse levelled out did she allow herself to open her eyes. She knew if she'd looked at him and seen the desire on his face that she wouldn't have been able to stop herself from getting lost in him again.

Alex's stomach convulsed as she watched plumes of dust follow the car up her driveway. Again? Brandy had run from the window and into her room, and Sabrina was still in bed. She met Edward in the driveway this time. He couldn't cage her in the open.

"Alex , you look beautiful as always." he drawled, leaning in for a kiss. She stepped back and turned away, his wet mouth sliding briefly over her cheek. The cool breeze burned the contact like dry ice.

"Edward. What are you doing here again?"

"I came to visit you. Why don't you invite me inside, Alex? I want to see your kid." She winced at the thought.

"She's down for a nap" she lied. "Why did you really come?"

His handsome face twisted in a smile that didn't reach his eyes. He looked like a snake about to strike.

"I heard there was someone hanging round here, and wanted to know if you were okay. I gotta keep my girl safe." Alex's skin crawled.

"It's just a mechanic, Edward. Old John packed it in and he's here to get him running again."

"Who?" His eyes narrowed.

"I don't know. A new guy. I hadn't met him before." She carefully avoided saying his name.

"What's he like?" He demanded. Alex took a step backwards when he moved closer. He glared at her, and when he took another step she held her ground, hugging her waist.

"I don't know, Edward. I've been busy with my daughter, and he's been in the paddock."

"Don't lie to me, beautiful. A relationship shouldn't be built on lies. I won't tolerate it, you *know* that."

Alex drew a shuddering breath, clenched her teeth and met the hard ice of his glare.

"He's the mechanic, Edward. I don't know anything else. He's not coming back, either. I told him I couldn't afford it." She hated revealing her financial situation, but he already knew. He'd sharpened his blade on the debts and held it to her throat. He'd made it his business to know her finances.

Edward shot her a hard look.

"Then come out for dinner with me tonight."

"Not tonight, please. I've been sick and I still don't feel great."

"Tomorrow then?" Alex's heart sank. She knew she couldn't avoid him forever. Eventually he'd get tired of waiting and...well, she didn't want to think about that.

"Friday?" Her voice small and tight.

A smile spread across his features. Not happiness, she noted. Victory.

"Jesus, Lex! Why would you agree to that?" Sabrina grated, handing her a steaming mug. Alex sighed heavily. She couldn't add to her mother's stress.

"Maybe I just need to give him another chance." Lexi reasoned.

"Don't give me that bull. You can't stand him. Brandy can't stand him. You know he's not good for you."

Fear and frustration battled in her stomach.

"It can't hurt." She didn't even sound convincing to her own ears. Sabrina's lips pinched.

"It's only for a while, Mum. When the weaners go in, things will get better. It's just a few weeks or so. I'll check them out tomorrow to see if they'll be ready. Damn. I'll need to speak with Pete again about running them through his yards. I haven't had time to fix ours yet." After the bull ran through his fence, that had become the priority. She would still need to get that done first, but to do that she needed Old John running. She groaned. Maybe she could ask Pete if she could use his tractor until hers was fixed.

"You'd better see Pete soon, then. I hear he's sold the farm." Sabrina spoke gently. She knew Alex was trying to put together enough money to buy the rest of the old farm off Pete, but she couldn't see that happening. The money wasn't there to fix a tractor, let alone purchase a second farm. With Pete's farm sold, Alex would have to accept that it would never be hers.

Alex pinched the bridge of her nose as she digested the news. Pete was too old to keep running the farm. He'd been talking about selling up and retiring for years. She couldn't blame him.

"I'll speak to him this morning before I look over the calves."

* * *

Alex greeted Pete in the front paddock. His pastures were spotless.

"Looks great, Pete! Another good year for growth." She smiled her approval. Guilt washed over his welcoming expression.

"It's okay, Pete. You need to look after you, and we all know I wouldn't be able to buy it back for a few years, anyway." She laughed lightly. Pete smiled his relief.

"Yeah. I'm so sorry, Alex. I just couldn't go through another winter here. The new owner wants to keep it pretty much the same, which is nice. I'd hate to have someone stick a feed lot here."

Alex knew Pete had been approached by a company wanting to run a feed lot. She'd seen them scattered across the land here and there, paddocks thick with cattle standing in mud, waiting for their quota of grain to be fed to them and not a blade of grass in sight. They looked awful, and the sounds of cows lamenting a pasture would have carried through the valley.

"So, who's the new owner? Have you met them?" She quizzed.

He glanced at the sun, and then his watch.

"Actually, they're coming to sign paperwork in about half an hour. Want a coffee until they arrive?"

"I'd love to, Pete. Thanks. I was actually popping over to see if I could lend your tractor for a bit? The bull broke out, and then I need to fix up the yards if I have any chance of getting the weaners off to market."

"Bring them through my yards. You know you can do that anytime, Alex. As for the tractor, I sold the farm with all equipment, so you'll need to pass it by the new owners, I'm afraid." She nodded, then the two fell into an easy conversation. Horace wandered off to roll in the garden when Alex and Pete went inside.

Pete's farmhouse was a newer building than Alex's home. It was lovely and cool, the large windows overlooking the winding creek and the rambling hills.

Horace called from the garden.

"They're here" Pete announced, and a shiny new four wheel drive rolled to a stop at the entrance. Horace was always delighted to meet new people, and she nosed the driver's window.

"Horace! Leave them be!" Alex laughed. Horace dropped her head in shame, backing up and giving the driver space to get out.

The man was alone, and a little apprehensive of the horse dancing in front of him.

"Just let her sniff you. She just wants to meet you, then she'll leave you be." Alex explained.

The man did as he was told. He was tall and toned, his dark hair styled close to his head. There was something familiar about him that called to Alex. Confused, she held her breath until he turned towards them. When she saw his face, she relaxed. He was attractive, strong features and masculine beauty, but not Alex's type. Alex's type had set her body on fire hours before, then left forever. But the way she'd reacted to this man's body...she shook her head. Her heart wanted it to be Jay. She'd almost believed it was him for a moment.

She realised suddenly that the man was staring at her. More than that, he was scrutinising every part of her, slowly, as he made his way to the porch. Instinctively, her arms dropped to hug her waist, and his eyebrows lifted. He caught her eyes with a flicker of recognition, before turning towards Pete. Alex frowned.

"Pete, thanks for agreeing to meet with me today. My, uh, brother couldn't make it, I'm afraid." He shot a guarded look at Alex .

"No problems, Daniel. Daniel, meet Alex. She's your new neighbour."

Alex took the offered hand, nodding a greeting.

While Pete and Daniel shuffled through paperwork, Alex poured them coffee and found a pack of biscuits Pete kept in his cupboard, arranging them on a plate.

When they'd both signed off on the documents, Daniel turned his attention to Alex.

"How long have you been farming here?"

Alex's chin lifted."Six generations. The land's firmly lodged in my blood." Her eyes blazed with pride.

"Nice place you got there, Alex. Just you and your man run it?" He asked. Something in his tone made Alex not want to answer. She didn't have to, as it turned out.

"Alex does the lot herself, and she docs a damn good job of it, too. Works too hard if you ask me. Wasn't so tough when Ryan was alive, but she's more than capable." Daniel jerked his expression to hers.

"I, uh, have to go." She stood, gathering empty mugs from the table.

"Alex, didn't you want to speak to Daniel about something?" Pete reminded her. She clenched her teeth and turned warily to Daniel.

"Oh, yes. Daniel, I was hoping I could borrow the tractor you bought off Pete with the farm. Just for a month, if possible. My tractor died and I need to get some fencing done."

Daniel's voice was warm and curious. "Aren't you getting it fixed?"

"No. I mean, I was, but repairs aren't in the budget this month, and I need the fence urgently." Was it her imagination or was Daniel asking some pretty intrusive questions? She frowned, her arms instinctively wrapping around her waist.

"Of course you can use it for as long as you need. We will settle here in a month, so we won't be needing it until after we're moved in. As long as it suits Pete, here."

Alex sighed in relief. She smiled her gratitude and shook Daniel's hand again.

"I'll see you again real soon, Pete. Thank you, too. It was lovely to meet you."

Odd compassion padded out his tone. "Likewise, Alex."

Once outside, she wound her arms around her mare's warm neck. Horace snorted her agreement.

"Maybe we can actually do this, Horace. Luck seems to be on my side for once."

# CHAPTER 10

## JAY

*J*ay's stomach was heavy with excitement and trepidation. He knew Lexi sent him away and expected him to stay away, but he also knew that the chemistry between them might just change her mind. He weaved around the potholes and locked his expression in readiness. He'd come with a plan. He'd tried to approach her with kindness, and that didn't work. Now he'd try logic on her. He drove towards the house before veering down the laneway to the John Deere.

As he worked, his thoughts kept straying to Daniel's account of his meeting with Lexi at Jay's new farm. He'd have to tell her about the farm eventually, but right now all of Jay's actions were focused on her opening up to him. Daniel revealed that although it was obvious she and Pete had been friends for a while, she'd been guarded with Daniel. Jay couldn't afford to give Lexi anything more to be wary of about right now.

He'd been working for half the day when he heard a tractor rolling closer. From the corner of his vision he could see Lexi at the wheel of a Kubota tractor, Brandy leaping up and down beside her as she spotted Jay. She lowered the hydraulics and shut off the engine, fury pouring from her. Jay braced himself as she approached. Her honey halo was pulled back into a single braid swinging halfway down her back. It gave her a fragile appearance, and Jay fought the impulsive urge to press her to his chest to ensure no harm ever came to her. Fragile, that was, until she loosened the fire inside.

"I told you to go, Jay! What are you doing here?"

He detected more pain than anger. His heart lurched.

"Jay!" Brandy wriggled from her mum's arms, landing with a warm flop against Jay's legs. He bent and planted a kiss on her head.

"Sorry Sass, I can't give you a hug just now. Look at my hands, I'm filthy." Jay apologised.

"Fiwfy!" She grinned up at him. He grinned back. He ignored Lexi's glacial expression.

"I'm a man of my word."

Lexi snorted her mistrust.

"The deal is I fix Old John, and you teach me what I need to know."

"I don't know if that's a good idea any more, Jay." Her lips thinned as she crossed her arms over her chest. He loved that she was so stubborn. So insanely independent she would forego the repair of an important farm implement to stand her ground.

"It's too late, Lex. A deal's a deal." He sounded calm, but his heart was pounding.

"I'm revoking the deal. I can do without a tractor for now. I'll get it done when money from the markets come in next month." Jay

73

gritted his teeth. He was prepared for this, but he'd hoped he wouldn't have to. He forced a cold expression and turned to face her, rubbing grease off his hands with an old rag.

"Problem with that, Lex. I've already done two days of work, and I've ordered the parts I need to get finished. They aren't cheap for an old boy like this. So, you have a choice. The way I see it is that you either stick with the deal you agreed to two days ago, or pay for the parts on order and a couple of days of labour."

Guilt gnawed at his gut as he watched her digest her options. That frightened rabbit pose hunched her shoulders, and he hated that he was the cause of that. But there was too much at stake. He was hoping she wouldn't have the money to pay the bill, because he knew she'd find it if she had to, even if the lot of them ate baked beans for a month.

"Stay, Jay! Please?" Brandy danced around Jay's legs. At least she was on his side. He gave her a grateful wink. She giggled and squeezed her eyes closed, trying to imitate him. He chuckled at her, winking again.

"Mummy, make him stay!"

Alex ground her teeth. *That's my girl*, Jay thought with pride. *She'd never give in easily. She'll go down fighting, even though she secretly wants this.* Her decision lifts her chin and stiffens her shoulders. Her strength, her defiance, her ferocity knocked the breath from Jay's lungs. He locked his jaw against the roaring desires it stirred up and remained nonchalant.

"Don't you have a paying job you need to attend?"

"Nope. I have leave owing. Jimmy already approved it."

"Fine." She snapped, and walked away.

For the next two days Jay worked on the repairs. Lexi didn't come down at all to see him, and he was able to finish the work early with the help of another of Jimmy's men he'd called on for the lifting component. His body was sore and tired, the muscles screaming in his back in protest. When he'd tightened the last bolt, he sat back and sighed in satisfaction. Now to see if he'd managed to breathe life into it.

The engine fired, bursting a plume of soot from the stack. Jay smiled at the sound. He revved it a few times, trying out all the levers and functions to make sure it was in good working order. With this job done, he could begin spending time with Lexi.

Three weeks, they'd agreed on. He hoped that would be enough time.

He soaped up his hands in the back of the van, and stripped off his overalls. He felt like a real farmer for a moment, powerful legs clad in tight denim, a plaid shirt in grey with the first two buttons popped, and his old battered Akubra to keep the sun off. The hat was an extra he added, hoping he would look like he belonged to the farm life. Her farm. Her life. If she wanted a cowboy, he would give her one.

He chugged up to the house at a crawl, taking in Lexi's farm. She owned hills and valleys covered in green waving pastures, and he was impatient to be working in them with her. He'd been disappointed when she'd kept away from him, and although he generally enjoyed entertaining his own thoughts, he was eager for the distraction. The many layers of Lexi bounced around in his thoughts and wouldn't let up. He was struggling to piece together the fragments of mystery and fear, and it bothered him. There was a threat he couldn't see. Or several. He huffed out his frustration.

Sabrina's warning haunted him *"You don't understand what's happening here, Jay. Everything is so messy. You shouldn't be here inside our home. You shouldn't talk to Brandy. You shouldn't be here at all. She won't tell you, either, so don't bother asking."*

She was so guarded, so suspicious of everything. Something huge had happened in the three years that changed her on a molecular level, and he needed to find it and eradicate it. His girl was still in there, fighting to get out. His lips twitched, remembering the laughter and playfulness five days ago. And the way her eyes darkened and burned into his very soul when he kissed her. When she kissed him back. That told an entire other story than the words she spoke.

Jay's knuckles whitened as he gripped the steering wheel. The house was in view, Horace watching him approach from her wood shed bed, her rump slightly dipped to one side in tranquillity.

Sabrina met him at the door, leaning against the frame, her stance ready for battle. Jay's heart sank. He didn't expect this to be easy, but he never counted on the gatekeeper.

"Sabrina, good to see you're feeling better."

"Jay!" Brandy squealed from the depths of the house and the sound of her tiny legs built until a small figure leapt into his arms. Jay caught her and swung her up, snuggling into her hair. She smelled of innocence and light, and it filled his lungs.

"Hey, Sass! You been up to mischief today?" He poked her soft belly and she collapsed into giggles. She pressed a warm palm against his face.

"Not fiwfy." She noted. His grin faded as he met with Sabrina's stony glare. He slid the toddler to the ground.

"Hey Sass, can you ask Mummy to come out, please?" By Sabrina's icy expression he knew the woman wouldn't oblige.

"I thought I told you to keep away, Jay. Alex did, too, if I understand correctly."

Jay forced a light smile. "You did, and she did, but we made a deal, and I intend to collect. I'll be around for a while. I kept up my end of the bargain. Old John has been resurrected. I was hoping to celebrate over dinner tonight."

Did he imagine a hint of respect in the woman?

"She won't go with you." She dropped her glance. Her words were heavy.

"Why not, Sabrina? I haven't even asked her yet." Jay crossed his arms.

"She's going out on a date tonight."

Her monotone knifed him in the stomach. Everything faded but for her words. A date? The lump in his throat threatened to choke him and he heard the sound as he swallowed it. Perhaps he read it all wrong. He'd never asked if Lexi was seeing anyone. Maybe the signs were there but he'd refused to heed them in his need to hold her. Sabrina watched him intently and he struggled to regain composure.

Like a nightmare, Lexi's footsteps brought her to the doorway, and Jay's mouth dried out. He'd been hoping Sabrina was lying to get him to leave, but there she stood, like a dream in a neat bun, a figure-hugging dress and a dusting of makeup. She had the grace to look guilty.

Jay opened his mouth, thought better of it, and turned away. If she had a boyfriend, he could almost understand her breaking their kiss. But she *had* kissed him back, and that would mean she went behind her boyfriend's back. Perhaps this man was about to have the night of his life, and then be discarded like Lexi did him. Jay's fists balled at his side. She might be adding another notch to her belt tonight, but all he could think about was the image of another man running his hands over *his* woman.

He could hear the tight catch in his own voice as he climbed into the John Deere, his entire body shattered and weak, his chest throbbing painfully.

"I'll see you Monday, Lex."

He couldn't look back.

# CHAPTER 11

## ALEX

"I told you before, Lexi, stop pretending I'm an idiot." Sabrina ushered her inside, ripping a tissue from the box on the hall stand and handing it to her daughter.

Alex pressed it to her eyes gratefully. Her sigh trembled. With slumped shoulders she relented, slipping onto a kitchen chair.

"Oh, Mum. This is so messed up. I finally got over him, and now he's appeared I feel myself sliding backwards again." She caught another tear before it fell.

"Rubbish, Alexandria Arlington! Will you just *stop* lying to me. You are right in front of me. You can't hide it. You *never* got over him. The question now is what are you going to do about it since he's determined to be here for as long as he can." Sabrina's tone was brutal.

She choked on the thought. Her pulse throbbed in delight at the prospect of Jay being close, but her heart wasn't safe, and neither was her family. Through it all, Sabrina had been a wonderful support, holding her through her heartbreak, encouraging throughout her pregnancy, but now it seemed she was fighting her.

"You like him!" It wasn't a question.

Sabrina thinned her lips."I'm just saying, perhaps you should hear him out." Her voice softened.

"But you know what he did, Mum. He's still that guy. Being nice doesn't erase that. I can't trust him, and I can't trust him around Brandy. What if she gets attached and he hurts her, too. Leaves us again. Or takes her away?" Fear exploded inside her. Images of him walking away, grey eyes in cruel slits, Brandy in his arms.

Sabrina snorted. "It's too late for that, Lex. Your daughter - *his* daughter - is besotted with him. And she lights his world. Isn't it obvious? As for him leaving you, stop worrying about the ridiculous. I told him to leave. You told him to leave, and he's adamantly refusing to listen. I'm not saying forgive the man. That's not my call, but I get the impression he's not the big bad ogre you need to believe he is. He might be good for Brandy, too."

Alex stared hard at her hands as she sought the words.

"I don't know if I can trust myself around him, Mum. I mean, its like I just look at him, or he says something to me, and everything inside gets all jumbled up and all my logic and purpose flies out the window. With everything going on, just being able to focus is all I feel I have control of, and he messes with that." She felt her throat constrict again, and fell into silence.

"What else is going on, Lex?" Sabrina's words were low and edged with misgiving.

"I…I can't tell you. You have enough to worry about. It's…nothing really." She hated deceiving her mother, but this was something she needed to work out on her own. Sabrina pursed her lips.

Brandy ran from the front room, past the two women and into her bedroom. The faint stamping of Horace's hooves thudded outside.

"Edward is here." Queasiness lumped in her gut. Sabrina stood with her, then took her daughter in her arms.

"I love you, sunshine, but you need to stop *that* nonsense before it goes too far." She jerked her head towards the approaching footsteps. Alex nodded stiffly.

"I love you, too, Mum."

Edward was dressed in his police uniform, and Alex's stomach twisted. He lived in those clothes, flashing them around like a badge of power. He grinned smugly at her as he helped her into the police car. It felt wrong to be sitting there with him, but she was running out of excuses to hold him off. She knew he was capable of tearing her life apart, and was constantly on the precipice of wielding that power.

"You look good enough to eat tonight." He leered over her, resting his appraisal on her chest. She crossed her arms tightly, trying to make it seem natural.

"You could at least give me a smile." He ordered tightly. She summoned a faint smile, and he showed his teeth at her.

"That's better, darlin'. We're going to have ourselves a great night."

He slowed his car as Jay's van crawled out from the lane way. Edward waited a moment, then accelerated hard, cutting off Jay, and causing Alex to grab the door handle to steady herself. Edward's lip curled. Alex peered into the van, but the tinted windows wouldn't allow a glimpse.

"See that? That idiot was going to ram me!" He snarled. Alex shrunk into the seat. Her stomach was boiling with unease.

Edward looked at her sideways as he bounced down the driveway.

"What the hell is he doing back here anyway? I thought you said he wasn't coming back?"

"He wasn't, but Jimmy said he could fix it, and I could pay it off later." The lie slipped easily from her tongue.

He grunted in response. He turned up the volume of his police scanner and spent the hour's drive into town explaining what all the codes meant. Alex was grateful he was happy to do the talking. She tuned out as the farms flashed by, contemplating her Mother's words. Jay *had* been told to leave and insisted on staying, he did seem to genuinely enjoy spending time with Brandy, too. She couldn't remember Edward making an effort with Brandy at all. He didn't even try to build a relationship with her. He seemed to happily ignore her existence for the most part. Not that Alex had ever considered a future with the cop. Or anything for that matter.

"Do you understand, darlin'?" Alex was ripped from her thoughts and she whipped her head around.

"What?"

"Where's your pretty head at, girl? When I ask you on a date, I expect that your focus will be on me, not farm work."

She clenched her jaw."Sorry, Edward, I was listening, but I got distracted by your scanner, and missed what you said."

He laughed, loud and harsh.

"It's hard to have two things to think about at once, isn't it, beautiful?" The condescending bastard. He leaned across and switched off the scanner, probably assuming Alex was impressed enough.

"I was asking if you understood that any wife of mine won't work. She wouldn't need to. I'd provide completely for her and my sons." Bile rose in her throat. She was feeling more and more like she needed to escape. His eyes cut over to her.

"Yes, I understand. You must be on good money if you can do that." Edward flashed her another oily grin before launching into how fast he climbed the ranks in the force, and how he is certain he will be sergeant before long. Alex chewed the inside of her mouth, nodding and exclaiming at each pause. It was already a long night.

Of course he took her to the pub for dinner. There were other restaurants in town, but he couldn't show off his prize there. He was pissing on his territory, showing the town Alex belonged to him. Nobody would dare approach her when Edward staked his claim.

They were shown to a table positioned against the window, intimate enough to display the nature of their dinner. Edward ordered a red wine and steak for her, without bothering to ask. Rage bubbled inside and she fought to appear neutral. She didn't like red wine at all, but alcohol was alcohol tonight, and she was needing a little something to help take the edge off her fury and disgust.

When the wine appeared, she grabbed it and took a gulp.

"Whoa up, girlie! We haven't toasted yet!" He chuckled obnoxiously. His lecherous eyes devoured her, lingering hungrily on her chest. In the generous sized room, Alex couldn't help but feel claus-trophobic as she shuddered. If she could just get through tonight, it would buy her some time before he hounded her again.

He raised his glass and tapped it to hers like a shrill death knell "to us, darlin'. To a night we'll never forget."

Alex choked as he sipped his, icy blue eyes boldly conveying his intention over his glass.

Cold sweat broke out over her body. She knew what he wanted, and that she wouldn't have a choice but to let him take it one day. She hoped it wasn't tonight. She scanned the pub for exits. She wouldn't give in without a fight. As she searched, she was drawn to the man staring at her from near the bar. Her new neighbour, Daniel, sat alone on a stool, beer in hand, a frown directed at her. She threw an attempted smile at the familiar face and raised her hand in greeting.

"Who is that?" Edward bit out.

"He's just my new neighbour. I met him the other day. Pete is moving him and his wife…"

"He's a bit young to be buying a farm. Probably drug money. You'd best keep away from him." He dismissed her.

Edward continued talking about himself over dinner. Alex toyed with her steak, unable to stomach it over the tumbling dread. Edward didn't seem to care, or even notice. When their dishes were cleared, he reached out and grasped her hand. Her skin crawled.

"What did you want for dessert?" He asked. Alex blinked in surprise. It was the first time all night he'd asked what she wanted.

"I, uh, I'm not hungry." She murmured. Edward leaned forward, a predatory look on his face, his lips pulled back.

"Oh, darlin'! You're as keen as I am." He tightened his grip on her hand and yanked her from her chair. She pulled at her hand, but his clasp was crushing. Her lungs heaved in horror. She sought out her neighbour, who was watching warily from the stool, his mouth a hard line. She watched him tap the shoulder of a man walking past him, speaking in his ear without dropping his gaze from hers. Who was she fooling? Alex knew that nobody would be brave enough to question the motives of a policeman.

Alex's knees wobbled as Edward dragged her out onto the front porch, opening the passenger door without releasing his hold. Nausea rolled in her stomach.

"Edward! We need you back in here. There's a fight." The door burst open and the publican hollered above the sound of crashing tables and breaking glass. Edward cursed, pain shooting through Alex's hand as he tightened his hold. He appeared indecisive until the sound of a woman screaming rolled out. Alex leapt on the opportunity.

"You have to help them, Edward. They need you." She prompted, appealing to his ego.

"I'll be right back, darlin'. Don't go anywhere." She watched him disappear into the bar, and sagged with relief against the car, holding the fronts of her thighs to keep steady.

"Alex, right?" She lifted her face. Daniel moved cautiously towards her, brows furrowed.

"Yeah. Hi Daniel." She didn't really feel like making small talk, she just wanted to escape the nightmare she was trapped in.

"Apparently, the fight was difficult to get under control. It took so long, the policeman had to call for back-up. The publican told him afterwards that his date was frightened, and was taken home by a neighbour and his wife." Daniel grinned.

Alex absorbed his words slowly as the sound of tables crashing and glasses shattering tumbled from the pub. Her knees and lungs were paralysed, and she couldn't summon her voice.

Daniel stepped closer to her.

"Did you want me to take you home?" he clarified gently. Relieved at the sudden turn of events, Alex nodded furiously, tears of gratitude shimmering.

Daniel took her hand and led her to his car. Her knees still wobbled, but she hesitated, looking between Daniel and his empty vehicle. Was she stepping from the smoke and into the flame? She'd met Daniel once, and although he seemed kind, she didn't trust her own judgement at that moment.

Daniel lifted an eyebrow, and held his left hand up, a gold band nestled tightly around his finger.

"Married. Happily, too. Two years now. I promise I have no ulterior motive."

Alex nodded stiffly.

"Thank you." she whispered, forcing her reluctant body to climb in.

Daniel drove in silence for a while, allowing Alex to settle the rising panic.

"You didn't want to be there with him, did you?" Alex shook her head at his rhetorical question.

"Why didn't you tell him you weren't interested?" That one ripped a huff from her.

"Sometimes we do things we don't like for a reason." She whispered. Daniel studied her for a while. She didn't want to think about it, and certainly not discuss it with a stranger.

"Lucky a fight just happened to break out, then, huh?" He smirked.

"That was you?" Alex gasped, then realised. "Of course it was. I'm truly so grateful, Daniel." She managed a weak, but genuine smile.

"I don't want to pry, but that cop made it crystal clear that you were his property. You realise he will chase away any other blokes who might be interested in you?"

She stiffened, and Daniel waved his wedding band again and she relaxed.

"I don't care about that. Love is overrated. I just wish Edward would just leave me be. I can't get rid of him." Out the window, spots of light from farm kitchens whizzed past.

"You've never been in love?" His mocking gasp of shock made her mouth twitch.

"Once," she whispered.

"And?" he pressed.

"I fell in love with him, and he tore out my heart, ripped it to shreds and wiped his feet on the remains."

"That's brutal! Sorry to hear, Alex. Was it a long relationship?" He queried, his tone lifting suspiciously.

"No." She breathed. She didn't want to go back there. Especially not after tonight.

Silence hung comfortably between them as the farm slid into view.

"Look, it's probably way out of line, but I think you need to know. That cop's been up at Pete's farm almost every day he tells me, and its not to look in on him, either. He's flattened the grass in the lower paddock. The one that…"

"Overlooks my place." She finished for him, her brown orbs impossibly wide.

# CHAPTER 12

## JAY

*H*e paced a path through the hotel room. Lexi was out, with a cop. On a date. He'd watched as they passed, the prick of a cop cutting him off intentionally. They looked like a good pair, he had to admit. With her stunningly gentle look, the handsome young cop matched her perfectly. And Jay was helpless to do anything but let her go with him. His Rolex told him it was 10.30pm. They would have finished dinner by now. Where would they be? Was Lexi tucked away in bed, resting up for tomorrow, or was she..?

He couldn't go there. Jay sat heavily on the side of his bed, raking his fingers through his hair again. Was this what she did? Led a man on only to ditch him the next day, broken and empty and pining for her like Jay was? It didn't sit right with him. And that look on her face as they drove off? He knew they couldn't see him through the tint, but he was positive she looked like a trapped kitten.

He didn't trust the cop. Maybe it was because he was insanely jealous of him, or maybe there was something worthy of distrust.

He'd be sure to find out. He'd ask Daniel. His brother had contacts everywhere that could check him out. If only Daniel would return his calls. He peered at his phone for the hundredth time that night. No messages. No missed calls.

Jay opened the door at the gentle rap.

"Service" the man announced himself, handing over a bottle of brandy and another of cola.

Brandy, he mused, was what Lexi drank that night. He poured himself a glass and took a sip. It was sweeter than Jay liked, but he drank it anyway. Lexi apparently loved the stuff so much she named her daughter after it. By the bottom of the glass, Jay decided Lexi could keep her drink, washing the sugary taste away with the swirl of straight whiskey.

Daniel's name flashed on his phone. Jay snatched the device off the bedside table and scrambled to answer.

"Daniel! What the hell?" he rasped frantically. The whiskey lapped at the sides of his brain. He'd feel that tomorrow.

"Calm down, man. It's okay. She's at home. *Alone*." Jay lay back on the bed in relief as he emptied his lungs.

"I took her home."

Jay was immediately sober as his brother explained what he'd seen.

"Jesus! What the hell is going on?" His jaw hurt from clenching, his fists ached from flexing.

"She wouldn't tell me. She had that look like she was a captive. But there's something else, Jay. I don't think she makes a habit of bedding and ditching guys. She was so terrified she could hardly stand, but she wouldn't get into the car with me until I flashed my wedding ring under her nose."

Jay's heart warmed at that. Maybe there was more to her story, then. Luckily, he had three weeks to find out.

"Do you think you can look into this Edward douche for me? It might be just me, but I just don't trust the guy. If she acted like you say, he must have something big to hold over her. She didn't hesitate to tell *me* to get lost."

"Have you thought that maybe he's the father of her kid?" Jay's brain threatened to pound right out of his head.

"Jay? Jay? Shit, I should have thought before talking. I'll be at your room in ten."

When Daniel arrived, he took in Jay's swaying frame, and the empty bottles on the table.

"You're drunk." He observed. Jay looked at his hands. The fine cracks that had appeared over the last week still held grease. He grinned idiotically at his little brother and held them up to him.

"I'm a mechanic now, Daniel. I'm a farmer and a mechanic, and I haven't been this happy in…ever."

Daniel smirked back at him.

"You still carry it around with you, don't you?" He was referring to the tiny worn bag that held all his hopes and dreams in the front pocket of every pair of pants and jeans he ever wore. Jay patted his hip with an overstated movement. His brother shook his head and grinned.

"You've got it bad, Bro. Look, I have to get back to Tilly, and touch base with my contacts about this cop. You're not needed back here until Monday morning, so you and I are going home."

"What if I want to stay?" He countered, swaying gently. Daniel shook his head.

"She won't have you back til Monday, and if you push it, you might break it. What do they say? Absence makes the heart grow fonder? Let her miss you a bit. Play it cool."

*  *  *

It was healing to sit around the oak table with his family. They had always been close knit, and Joseph and Lydia were the epitome of the happily ever after their sons modelled their own ideals after. The laughter and chatter distracted Jay from his over active imagination, the kilometres between him and Lexi enabling him to keep a firm grasp on his urge to run to her. Daniel was right. She needed a chance to miss him, and if she felt remotely close to the torture he was experiencing, they had a good shot. Daniel had his wife lodged hard against his side, evidence of how difficult he found it to stay apart from her. Jay realised then that Daniel understood how it was for him, too. He watched his little brother appreciatively, wondering how he missed noticing that leap between sandpits and marriage.

Daniel speared Jay with a wide secretive smile, and slowly rose from the table. The conversation dried up and all eyes gravitated toward him.

"We wanted you all to be the first to know." He began. Tilly stood beside him, arm looped around his waist. Lydia squawked, her fist jammed against her mouth, eyes sparkling eagerly. Daniel shot her a wink.

"Tilly and I are officially expanding our family!"

The excitement cascaded over them as they were rained with kisses, hugs and slaps on the back. Jay planted a delighted kiss on Tilly's lips and hugged her tightly.

"I'm so happy for you!" He whispered in her ear. She grinned at him. The moment was bittersweet. As the oldest, it was naturally expected that Jay be the first to marry, settle down and raise a family. Perhaps it could have been him, had he just remained in bed that morning. But for that moment in time, *he* might have been the one floating on air right now. Daniel grabbed him in a firm embrace, slapping him on the back.

"You'll get your happily ever after yet, big brother."

Jay squeezed back. "You'll be an amazing father, Daniel."

Their bellies and their hearts full, they congregated in the comfortable couches in the den. Tilly hurrumphed when a lemonade was passed to her instead of the usual whiskey. Her husband raised an eyebrow at her.

"I'm just practising lamenting all the things I can't enjoy" She muttered sheepishly.

Jay joined them in laughter.

"Jay bought a farm."

Jay glared at the audacity of his brother. He listened as the rattle of the ice in his hand broke the silence, and sighed.

Lydia pounced. "Joseph Junior, where is this coming from? You're supposed to be the predictable one, and you haven't even mentioned it to us." She glanced at her husband who shrugged his agreement.

"You know I've always loved the farm we had, and figured it would be a good investment at this stage. They're not making any more land, so I wanted to find a good slice." Jay reasoned.

"Its a girl" Daniel betrayed his brother with a smirk. Tilly leaned forward.

"It's not just *a* girl. Its *the* girl" She whispered, expression twinkling mischievously.

"Oh, sweet Jesus! Jay, why didn't you tell us?"

Jay shifted awkwardly. "It's not that simple. There's some things I need to find out, and there's a few fences between us yet."

Jay spent the night discussing Lexi at length, and as he lay on the edge of sleep, his thoughts turned to Brandy. He entertained the image of waking up with Lexi's sweet breath curling around him, his arm resting possessively on her hip as Brandy climbed onto the bed and snuggled sweetly between them. His cheeks lifted in the dark. They were a package deal. Lexi, Brandy and Sabrina. His love for Lexi had organically overflowed to incorporate her daughter and mother without him realising.

Jay turned to the left, studying his day's growth in the bathroom mirror. He'd wiped away the condensation, but the reflection was still blurry. He tucked the towel tighter around his hips seconds before the door slammed open, and Tilly tumbled into the room, barely making the toilet bowl before emptying her stomach.

"Shit, Tilly! I could've been naked!" She gasped around the waves of nausea.

"Right now, Jay, your penis, or anyone's for that matter, is of absolutely no interest to me, whatsoever. Besides, with Daniel locked in our ensuite, it was either here or the kitchen." Jay curled his lips in distaste.

Tilly gave him a hard look. "Were you just checking yourself out in the mirror?" She scoffed.

Jay's face burned. "Maybe" He admitted warily. Tilly laughed.

"I'm worried she doesn't like what she sees." He searched his hazy reflection for the man Lexi saw.

"You are the hottest man I've seen in my life besides my husband, Jay. You have the body of a god, the face of a sinful angel and your heart is bigger than all of it. You are the complete package, if you haven't worked it out already with the women piled up at your feet." Tilly gave him a once over. "And yes, give her a day's worth of stubble to get her pulse racing here and there. I can't wait to meet this woman."

# CHAPTER 13

## ALEX

The usual Edward-induced migraine wasn't as bad as Alex expected this time around. Her frown deepened as she mulled over her dinner with him, and the fortunate escape, thanks to her new neighbour. As promised, he'd left the security camera box at the front door for her. He couldn't install it himself, he said, because he had an early flight that day to meet up with his wife. Alex wasn't great with electronics. Her strength was in the twist of barbed wire and the herding of cattle, but she never backed down from a challenge. She'd managed to raise an image of the entire kitchen, and the front door, but the intricacies of the program used were a bit beyond her. She'd ask Jay to set it up when he arrived Monday. She silently berated herself for allocating tasks to a man she was supposed to be removing from her life, not solidifying his presence with jobs. She dumped the net of cables on top of the camera and met her mother in the hallway.

"Are you ready, Mum?"

Sabrina nodded happily, tugging guiltily at Alex's insides. She'd looked over the herd, finding they were in better condition than she'd initially thought. Only another few days and the cattle could be sent to market, and she hoped it would be enough to finance another term at the care facility for Sabrina. Brandy was old enough to come with her to work, and just like Alex would grow up riding the tractor.

"I know what you're thinking, Lex. Don't go there. I love watching Brandy grow. Most grandparents don't get to see as much of their grandkids as they'd like. I consider myself fortunate." She leaned over and squeezed Alex's hand. Alex chewed her lip, offering a gentle nod to hide the determination in her jaw.

The journey into town was uneventful. Alex found herself scanning the roadsides and main street for a certain dark haired god, with a blend of anticipation and trepidation.

"You're thinking about him, aren't you?" Sabrina smirked.

"Nope. I don't know what you're talking about, Mother." The formal chill in her voice brought Sabrina to laughter.

"It's almost a pity I won't be back until Tuesday night. You'll have to catch me up on what I miss."

"There will be nothing to tell." The retort pushed through clenched teeth.

Alex rammed the last of the posts in with Brandy bouncing around in excitement in the cabin of the tractor. There was something grounding and fulfilling about her daughter constantly being in her space. She felt like she spent too many hours away from Brandy, and she needed this time with her as much as Sabrina needed to socialise with someone outside of a 2 year old. She picked up the rolls of wire and extra posts with the tines while Brandy pointed excitedly where they needed to be taken. She was all set for the repair of the bull paddock, so she took Brandy over to the ancient cattle yards. She could use Daniel's yards to load her marketable beasts, but she still needed halfway decent yards to bring the calves in to tag, immunise and castrate them. She grinned at her daughter who was climbing through the long grass beside the cattle race.

"Jay is going to regret asking for my help, isn't he, Princess?"

"Jay?" Brandy's head bobbed up as she searched for him.

"He's not here yet, Princess. Tomorrow." She was hoping she wasn't building her daughter's hopes needlessly. He'd stiffened up, the cords in his neck tight when he saw her dressed up for her date. His biceps almost tore his shirt. Maybe he'd decided that it wasn't worth the effort after all, and not show. Somewhere in her soul, Alex knew he'd be there. She just hoped he wouldn't be irritated by Brandy dancing about them all day. She was vaguely aware that it was more important than it should be that he like Brandy. She mentally shrugged it off. After all, Brandy would be an effective barrier between them, ensuring Jay behaved himself, keeping out of her personal space, and even further away from her heart.

Alex gave Horace a hug. The mare rubbed her chin on the girl's shoulder.

"I don't know what I'd do without you, girl."

Horace had dragged the low cart into the barn, loaded with tools in preparation for the morning. Brandy giggled and squealed in delight as she ordered Horace about.

"Walk on!" She demanded, mimicking her mothers instructions. Horace obliged instantly, drawing laughter from the toddler.

"Woah up!" She cried, moments later. Horace complied. At the sudden halt Brandy unbalanced and tipped onto the floor of the tray, her tiny body convulsing in laughter that was bigger than her. Alex laughed until her belly ached. There was no doubt Brandy was the best thing that had ever happened to her. After unhitching the mare, Alex swept her daughter up, depositing her on Horace's bare back and headed for home. Brandy clutched a fistful of mane to keep her balance.

Alex frowned at the storm clouds building in the north west. They billowed and growled from the horizon in the eerie stillness of twilight.

"Storm, Mummy."

"Yeah. Looks like I'll be snuggling up with you tonight, Princess." Brandy's grey eyes sparkled. Alex expelled the emotion in her lungs. She missed spending time with Brandy. The days never appeared quite so long when her daughter shared them. Alex slid Brandy off the mare and frowned with unease as she watched Horace clop slowly towards the barn. If the horse was taking cover, they were in for a wild night.

It was just past midnight when the old redgum beside the house lost its footing to the wind and toppled over. The progressive crack and snap as the wood fibres battled and lost echoed past the wall of raging wind. The ground shuddered, and the high pitched twangs of wires stretching and separating ripped Alex from sleep. Brandy whimpered in her arms.

"It's okay, princess, it's just a tree fallen over." In the light of the moon, Brandy's eyes were wide with fear.

"Is it going to get us?" Her voice wobbled. Alex brushed a loose lock of hair from her forehead.

"No, sweetheart. It can't fall any further." The toddler blinked, unconvinced.

"How about we have a look?" Tiny fists crushed Alex's shirt as she nodded. Pulling a blanket from the bed and wrapping it around the both of them, Alex lugged her warm bundle onto the verandah. The wind roared like a demon, raging over the hills and through the valleys, the mighty gums scattered throughout her paddocks bowing in surrender in the half-light. Loose roof tin shuddered and clacked around them. The silhouette of the fallen gum made Alex's heart sink.

"Honey, the tree broke the wires. I'm going to have to cut it off the fence and fix it."

"Do it in the morning?" The child implored.

"I can't, love. See how it broke the fence? That's where the cows are, and if I don't fix it, the cows will get out. You can watch from my room where it's warm" Tiny red lips pouted, but sleep was already creeping back in. She knew the herd would have run from the noise of the falling tree, but their curiosity would win them over before long, so she didn't have much time. She popped Brandy into her bed with instructions to use the torch to get her attention if she needed anything.

Alex fetched the chainsaw from the woodshed and pointed her ute lights at the tangle of limbs and leaves. She shut off the power to the fences and drowned out the storm as her saw roared to life. After a while she couldn't feel the wind. The smaller branches fell away under the hungry wail of the chain. She stopped only to refuel and re sharpen the teeth on the chain. Horace plodded out of the barn to watch, ears back against the noise, and kept warm darting at the cattle to keep them penned.

Lightning drenched the farm in light. The crack of thunder broke above the hills. Alex gritted her teeth as the last of the canopy fell away from the fence line. Hastily, she snagged her spare set of wire strainers and set about repairing wires. Once the first strand was secured, Horace took shelter in the woodshed. Her work was done. As Alex reconnected the last strand, the first drop of rain splashed against her hand. She looked up into a sky that swallowed the moon, and lightning flickered. Alex saw the wall of rain closing in and grabbed her tools, almost throwing them in the shed before she flicked the power back on and scrambled up the verandah. She heard it pounding into the paddocks behind the homestead.

Hail.

"Horace!" She shouted. The mare's head yanked up.

"Over here, girl." Her head swung around, and she casually strolled up the steps and into the kitchen as the hail bashed against the tin roof. Alex moved aside the table to give her more room, Horace folding her feet beneath her and sank to her belly on the wooden floor. Alex grinned as the mare settled in for the night, then slipped in to check on Brandy. She lay curled in the centre of the bed, blankets swamping her, a light snore bubbling in her throat. Sound asleep. Removing the torch from against her forehead, Alex felt her own body sagging in fatigue. She made her way drunkenly to the lounge room, pulling the throw over her as she slumped into the cushions of her couch.

Around her, the storm raged and burned out. The hail eased, and the clock ticked 5am.

# CHAPTER 14

## JAY

The clock flicked over to 5.30am. Threads of excitement wormed through his veins. He would be seeing her today. All day. The memory of her lips pressing against his with a hunger that rivalled his own brought every molecule to life. He rubbed a hand over yesterday's growth and grinned. He wouldn't be shaving today. He pulled on his shirt, tucking the tails into his worn jeans. Tilly had picked them out for him especially. His reflection practised casually rolling the Akubra in place. He snorted at his nervousness, and grabbed the lunch bag he'd rummaged up last night.

Jay breathed in deeply, snatched the keys from the counter and headed for the ute he'd borrowed off Jimmy. His own car wouldn't handle the potholes. He'd already decided to trade it in for something more worthy of a farm.

6am. An hour to get there. He was sure farmers rose with the sun.

Horace didn't come to greet him, and he paused uncertainly. They hadn't discussed a time, so there was a possibility she was already out in the paddock. With the storm last night, there was likely fences down. An odd thud sounded softly from inside the house, enticing Jay to the door. He turned the handle and almost leapt from his skin as Horace pushed the door wide, bunting the man aside as she made her way to the garden and lifted her tail. Jay stifled a chuckle and shook his head. The woman was crazy.

He located her sleeping form sprawled out on the couch as if by instinct. The excitement of breathing her air again slowly contorted into something more carnal as he lowered to his knees, hungrily studying her. Wood shards decorated her hair like burned out stars, buried in the honeyed tangles resting around her. Her long lashes caging in the mysteries of her dreams, her luscious pout open around her soft breaths. Jay's pulse picked up. He'd kissed the creamy decadence of that graceful neck. He'd explored that body hidden beneath the blanket. He'd felt how they fitted so perfectly together, without a breath of space between them. He'd revelled in the light shudder of her skin as his fingertips had teased, worshipped, loved. Love. It was in everything between them, set in stone, locked in the certainty of their DNA. Their fate woven intricately together through the fibres of space and time. She was his.

He gasped when he saw her eyes were open and locked on him, and Jay realised he was laid bare before her. Everything he felt, the truth of what he knew was in the raging heat of his stare, open and vulnerable and spilling out for her to see. His heart hammered in his chest, trying to reach her through his skin. Flesh prickled and heated with the intrinsic need to touch her. His swallow shifted loudly. She didn't break contact, courageously digesting everything he wasn't saying. He gave it all to her. He was helpless to do otherwise. He showed her the years he searched, the desperation, the agony. He showed her everything that made his heart beat. His unwavering certainty of her. Of them. She blinked languidly and a ruptured tear slid free. He watched its path, his lungs tearing with the need to ease her pain. It was too big to resist. With a low growl he dug her off the couch and pulled her close against his chest, the exquisite agony as her arms, warm from sleep locked together around his back. The air hissed between his teeth with the magnitude of her perfection. He dipped his head and touched his nose to her neck, nostrils flaring as her vanilla scent lodged in his lungs. He snaked his fingers into her hair, possessive and protective as she nestled against him. His muscles strained with the force of his need to touch all of her to all of him, to etch every inch of her into his very chromosomes.

He felt her slack as she relaxed. Reluctant to release her, he didn't loosen his hold. The feather-light stroke of her fingertips inched down the valley of his spine. Jay's throat bobbed. His body coiled as hunger boiled in his veins. She landed a finger on the belt, then fisted the cotton shirt slowly from his jeans. Jay's head dropped back, air rasping from his parted lips, grey steel dimming to black.

A shudder ripped through him as her warm fingers connected with flesh. She traversed his ridges and edges with excruciatingly cautious tenderness.

"Christ, Lexi, what are you doing?" He didn't want to break the spell, but he had no control when it came to her.

She sunk to the ends of his embrace like a feline, hooded eyes conveying what her touch already told him. She lifted one hand, feeling the texture of his stubble, then followed his jawline grazing his lips as she moved. He groaned softly. She dropped her eyes to his shirt, her fingers freeing the buttons as Jay held her to him. He matched her heavy breaths, the sensation of both her hands on his bare chest sending shock waves through his brain, the animal within rising wild and wired over any rational thought still prevailing.

She reached the line of soft hair thickening beneath his navel, leading below the band of his jeans, following the trail nature mapped out for her. With the last molecule of control he had, Jay caught her wrist. Jaw twitching, breath hissing he warned her.

"Lexi, if you go any further....I won't be able to stop. It's been three fucking years, Lex. I can only bear so much."

Lexi snatched her hand away suddenly, pushing away from him in a flurry of arms. Pain scrunched her beautiful flushed face.

"You *knew*?" Damn. He stabbed his fingers through his hair in frustration. Him and his idiot mouth. His entire body heaved in objection at the loss of her touch. He wanted to scream. He was so close.

"Lex" he pleaded, but her chin lifted, and the warm fire that burned before was replaced by a barren wasteland of cold fury.

"You knew it was me the moment you saw me, and you pretended I was a stranger? Was it that embarrassing for you, Jay? A regrettable hook-up? And what did you think this was going to be? Huh? Round two because it had been a bit too long between drinks for you. I guess since I was a sure thing back then, that it's a given I'd be up for another tumble?" The acid in her voice poisoned his lungs. Her rage settled over her entire demeanour. Her fight, her spirit, they made his heart hum. Part of him was shattered that he'd opened his mouth and taken their relationship backwards, but this part of him, the one that acknowledged her defiance, brought him closer to her. Lexi riled up was breathtaking. His response trapped in his throat.

"Mummy?" Their eyes darted over to the toddler standing swaying with remnants of sleep in the doorway. Her face lit up suddenly.

"*Jay!*" She squealed at him, laughing around delighted tears as she launched at him. Jay caught her and swung her into a snuggle.

"Hey Sass! I missed you." Thin arms threatened to cut off his airways. His admission took him by surprise. He missed Brandy. The weight of what that meant wasn't lost on him.

"A tree fell down, and there was a big storm and lots of rain!" Brandy chattered. Jay laughed at her. Even with the destruction he'd created, Brandy could still make his heart sing.

Ignoring the icy glare from Lexi, Jay carried her to the kitchen.

"Okay, Sass, you tell me about it while I make you some toast." He could almost hear Lexi gnashing her teeth at him. He cocked his head at her, watching as passion flared up, engaging her wrath in battle as she stormed through the doorway to shower.

Brandy danced around the kitchen as the smell of toast wafted through the room. Jay was awed by the boundless energy exuding from her even though the shadows under her eyes revealed her exhaustion. She bounced to the fridge, ricochetted to the table, and flung herself over to the hall stand where she came to a stop. With the finesse of habit, she brought two fingers to her lips and pressed them against the framed picture. Jay froze against her action. He glanced up the hallway, and seeing no sign of Lexi, he crouched before the girl.

"You love him, don't you?" It scratched at his throat to utter the words. Her response stabbed him in the heart.

"Mummy and me love him this big." And she flung her arms as wide as she could, her lungs bursting with effort. Jay's neck bobbed thickly. He offered a weak smile, then went back to smear peanut butter on her toast.

# CHAPTER 15

## ALEX

She felt like a naive fool. She'd wanted him with a need that shocked her. He would have taken what she offered, too, and no doubt be gone before the sun set that night. She groaned and bit down on her lip in frustration. She'd started it, really. She'd taken a comforting embrace straight into foreplay. But he was so hard. The flexing, twitching power of him. It was more than his muscles. He was pure masculine strength in the shape of a sinful god, enticing her to return to that night with wanton abandon, and she would have gone there in a heartbeat. Then that rumbling velvet tumbled over the truth. He'd remembered her. He remembered, and he hadn't responded until she'd thrown herself at him. Ugh! When she broke through the humiliation, she gave it deeper thought. The way he looked when he thought she slept was arresting. She didn't know what it meant, but it completely saturated her. The bunch and lunge of his craving liquefied her, but the way he didn't just look at her but reached out across the air with grey fingers and ran them through her heart… that was the greatest aphrodisiac of all. In that moment she almost believed in forever.

Alex closed her eyes under the water jet. It was going to be a long three weeks.

\* \* \*

As she padded down the hall, the warm sounds of conversation indicated Jay and Brandy were still in the kitchen. Jay's nostrils flared as she approached, raking his gaze down her old pale blue shirt and fitted jeans. He subconsciously licked his lips as his gaze lingered on the rip spanning her upper thigh. When the cattle sold she'd replace them, too. She glared at him, reminding him that she wasn't forgiving him just because he fed her daughter. He quirked an eyebrow and handed over a plate with two slices of toast.

"A chef, now, are we?" she bit out. Amusement sparkled in his incredible eyes as he dipped to a bow.

"Anything for the lady." His drawl tingled. His unshaven jaw and hair tousled from earlier completing the picture of a wicked Prince Charming come rugged cowboy.

"What else do you cook?" she challenged.

"I can cook up a mean cereal in the blink of an eye." He threw her a lopsided grin. Damn but he fired up her pulse. She rolled her eyes and scowled to hide her smile.

With a curl of her finger, she led Jay and Brandy outside. Passing Ryan's photo, she pressed a two fingered kiss to it.

"Brandy misses her dad, huh?" His voice was tight and it pulled Alex up short. She caught her breath and shot a look of confusion at the man. He stared at Ryan's photo, the one where he was hugging her with Brandy in her arms. He thought her brother was Brandy's father? Her pulse clattered. She really looked at the picture then, noting how different her and her brother were. Ryan was the spit of their father, dark hair, darker complexion, different shaped face. Except for their eyebrows, they could have been perfect strangers. She hovered on the edge of honesty and self-preservation. Reluctant to spin a web of lies, she was also remiss to reveal the truth. That would open her up for more questions she wasn't prepared to answer. She stared at the back of her daughter's hair, dark like her father's. She chewed over the many times she had asked if Jay was coming over. She did pine for Jay when he wasn't around.

"Yes, she does." Fact. Deadpan fact, her tone indicating she didn't want to discuss the subject.

"You miss him, too." Statement. She saw his shoulders tighten. She looked at Jay and brought up the memory of her and Jay in the bar, dancing so close their flesh merged, when their expressions were free and honest, and so deeply *inebriated* with each other. Yes. She missed that Jay so much her heart ached. And Ryan. Alex missed him so so much. She nodded tightly and stifled the twinge of guilt.

She took in the damage from the tree she wasn't able to see clearly last night. The root ball had torn from the ground, leaving a pond in the crater it left. The wood could be cut up and be dried ready for next winter, which was great, but filling in the hole, cleaning up the branches - it all required time she didn't have.

"I can help you cut it up if you like." The offer grated. She didn't need help. She needed more daylight hours.

"Don't have time. I have to get the bull paddock fenced off."

Jay hadn't moved. He took in the debris, the reconnected wires, the scatter of discarded branches. There were hours of work in those piles.

"Did you sleep last night?" She shrugged and shook her head.

"Now I feel like a complete jerk waking you up. Did you want to have a rest?"

The concern in his voice riled. He wasn't in a position to be able to offer compassion. That was the right of someone who actually cared, somebody who wasn't in the business of traipsing across her heart to scratch an itch.

"If I took a rest every time I needed one, Jay, nothing would get done."

Horace walked along beside them, the sound of her hooves against the packed lane way soothing. With the sun beginning to burn the moisture off the grass, Alex couldn't help but smile. The further from the house they got, the more liberated she felt. Jay slipped into thoughtful silence since leaving the house, and used to her own company, she fell into a gentle hum. She began to chatter to Horace about the work needed in each paddock, the schedule for the day, and tools she must remember.

She glanced back and felt her face flush. Jay was watching her closely as he struggled to keep up, Brandy heavy and oozing in sleep over his broad chest.

"I'm used to it just being Horace and I. I forgot you were there." She apologised.

"You talk to yourself?" He quizzed.

"All the time. It helps me think, even if it's only a horse I bounce my ideas off."

His lip twitched. "Argue much?" Jay grinned lightly.

Alex laughed. "Actually, Fighting myself is one of the negatives about a solo conversation. When I fight my own ideas with logic, it can get nasty."

"Which wins?"

"Unfortunately, it's always the ideas pushing past the logic. I won't tell you some of the horrendous mistakes I've made. I always bury them out in the paddocks and never mention them to anyone. It's why I'm grateful Horace can't talk. She'd probably have me locked up in a loony bin by now if she could."

Jay's chuckle rumbled. Brandy was slipping further and further down his chest.

"I'm sorry you were left to carry Brandy. I know better than most that she can gain fifty kilos the second her eyes close. We're here now. Put her in the shade next to the fence and Horace can watch her." He looked down at her face, slack and angelic in sleep. He shuffled her carefully, arranging her softly on the patch of soft grass. Alex's hand clutched her chest. Watching Jay handle his daughter with such fragility touched her on a primal level.

"She's no trouble at all, in fact..." He looked sheepishly down at her sleeping form and rubbed the back of his neck "She's pretty amazing." Alex didn't know how to respond to that so she pressed her lips together.

"I'll bet you were delighted when you found out you were pregnant." His voice held a warm tenderness. She snorted and Jay's eyes narrowed on her.

"She was actually a...surprise. A big surprise. I was so careful. Took precautions, you know. Never even contemplated a baby. Figured I had all the time in the world to worry about motherhood."

"What changed?"

Alex blew out a breath. "I had no symptoms at all. By the time I found out, I'd passed the first trimester, so I didn't have a choice in it. Not that I mind now, though. If I could go back in time, knowing what I know now, well, I'd still do it."

"Why Brandy?" His voice held a soft curiosity.

"I'm not great at names. Exhibit A" She gestured to Horace standing guard over the girl.

He grinned. His amusement touched his eyes, almost hidden beneath the sexy tilt of his Akubra. Her lungs stuttered. He appeared to fill the air with his presence. So big, so broad. A creation of strength and masculinity in tight jeans. The ultimate cowboy specimen. All he needed was a bull he could wrap those powerful legs around. His focus on her tightened. She wet her lips with the tip of her tongue and Jay smirked as his gaze heated and darkened. He'd caught her staring again. She turned her back on him, squaring her shoulders.

"Her father didn't help name her?"

Her mouth dried out. *Don't lie, Alex.*

*He slid the drink over in front of her. His deep murmur shot shivers through her body.*

*"Brandy?" He invited. The way his mouth formed around it had her lungs hitching. He was the most incredibly potent and attractive man she'd ever seen, and although whiskey was her drink of choice,*

*if he'd asked her to drink straight vodka all night she would have. Never had a word sounded so perfect.*

"He kinda did…enough talk. Lets get to work."

Teaching Jay was easy. He listened intently, watched carefully and asked intelligent questions. He learned how to use the wire strainers to pull the wire taut, as well as utilising the contours of it to fasten the stay sets. The stay sets were two uprights, connected with a post between them, fastened and tightened to create a strong frame to tension the wires off. Without stay sets, the tight wires would pull the fence posts sideways.

She taught him to measure and mark where the wires would sit up the post, and asked him to attach the insulated ratchets used to tighten the wires when they sagged and loosened in the summer heat. She was lulled by the soothing timbre of his voice as he told her about his family, and how his brother and sister in law were expecting their first child. His pleasure was organic and honest. Jay was a man who would adore a family of his own, chatting over a beer on the verandah in the summer twilight, throwing the footy around with his kids, or snuggled up in front of the warm fire with them curled around him in winter.

Sadness crept in knowing that one day he would have the family he wanted, and disappear from her life again. This time forever. Edward wouldn't allow her to pursue a future with Jay, but she was becoming increasingly reluctant to let him go.

# CHAPTER 16

## JAY

*I*t was painful trying to suppress the queasiness rolling about his stomach hearing about Brandy's father. He had to know, though. He needed to know who his competition was. Lexi seemed hesitant to elaborate, and he'd really learned nothing about him. Clearly, his death may have occurred a year ago but was still so fresh and raw. Blended with her pain of her absent husband were the obvious signs of her attraction to him. It was becoming increasingly difficult to retain his mask of indifference when her body screamed for him to touch, to taste, to love.

The thick wire was hard on his hands, but it felt good to bend it, twist it, tighten it and turn it into something useful. His efforts would be part of the soul of Alex's farm forever, and that was a comforting thought. They worked easily and fluidly together. She was a competent teacher, explaining before he asked the reasons behind her methods, and considered his questions and suggestions with seriousness and excitement.

A sudden heavy huff caught his attention. She stood so close he could scent her but her mind was far away. Her tidy ponytail had loosened and been caught roughly in a bun on the top of her head. He saw the perfect arc of her spine straightening out the stiffness. Her face glowed slightly from the kiss of the sun, and her tantalising mouth was drawn in a line. Her brown eyes were firm and flickered with annoyance. Horace stamped behind them, and Alex tightened her jaw towards the house. The sun glinted off those same red and blue beacons he'd seen rolling in before.

"Are you okay?"

She shuttered her expression, shoving a packet of insulators at his chest. "Just hammer these in on the marks we made." She ordered tersely, bending back into work fiddling intently with the ratchet fittings. She wanted him to be far away from her, and until he knew more, he would oblige.

Jay positioned himself so that as he hammered, he could watch from his periphery.

Alex stood straight and sudden like she'd just noticed the car pull up. He noticed her chin drop, and her arms wrap around her waist protectively.

The cop prowled from the drivers side, focusing on Jay's figure. He called out to Jay, not a greeting, but essentially a command to acknowledge his authority. Jay bristled, but ignored him, continuing his hammering. When the cop barked louder, Jay made a show of startling before touching his hat in return without revealing his face. The less that scum knew of him, the better for everyone.

Unable to hear their words, Jay listened to their tones. He dominated her, demanding her response, her attention. Her voice tight and wary. Jay's fists itched as he watched the cop move further into her space. He reached out to touch her chin, and she flinched, but allowed his hand to lift her face level with his. He stepped forward, wedging her against a post. Lexi stiffened, lifting her hands to his chest, forcing distance between them.

The hammer slammed to the grass, and Jay's teeth ground, Couldn't he see Lexi didn't like it? Before he was aware, he was standing beside them, fists clenched.

"I don't think the lady is comfortable with you up in her space." He growled. Shock wrenched Lexi's face to Jay's.

"Who the fuck are you to tell me what I should and shouldn't be doing?" Arctic blue locked on silver. Lexi slid away as the officer turned on Jay.

"Someone who understands what sexual harassment means."

The cop stepped towards Jay, hand dipping to rest on the gun holstered at his waist, teeth bared. Eyes narrowed to slits. Jay stood firm, refusing to be intimidated. He kept his gaze hard and steady. He could smell the adrenaline between them. The cop might be armed, but Jay was confident he was faster, stronger, and ready to do what was needed to ensure his Lexi was safe from this man.

The two men stood locked in silent battle. The cop was the first to back down. He snarled his loathing, then stalked back to the patrol car, snatching at Lexi's arm possessively as he passed.

"Get rid of him." He squeezed his order into her flesh.

Jay sidled up to Lexi, offering wordless support as the dust plumed behind retreating wheels.

"You shouldn't have done that" Her voice thin and guarded.

"He was all over you, Lex. It was pretty damn obvious you didn't like it."

"That's not your call to make!" Her words trembled.

"What's going on? Don't lie to me. You're the strongest woman I know, yet you let that tosser touch you. Something's up, and you need to tell me." A fire engulfed her. Her delicate chin lifted and anchored in magnificent rage.

"And why is it that you think yourself so special that I confide in you? You are no better than him, turning up when I tell you to leave, making your own rules without consulting me, and do I even need to remind you that until this morning, you refused to admit you remembered...." Her fury heaved in her chest. Her next words laced with pain.

"I mean, why DID you leave? If you didn't want me any more you could have just told me. To wake up alone, after you made me feel so....safe and cherished. That hurt, Jay. It was the only time I gave myself to a man on an impulse, and you left me feeling like a cheap whore!"

Jay's chest ached, the layers of regret engulfing him. His neck bobbed as he drank in her honesty. Maybe it was time to explain. Not all of it. She wasn't ready for that. They weren't ready for that. Yet.

"I didn't leave, Lex. Not really. I stepped out to get...coffee. When I came back you were already gone. I must have woken you when I shut the door, because I wasn't gone more than ten minutes..."

"Rubbish" She snapped. "There was coffee in the room, Jay, I'm not an idiot. I know I meant nothing to you, because..." She broke off as grief clouded her expression. Her accusation irritated him. She had no idea how she'd haunted him for three damn years.

"When I found you gone, Lex, I looked for you. It wasn't like that, I promise you. It wasn't a cheap hook-up for me. You have to know that."

Her rage took flight. "Would you just shut your goddamn mouth, Jay? The more you speak, the more you reinforce how full of shit you really are. You'd say anything if it means you'd get your dick wet again."

The injustice rankled. His own temper rose. "You don't know me, Lex. You can't tell me what I did when you weren't there, you can't assume my motives. It meant something then, and it means something now."

Exasperation surged through his veins. She was too stubborn to see reason. She tested the boundaries of his restraint. The disbelief curled her lips, the ferocity of her breaking his resolve.

Jay closed the space between them, pinning her head with a fistful of hair as he crashed his mouth savagely on hers. Sweet Jesus, the taste of her! He groaned into her mouth as her hands slid up around his neck, fingers buried deep in his hair, tipping his hat to the ground. There was no resistance, her hunger as great and as large as his. He swallowed her whimper, her lips parting for him. He dipped and teased, swirling his tongue against hers until he ran out of air. He bent down, letting his lips explore her jaw, flicked his tongue against the thundering pulse in her neck. She gasped when he reached the base of her neck. *Christ.* He had to stop now... before he couldn't.

He stepped back, on the razor's edge of control. Her head tilted towards the sun, her mouth parted in amorous sensation.

"Look at me, Lex!" He rasped. "And tell me you mean nothing to me!"

# CHAPTER 17

## ALEX

From her swollen lips, through her pounding heart and into her very soul she felt him. Her knees threatened to give way, and her inhales were short and shallow.

His maleness was so erotically savage and brutally arousing that her brain refused to function. She was compelled to press herself against him, keep heading down into that abyss she craved. She remembered how he made her body react, and she wanted to feel that again. To lose herself in the hot embrace of delicious sin.

He stood facing her, his wide chest straining for oxygen. The pulse at his neck thundered like a raging bull. She swallowed and dropped her gaze. His erection pressed painfully against his zipper, and she licked her lips. She burned to reach for him, release him from his jeans and feel him deep inside her body. She forced her head up. His beautiful mouth was puffy with passion, his hair in a sexy tousle. But his eyes! Black and wild with arousal, they blazed with more than lust, something deeper than desire. Alex was drawn into them, heat surging between her legs. They held an intensity that spoke to her soul, called to her on a primitive level.

"Do you see it, Lexi? Do you see what you do to me?" His thick voice rolled over her in a caress of liquid fire and air. "I don't just want you in my bed, Lexi. I want you in my life. I think you want it too, but you need to let me in."

Things were getting too complicated. Edward wanted Jay gone, and if he wanted Jay gone, she had no choice but to make that happen. But Jay was still poised before her in all his primal beauty, begging to be touched. She realised she didn't want Jay to leave.

"I can't." Her voice was a mere whisper. He brought his intoxicating heat against her again, and she couldn't hide the groan that escaped her.

"Can't what? Be with me?" She looked into his face and saw the fear, the desire, the uncertainty etched in every muscle and line.

"I can't tell you, Jay." He'd been bracing for rejection, and he let out a soft sigh of relief.

"Okay, Lex. I'll let it go for now, but I hope you will trust me enough to tell me soon."

They stood in the long grass in a tight embrace, pretending that they didn't want to tear each other's clothes off.

Brandy awoke full of energy. As if she'd expected him gone, she squealed when she saw Jay and flung herself at him. Alex tried to clear her head. Jay was already planted so firmly in her heart that she couldn't consider letting him go again. And he wanted more than just a fling? She watched him as he lifted her daughter, his daughter, and perched her on his shoulders like they'd done it a hundred times before, her chirping giggle colliding with Jay's chuckle. Alex caught her breath. This would have been perfect, the three of them, but with Edward in the picture, she wasn't destined to be happy. She was destined to play his cruel game until he grew tired of her. Unless he never grew tired of her. Cold dread formed in her stomach. Her pain was Edward's pleasure. She'd seen it in his eyes that night. He'd turned up to deliver the news that Ryan had been killed, but it was excitement, not empathy, that danced in his eyes. She felt him slide his oily gaze over her like he was surveying a meal.

It seemed appropriate that the clouds shifted across the sun at that moment, cloaking everything but Jay and Brandy.

"The last two pieces of my heart." Her whisper caught on the broken shards inside her.

They headed to the barn and hooked Horace up. Brandy rode on the cart as Alex and Jay walked behind, slipping the wires into the insulators on the posts from the two wire spinners Horace pulled. Alex ratcheted the first wire tight, watching Jay do the second one.

The sun's position told her it was after 2.00pm, but the long night and Edward making an appearance had her wishing it were bedtime. Sabrina would be home soon, too. She'd be happily exhausted from spending time with her friends. The fencing had been completed faster than expected, so perhaps Jay would help her fix up the yards to be able to do the castrating and ear tagging.

"Are you alright, Lex?" Jay was suddenly at her side. She must have dozed off for a second with her back resting against the cart.

"Yes, just a power nap."

"You look wrecked. Did you want to get back up to the house?" Concern crinkled his forehead.

"I'm good. Just a little tired. I need to get the bull shifted and test out the spray rig. It's been a while since I've used it, and the front paddock is full of weeds. Rain is due by the weekend, so I'd like to get it out tomorrow."

"Lex." Jay shifted Brandy to the ground. "If you don't take a breather you'll burn yourself out. The bull can wait until tomorrow, I'll check out the spray rig first thing in the morning, and we can leave the cart in the house yard until then."

"It's okay, I just-"

"Lexi, let me help you, please? You don't always have to be so damned independent. It doesn't hurt to need or accept help every now and then. You don't have to do all of this on your own." She sighed. Behind his stern expression, concern stood firm. He looked tired, too.

"Fine. We'll get this cart unhooked and head back. Mum will be home soon and will want to see Brandy."

On the way back to the house, Brandy riding happily on Horace, the gravity of the week before pressed against Alex. Jay in her life again triggering a tornado of emotions, the secrecy of Brandy's parentage, the date and constant underlying threat of Edward, and the ongoing fight to keep on top of the farm. Jay noticed her fatigue, quietly slipping an arm around her waist in support as her legs grew heavy. The heat from his touch revved up her pulse, but she was too tired to do anything about it. Instead she relaxed into him, hip rubbing against his thigh, feeling so secure and…right.

*"I've waited all my life for you, Lexi, and now I have you I will never let you go."* Words curling with his hot breath against her neck.

His words threaded with her veins. And in the morning he was gone.

She'd tasted his sincerity. She'd believed it. Then she'd rolled over to empty sheets. She wondered if he was just a con artist. But that didn't make sense, either. He wouldn't know that the farm was hers and not Sabrina's, and the farm wasn't really worth anything, anyway. He knew she didn't have money. But he'd promised her he wouldn't let her go, and still left. And then when she saw him the following weekend and he... She stepped out of Jay's hold. His head whipped down, frown deep, lips thinned. She lifted her chin at him and walked ahead. She wasn't sure what was going on with him, but she needed to keep some distance.

Her thoughts turned back to Edward. He'd ask her out to dinner again. She was fortunate last time that Daniel turned up to help. She knew that wouldn't happen again. Bile rose at the thought of his hands on her, and she wished in that moment that she could confide in Jay. Maybe he could help her. But Edward was a cop, and Jay was just a mechanic. She knew Edward would go to any lengths to remove Jay from the picture, even more so if he knew Jay was tied to her through Brandy.

It was safer for Jay that he not discover the truth about his daughter.

# CHAPTER 18

## JAY

*H*e couldn't understand why she was so hot and cold with him all the time. He'd laid his heart on the line, told her what she meant to him, and put the ball back in her court. When she shrugged him away on the way back to the homestead, frustration sizzled inside. Perhaps it was Ryan, haunting her, preventing her from accepting him the way he knew she wanted to. His Lexi, so responsive. Had he not broken their kiss, he was sure she would have given herself to him. He tensed his stomach in regret. Perhaps he should have. If she wouldn't let him in, he would just have to wait until she worked through it on her own to come to him. He smiled inwardly. He'd waited for years, a few more days wouldn't kill him. He didn't have to make it easy for her, though.

Lexi was still in the shower when Sabrina returned. After folding a squealing Brandy in her arms, she met Jay's grey stare.

"Jay. It's good to see you again." Warmth emanated from her grin.

"What have you done with Sabrina, you know, the one who demanded I leave last time we talked?" He drawled as he leaned against the door frame, crossing his arms over his chest.

Sabrina darted a look down the hall.

"She's in the shower."

"Listen, Jay. I know I did, but I'm worried about Edward. She won't talk to me, but it's something big. I was hoping she'd talk to you about it." Her low tone conveyed her concern.

"I don't know why you think she would, Sabrina. She's been hot and cold so often I don't think she's ever going to let me in." Jay dragged a dirty palm down his face.

"She needs you, Jay." This time fear flickered in her eyes. "She'll hate me for telling you, this, but there's something about you that makes her feel safe, gives her hope. There always was, and I'm hoping she'll come clean and go back to the strong and vibrant woman we both remember."

Jay's body stiffened. "*Always* was?" Realisation took his breath.

"You knew me the second I saw you out in the paddock, didn't you?" He stepped towards her, catching her shoulders in his hands. His stomach twisted.

"You hurt her, Jay. You have to understand that she never completely recovered. I don't understand why you did what you did, but I can see the purpose on your face when you look at her now. All the men in her life have been taken away, and she can't bring herself to trust that you'll stay. I'm telling you this because I need to know right now if you're serious about her or not. If you're not, you need to leave immediately." The woman implored.

"How did I hurt her, Sabrina? I don't know what I did, but she's using whatever it is to keep her distance from me. Help me, please."

Sabrina scrutinised him. "You moved on. She couldn't. She tried to find you."

Jay's eyebrows raised. "That's not true! I have been searching for her. She couldn't have been too heartbroken, though. She was the one who moved on and started a family."

It was Sabrina's turn to look surprised. Jay flung an arm out towards the stand where the pictures of Ryan stood like a shrine.

"Lexi told me how much Brandy misses her Dad."

Sabrina lifted her hand to her mouth. "She told you that?"

Jay dipped his head. Something didn't add up.

"What's really going on, Sabrina? What are you two keeping from me?"

The bathroom door creaked and Lexi's footsteps grew louder. Jay darted his expression quizzically over the older woman.

"Help me, please?" He pleaded.

"I promised her I wouldn't tell. You two need to talk, though. Badly. And Jay?" She clutched his forearm in urgency. "Ask her to tell you about her brother."

Jay stifled a groan as Lexi stepped into the room, a white towel encasing her hair, exposing the enticing lines of her graceful neck. The top she wore revealed the hard peaks of her nipples, sitting firm on perfect breasts, free from her bra. Jay wasn't sure if it was the cooler air after a warm shower, or if it was her reaction to him. He hoped it was the latter. Her tiny pyjama shorts exposing the satin length of her thighs, sending him headlong into flashbacks that heated his skin and played havoc with his pulse.

"Oh, Damn it, Lexi, I forgot. Edna is babysitting her granddaughter tonight. She's hoping I'd take Brandy and let the girls socialise for a couple of nights. She's set up one spare room for me, and the other for the two girls. I hope you don't mind. I was going to call and ask, but I figured you needed to get cleaned up after the storm last night, and Brandy would just get bored."

Lexi folded her arms at her mother, lips pursed in suspicion.

Sabrina shot her a look of innocence. "I just came home to get clean clothes, and this little ratbag."

Jay was immediately and deeply grateful Sabrina had suddenly turned ally. As a foe she would be formidable. He swallowed a smirk. The woman sure didn't waste time.

Lexi squeezed her daughter to her chest, covering her giggling protests in kisses. The little girl held her arms out towards Jay, and he pulled her to him, sprinkling kisses over her soft face.

"You be good for Nan, Sass, and have fun." He smiled.

With Brandy strapped securely in her car seat, Alex and Jay waved her off. The brake lights came on and Sabrina called.

"Jay, I need you to stay the night if you can. They were saying at the bar last night there's been someone breaking into farms recently. I know how stubborn Alex is, so I'm asking you to keep an eye on her. I need to know she's safe." In his periphery, Jay watched Lexi's eyes narrow and her chin lift. She was beautiful in her defiance.

"Will do, Sabrina. Have a lovely catch up." Jay called, struggling to keep the amusement from his voice. As she peeled out the driveway, excitement stretched his chest. They were alone. Finally. There would be no distractions, no daughter for Lexi to hide behind, nothing but the intimacy of dusk and time. He could begin the task of unravelling the secrets she was holding.

"You're not staying."

Jay turned slowly to face her. She looked small and vulnerable in the dimming light of day, and understanding chilled him. Her aggression stemmed from a steaming vat of fear deep inside. She was afraid to let him in, frightened of exposing her heart to more pain, if what Sabrina said was true. He needed her to quiet the noise in her head that fought him, that wanted him closed out.

"You're right, Lexi, staying here isn't a good idea. I'll just call your mother and let her know I can't stay." Lexi pinched the bridge of her nose and closed her eyes.

"She doesn't have to know, Jay." She snapped.

"No, but I gave her my word. I either stay, or I call her. Your choice." Jay reasoned lightly. He'd already won, judging by her defeated expression. But she wasn't going to go down without a fight, though. With a military tenacity his girl wouldn't relent. The battle of wits thinned his blood and strained against his jeans.

"You can't, Jay. She has an unlisted number. We both do." Her challenge was firm. Jay lifted one eyebrow and closed his lips.

"You have my mother's number? You don't even have mine!" Her mouth sagged, incredulous.

"Sabrina gave me yours, too." Jay gave her the full power of his lopsided grin. Her eyes darkened. He watched as she fought defeat. His smirk told her he'd seen her reaction, and he turned his back on her, opening the fridge.

"Now, what can we find for dinner?"

* * *

"The benefits of having a beast killed for the freezer is that even when things are tight, I can still pull out a porterhouse." She grinned at the meal, tongue running over her lips. Jay's cutlery clattered to his plate.

"Could you not make those noises when you eat? It's distracting." His request was tight with heat. He let her see it, watching for her response. He adjusted his jeans, watching her reaction rise and spread in a pink tinge from chest to face. Her tongue darted out again in an unconscious show of arousal. The warm brown of her pupils slid into lusty black. She fought it. Jay delighted in the stunning battle playing out before him.

"You can sleep on the couch." She whispered huskily.

Jay agreed with a nod, running his fingers lazily through his hair, watching her follow his movements.

"You don't mind if I grab a shower first?" His voice deepened, inviting her to imagine him naked. He heard her swallow.

"Towels are in the bathroom cupboard." she choked out.

The air around them was tangible with tension, so much so, that when Jay pushed his chair from the table Lexi gasped. He paused deliberately beside her, bending so close his breath tickled her ear.

"I'll help you with the dishes when I'm out." She nodded stiffly, but Jay was aware of her erratic pulse. He felt her lean towards him, allowing the barest touch of his lips to graze her neck, and it took all the self-restraint he had not to give her a taste. Instead, he backed away, watching the shivers track through her.

It was a matter of time before the undeniable spark between them would blaze into an inferno of passion inside of her. And he was hungry for it.

# CHAPTER 19

## ALEX

She had sizzled for him to kiss her. She thought he might, but instead he left her alone trying to regain control over the ferocious battering of her pulse. She couldn't afford to allow herself to be shattered by him again, but her body wasn't under her authority any longer. While Brandy was present and buffering his intensity, it was much easier to resist him. Her eyelashes fluttered closed as she drew a breath deep into her lungs. But without her daughter around, all Alex could do was picture Jay in the shower, water everywhere that she wanted to put her hands, her lips.

She sat back from the table and clenched her thighs together with a groan. She was so wired and turned on and it had been years… She tipped her head back as she felt one hand move beneath her shorts to rest on her inflamed centre, the other sliding up over her breast. She felt her legs fall open and ran a finger through her crease, revelling in the wet heat Jay had summoned. She was so close already. She just needed release to get her through the night, help her resist the insatiable pull she felt towards Jay. She slowly dragged her fingertip up, covering her nub in her slick. She slowly started working her finger in long strokes.

A low growl sounded from the doorway, and Alex's head whipped around, pulling her hands to her lap. Jay leaned against the door frame, gripping tightly as if to steady himself. His hair was wild, his gaze feral. Locked on her face like he wanted to devour her. His nostrils flared like he was scenting her, so primal was the act she groaned. The towel wrapped around his waist jutted towards her, straining to break free.

"Christ, Lexi" He hissed a savage warning. "Go to bed now if you don't want me to take you." He didn't move. Lexi stood slowly. She explored his naked torso with ravenous desire. Wide shoulders tensed with restraint, his thick chest rising and falling rapidly, his muscles stretched tight beneath his flesh. The hard wall of his abdominals flexing, the tantalising trail of hair disappearing beneath his towel. Her blood sang and reached, protesting the distance between them. Desire sparked through the atmosphere and enveloped Alex. She wanted him, She wanted to feel him move inside her with an urgency that wrapped around her soul and invaded her heart. She *needed* him. A throbbing, untamed desire so carnal she groaned her lust.

"Lexi!" His growl caused tingles to spread through her abdomen and pulse between her thighs. Her lips moved before her brain could process.

"Come with me."

His breath wooshed out. She heard his agony.

"I won't be able to stop, Lexi. I need you to be sure." His beauty was untamed and ferocious. He was wild testosterone, at his physical peak, an Alpha male with his sights charred on her.

"Please, Jay." She invited him with hooded eyes, pulling her lip between her teeth against a quiver. The silence stretched. Then it snapped.

The sight of Jay prowling towards her, predatory eyes like pools of ink, muscles rippling as he fought for control... Jesus he was beautiful. He scooped his large hands beneath her and swept her off the ground as he took her towards the bedroom.

Alex crawled her palms over the flaming contours of his shoulders, feeling the pounding of his heart vibrate through his body into hers. She whimpered her craving into the crook of his corded neck. The hollow sound of his lungs reaching for air betrayed the urgency of his lust. Her centre throbbed in response, his impatient growl reverberating when the scent of her arousal reached him.

Alex was vaguely aware of him lowering her to the bed. Her skin tingled when he rucked up her shirt and slipped it over her head, baring her breasts as he tossed the fabric aside. She felt his body cover hers completely, pressing her deep into the mattress, pinning her with his strength. The power she felt move within him sparked a wave of yearning so acute she couldn't breathe. After so long, it felt like coming home. So safe and warm. She rediscovered the ridges and valleys of his chest with every starving stroke and brush, the texture of silken flesh over hard steel, running her lips and tongue over the edge of his jaw, tasting the pulse firing in his throat.

He sought her mouth and forced his way in, diving with fevered hunger and rasping breaths. His kisses were wild and raw and primal. Dipping, tasting, teasing her with his tongue. Alex lost herself in the intensity, tangling her fist in his hair, pulling him closer, the other gliding over his back greedily.

Jay broke the kiss and pulled back, catching her arms. His blazing eyes found hers as he ran his hands slowly up to her wrists, pressing his thick fingers through hers, locking them above her head. Alex gazed up at him, stretched out beneath him, watching as he drank in her body, helpless and wanton in the grip of his hunger. Her body throbbed. She pressed her hips into him, and he thrust back, the steel of his cock teasing her through the cotton of her shorts. Alex whimpered.

"You're mine, Lex. You have *always* been mine." His voice was deep and harsh with lust. She quivered. He was sin wrapped in temptation, dipped in feral hunger. And she wanted it all. The air around them shuddered with desire.

"Please, Jay" His lips crashed on hers again, stealing her oxygen. He dropped her hands and slid his weight slowly down her body, sprinkling kisses and soft bites on her jaw, her neck, her collarbone. He tracked his lips to her hard nipples, his heated breaths stroking her breasts. He caught a nipple between his teeth, nipping gently. Alex jerked against him, arching her back, a cry escaping.

"Jay!"

He hissed and ran his tongue over the peak. Alex writhed beneath him, digging her nails into his shoulders to spur him on. He teased first one breast, then the other, his hands squeezing, caressing, worshipping where his mouth wasn't. His movements languid, savouring her every twitch, tuning into her every sound. Alex groaned into the air, her hips rolling against his chest. Her body sung for him.

He slid his mouth down, tasting the skin on her belly, wide hands firmly gripping her ribs.

The air was thick with sawing inhales and suffocating need. Her fingers gripped everything they touched finding endless waves of awe in the slightest of gestures.

Jay revered her with his touch; gliding fingers, tantalising nibbles.

Alex gasped and flexed as her shorts were yanked down, dropping roughly to the ground. She was bare. His tongue burned a path to her trimmed mound, and his body shuddered. He slid his hands roughly under her thighs, lifting her towards him. Jay fixed his dark stare on hers. His need for her ran deeper than this moment, she realised. He was ensuring she knew he was marking her. Dipping his head he watched her as he scented her, the ancient instinct so primitive and raw on his flared nostrils. Arousal ran down her thigh at the sight and she twisted needy fingers in his hair. Her heart tumbled over his. He held her there for a moment on the edge of combustion.

Then he slid his lips over her slit, skimming his tongue through her folds.

"Jay!" She unravelled underneath him, nerve endings detonating, head thrown back.

"Christ, Lex. You're so damn stunning!" His restraint snapped. Then he devoured her. His tongue teased and curled inside her, flicking around her hard node, back inside her. Alex was hyper-aware of him invading every cell, felt the waves of release rising, needing more.

"Jay, I need you" she panted through the mounting pleasure.

Jay answered by sliding a finger inside her and she was gone.

"*Jay!*" She screamed, her muscles contracted and pulsing around his finger. Her nails scraping, body bowed and writhing as he brought her down.

"Jesus, Lexi, I can't-" Agony deepened his tone, and Alex reached out to him. Watching him on the brink was intoxicating. She didn't care. She needed him however he came to her. His body landed on hers again, the urgency of his hands on her revealing the lack of control, his grip firm and crazed. His breathing lost rhythm.

He crashed his lips to hers, giving her a taste of her own arousal. He growled into her mouth, burying her groan.

Her legs moved instinctively around his hips shuddering and bucking as the heated tip of his cock nudged against her entrance.

"You're so slick for me!" He rasped. He locked his eyes on hers in a silver thrall that pinned her to the bed, carefully gauging every reaction with erotic intimacy. Like he found himself in a fantasy he wanted to carve into his memory. With a long smooth thrust he pushed inside her, and she cried his name as her body stretched and filled, the euphoric burn as her body struggled to accommodate his size. She squirmed, muscles contracting, gripping his girth.

"So tight" He panted. He snarled down at her, the fire in his eyes dangerous and predatory, and she saw the second his control shattered. She caught her breath at the sight of him, pure primal energy focused on her. He was magnificent. He was hers. He gripped her shoulder in one hand, the other buried in her hair, forcing her head back, and he started moving inside her. He dragged out of her, then plunged deep, deep, deeper with every thrust, each kick of his hips. She bucked her hips to meet him, groaning with the exquisite sensation of him inside her body, pressing against the very end of her. The vibrations quaked from her stomach, jolts of electricity building, spreading, His scent invaded her senses. He was all around her, on her. In her. Finally.

"I'm coming, Jay!" Jay fixed his potent attention on her, his slow, deliberate strokes burning hotter as she hurtled towards her peak. His jaw locked, neck corded, and every muscle strained and held as he sought the last of his restraint.

She contracted around him as she shattered, the carnal strokes short-circuiting her mind. Her nails scraped down his back in her haze.

Jay let go. He bent down, snatching the tender skin between her neck and shoulder in his teeth. She felt the sting morph into another rapturous wave, and she whimpered.

He shortened his own frantic pounds, the pressure building faster, harder, until she felt her lungs might explode. Her next climax shattered over her the same moment Jay roared his own release.

He collapsed on top of her, heaving into her neck. She laid lust-glazed eyes on the shimmer of sweat cooling on the pulsing muscles of his shoulder, and rode her steadying heartbeat into sleep.

# CHAPTER 20

## JAY

*H*e rolled off her gently, reluctant to break contact with any part of her. His head swam with images of her coming apart around him. It was so much better than he remembered, if that was possible. She fit him. She'd surrendered herself into the arms of their madness; stepped into the wild abyss with him and met his hunger with her own ferocious need. His cock jumped.

His mouth twitched in silent rapture as her gentle breaths whispered between them.

She'd had a big day. Her lips were slack and swollen, the flush of arousal slowly ebbing from her neck. Jay ran the tip of his finger over her mouth, tracing the soft texture of her chin, her neck. He followed the outline of her shoulder in awe, down her arm, explored the gentle curve of her waist before spreading his hand over her hip. She instinctively rolled towards him and nestled into the warmth of his chest, hanging an arm over his waist.

She was killing him. He knew the very instant he fell in love with her, sitting at the bar with a song on her lips, the tilt of her head and a drink in her hand. He'd smirked at her singing, and she threw her head back. The crisp sound of her laughter curled under his skin and into his heart. He knew right then he needed to hear her laughter more than he needed air.

If he was being honest, he thought he'd never see her again. The days had dripped into weeks, then months. Then years of nothing. Nobody seemed to know who she was. Daniel had joked about it, but there grew a genuine fear that he'd had too many drinks and imagined her. He groaned quietly and pulled her closer to his chest. He sunk into sleep to the rhythm of her breaths against him. He could never let her go again.

His eyelids fluttered open and collided with the warmth of her gaze. He held his breath, unsure of her reactions in the cold light of morning. She licked her lips and offered a shy smile. Jay flashed a wolfish grin in return. She pressed a palm to his chest, adding pressure until she rolled him to his back. Her eyes flashed as she fell on him with tongue flicking over his abs, hungrily nipping her way to the soft hair below his navel. His pulse hammered as her exploration led her further down. He watched as her honey waves, shaken loose from their passion in the night, tickled along the ridges of his body as her head dropped lower.

"Aaaahhhh, Lexi" A long groan vibrated in his throat. His cock twitched against her chin. Warmth surrounded the hard head of him, and she swirled her tongue around it, tasting the pearl of arousal. She hummed in satisfaction, torturing him with delicious vibrations. He gasped when she slid her mouth slowly down his shaft. She had taken half of him when he nudged the back of her throat. She slowly ran her tongue up and down the vein underneath while sliding up and down his length. A groan ripped from him as she built up a slow and erotic rhythm, firing up Jay's already erratic pulse. As if she sensed his building need, she wrapped her hand around the base of his cock, the other teasing his heavy sac. She increased her tempo, and his breath rasped to the tune. His hips jumped and his fingers snagged her hair, instinctively pressing her to him. He fought for control as she relaxed into his dominance, allowing the nudge against the back of her throat.

"Jesus" Jay hissed. Lexi moaned, her hot breath encasing him.

"I'm going to come," he warned through clenched teeth. He pressed her to his groin again, and she opened up to him. He felt the wide crown of his cock slide into the tight channel of her throat, so deep he felt her lips tighten around the skin above his balls. Light danced on the edge of his vision.

"*Lexi!*" He roared as he exploded down her throat. His heart slammed at his rib cage as he convulsed against the bed, bucking and panting.

His lungs burning, he reached down and hoisted her against him, wrapping her in his arms. Her hooded, sultry expression lodged in his throat.

"Don't you ever disappear on me again" His voice was choked with thick emotion.

The gorgeous siren smiled.

* * *

He watched in awe as she worked the calves. She walked among the small herd, bunching them into the race. She locked their heads still as she immunised them and pressed identification buds into their ears. Dust clung to Lexi's sweat. The honeyed bun had loosened into a sprawling mess. Her jeans earned a few more rips, and small cuts oozed scarlet. She shot Jay a grin that he felt in his groin. The spark in her eyes, she loved this. She loved the filth, the smell, the exhaustion.

Horace stood beside the yards, her presence having a calming effect on the worked up beasts. Her tail swished.

"Now it's your turn." She smirked. Not wanting to be outdone, Jay rolled up his sleeves and dropped over the rails into the yard. The calves scattered and hugged the fences. Jay imitated Lexi's example, stretching his arms and moving slowly towards them. The cattle bunched into the race to escape him. When he'd secured one in the head bales, Lexi handed him the syringe.

"Just under the skin" she instructed. Jay looked at the calf. It had twisted its head to the side trying to free itself, hooves piling up dirt as it tried to pull backwards. The yards clanged with the force of its struggles. Jay was grateful they'd repaired the yards earlier with extra reinforcements.

Taking a deep breath, he grabbed a pinch of neck skin and felt the needle sink in. The calf jumped, making the hold on the plunger difficult. Lexi exchanged the empty syringe for the ear tagger. He pressed the identification bud into a furry ear, and stepped back as Lexi released the bales and opened the gate. The calf shot Jay a suspicious look as it trotted into the holding pen with the rest of the finished beasts.

"That wasn't so hard" Jay smirked.

"Glad you think so. You've got another twenty odd to go." Her smile was overly sweet as she reset the bales. They fell into easy conversation around the bellowing animals.

"Tell me about the farm you grew up on" Lexi inquired.

Jay darted to the left and a calf ran into the race.

"It was similar to yours, actually. Beefers so my father could work through the week and catch up with the farm work on the weekends. I was too young to do any actual work, but I had a pony I used to ride after school. The farm was next to a creek, and my little brother and I would ride double and go swimming with the other locals. I remember the sun being bright, the air clear and the days longer. Sometimes, you just know where your heart wants to be. I was devastated when Dad moved us."

Jay lifted his Akubra to itch beneath it and frowned.

"Actually, my parents are in town on Monday, and I was hoping you'd come with me to see them." Jay focused his attention on snapping the bud into the calf's ear, keeping her in his periphery. She leaned against the rails and stared at the ground. She shifted her stance a little. Jay felt the silence stretch. Her shoulders squared as she reached her decision.

"Sure. Okay. Mum was talking about having Brandy again anyway, so I can organise to pick her up on the way home." He clenched his teeth to hide his delight. His heart soared. In a casual voice he didn't feel, he muttered; "When do these guys go off to market?"

"Tomorrow. We should be done here in another hour, and then we can run them up to Daniel's yards for pick up." Jay's lungs tightened. He was aware he and his brother looked similar, but so far it seemed Lexi hadn't made the connection. Jay hoped Daniel made himself scarce when they ran the cattle up. Side by side she'd spot the family resemblance immediately.

Sabrina's words stabbed in his head suddenly. *Ask her to tell you about her brother.* The brother Lexi hadn't mentioned to him. He glanced around the task at hand. Lexi admitted there was a few hours of work to do yet. And she needed his help. It seemed the perfect time to ask, but the cold knot in his stomach persisted.

"My parents will love you, you know. My brother should be there, too. You'll like him. He's a bit of a smart-arse, but he makes me laugh. He's a good guy. Your brother the same?" He forced himself to remain impassive.

"Yeah." She sighed. Jay's breath stumbled and he clamped his molars as he casually took the syringe from her.

"He loved me so much. We were inseparable, you know. This was our dream, to run the family farm together. We planned to extend the house to accommodate both our future families. He was so great and supportive when he found out I was-" He watched her muscles lock in place with a jerk. He felt, more than saw the shock, the fear shudder through her. He allowed the silence to fall then, trying to picture a man with the face of Lexi. He would have been a handsome man. He searched his memory for photos on walls he may have appeared in, but all he could recall was the images of Lexi and her ex in the shrine in the hall. The truth slammed in his guts, heart threatening to leap from his mouth.

*They were pictures of her brother!*

Why was she so set on leading him to believe he was her boyfriend? And why did Sabrina want Jay to know? He let the questions simmer as he worked the rest of the cattle in silence. Lexi's entire demeanour changed. She was stiff and wary and jumpy. Jay failed to comprehend the importance she placed on a simple detail. It wasn't as if the brother was a lunatic hell-bent on destroying his sister, or taking the farm from her. She'd described a beautiful relationship between them, so close they wanted their families to grow up together. She said he'd been supportive of her when he found out.....*when he found out she was pregnant!*

# CHAPTER 21

## ALEX

She watched him warily. She could tell from his tight jaw and locked shoulders that he was digesting the information that slipped out. If he was able to put two and two together… She swallowed thickly and mustered all her courage to keep topping up the immunisations and placing the buds in the tagger.

"Who is Brandy's father?" His cold query lifted bile from her throat. She drew a shaky breath.

"It's not important." She dismissed, hoping he'd accept it while knowing he wouldn't.

"What happened, Lexi?" His timbre demanded an explanation.

"There's nothing to tell. I found out he was seeing someone else. By the time I discovered I was pregnant three months into it, he had already moved on. I never bothered telling him."

"Jesus, Lexi. I'm sorry. Wouldn't he have at least helped raise her, though. If he knew?" She scrutinised his tone. He didn't know. Her exhale was jagged with tension.

"Jay, we used protection and the condom failed. He never would have considered a baby a possibility. He hurt me, Jay. There was no way I wanted him, or his help in my life after that. I can do it on my own." Her chin lifted in defiance.

"I know you can do it, Lex. You *are* doing it. But perhaps he could have helped maintain the house. You know the verandah is on the verge of collapse. That's not safe-" He cut off when panic bled the colour from her face.

"I'm going to fix it, Jay, they can't take Brandy away from me, I won't let them. She's all I have!" Her pulse bruised her skin. Her vision blurred.

Jay moved towards her, his wide chest blocking light as he wrapped her in his filthy arms.

"Nobody's going to take her away, Lex. They can't, and I will stop them if they try." She inhaled his heavenly ambrosia as her panic fizzed. She could almost believe it when his arms were around her listening to the hollow music of his lungs moving air. And the beat of his heart. So strong and sure, like Jay. She immersed herself in that moment. Still anaesthetised from their lovemaking, she could convince herself that everything would work out. He hadn't told her he loved her, but he'd showed it in the tender worship of her body, his unwavering attention, the way he reached out often to touch her. Just because he wanted to and it was what they both needed.

"Jay?"

He grunted.

"Jay, I need to tell you something."

"Okay?" She felt him stiffen against her cheek.

"I need you to keep an open mind." She cautioned. He gripped her shoulders and pulled back, His grey eyes patient.

Horace stamped her feet at the same instant the sun caught the metal of the approaching car.

"Shit" She pushed away hard from Jay, climbed the fence and dropped into the yards.

"Hand me the syringe, Jay. Quick." She knew he sensed her fear, but he passed her the shot without a word.

The car crunched to a halt, Edward bursting out of the car with his hand on his gun. His face purpled with barely restrained rage.

"I fucking told you to get rid of him, Alex. What the fuck is he still doing here? And why was he holding you?" Spittle sprayed from twisted lips. Jay held up his hands.

"Cool it, man. A calf stood on her and I was making sure she could still stand." Alex mentally thanked him. The cop shot him a murderous look, stepping into Jay's space.

"I wasn't talking to you, you piece of shit. But while I have your attention, allow me to be clear. Alex belongs to me, so the next time you lay a finger on her you and me are gonna mix. Better yet, fuck off right now, and never even *look* at her again." Edward's voice was ice and poison.

Alex watched as Jay bunched his fists. He was taller and broader, but she knew Edward could be cruel and underhanded.

"Edward, he came today to help out with the calves. I will send him away now if you want to take over from him?"

His lips curled in disgust. "Why do you even do this shit, Alex? You're covered in muck and fucking stink like these beasts. You'll never get me near one of those things! Once you're finished, Alex, he's gone." It wasn't a choice. Her head drooped to the ground in a defeated nod. She noticed Jay flexing his fists, fighting to remain silent.

Edward rounded on Jay, snapping his gun from it's holster. He lifted it slowly, pressing the barrel hard into the space over Jay's heart. The metallic crunch of the safety being released made Jay's nostrils flare.

"Don't fucking touch her. I'm not kidding."

He replaced his weapon and prowled back to his vehicle, turning it next to the yards with a rain of flying sod, scattering the calves.

"What's going on, Lex?" Acid dripped from wild lips. Alex clutched the rails to support her trembling legs.

"I…I have to do what he says, Jay." She felt her voice tremble.

"Why? What the hell is going on. I'm so tired of the secrets, Lex. I think I've made it clear I intend to stick around. And I *will* protect you. But I can't do that, dear heart, *if you don't tell me* what I need to protect you from!"

A sob burst from her. This was what she wanted. Her and Jay and Brandy as a family. It was within her reach. She'd watched her dream solidify and she had a tight hold on it. And now Edward was destroying it. And there was absolutely nothing she could do about it.

Jay drilled his plea into her, and watched, broken, as she closed down before his eyes, shutting him out once more. She winced as he spun away from her, drew back his arm and felt the yards thunder with the force of his punch. He turned back to her with pain crinkling his eyes.

"Is he the father?" His words hitched.

"Good God, no! I'd *never…*" She blanched involuntarily. Jay blew out his relief.

"Why won't you trust me?" Torment etched in the lines of his thinned mouth.

"There's nothing you can do, so all it would do is frustrate you."

"You don't give up, Lexi, you aren't that person. You face obstacles with courage and fire. Not submission. What is he threatening you with?"

Alex just shook her head, tagging the last calf and releasing it.

"Can you help me run this lot up to Daniel's?"

He nodded stiffly, silver eyes piercing her.

Alex retreated into herself. Trust was earned, not granted. Jay still had a long way to go there. While she hadn't caught him in deceit yet, she still couldn't completely trust him. While he'd shown nothing but honour, there remained this niggling doubt, a sharp memory that haunted her. One that refused to let her lower her walls completely.

Later, with the cattle yarded and ready for collection, Alex was elated. They all looked solid, healthy, and should fetch a good price at the market tomorrow. Alex hoped there would be enough for her mother to stay in town for a while. At least until the next lot of vealers went in, then she could pay for longer. Her mother had supported her so much that giving her happiness was the least she could do for her.

# CHAPTER 22

## JAY

"*I* want you to do something for me." Jay concentrated his focus on her. He watched her tense with his request.

"I want you to show me the farm." He saw her relax into surprise. He was consciously making efforts to reprogram her brain, teaching it to understand that she was safe, that she could receive an invitation from him without having to owe him anything. Tilly had armed him with ideas and suggestions, and he was determined to use them to bring his girl to him without barriers. It was working slowly, she was becoming less guarded in his presence. At first she'd gritted her teeth and retreated into herself, and now she was simply on edge. It was a strong indication that Lexi *wanted* to trust Jay. She didn't realise she was working with him so openly.

Her mouth widened over her teeth.

"Okay. I can check the fences in the far paddocks at the same time."

Lexi mounted the quad bike in front of him. The bike was made for one, but she didn't seem to mind the squeeze, and Jay quivered at her tight warm body pressed snug against his. He felt his jeans bulge immediately with the scent of her hair beneath his chin, and hoped he could restrain himself for the duration of the tour. Lexi indicated to the left and they were carried up a dirt lane way behind the house. The morning heat warmed their clothes and the breeze stroked their faces. Jay couldn't remember when he'd ever felt more contented. The long grass flashing past, the summer day stretching out before them and his woman between his legs....utter transcendence. He felt the grin change his face.

\* \* \*

At the end of the lane the old gate stood open, so Jay took them to the middle of the field and shut the engine off. He inhaled the fragrance of crushed grass and clean air, the birdsong and grasshoppers playing their melodies in unison.

"This is one of my favourite pastures." Lexi sighed as she flung her arms out to embrace it. Jay peered into the grass, noting the weeds growing among a scattering of clover, rye and other grasses that had crept in and made a home in the opportunity neglect offered them.

"It's full of weeds."

She grinned and cocked her head.

"Yeah, it is. But the cattle coming out of this pasture are more robust, healthier than in the sown paddocks. I like to run the marketable stock through here last when I can. The variety of native grasses that have overtaken, and the many weeds in here tap their roots into different depths of soil, accessing levels of minerals the cattle can feed on to sort out any imbalances they might have. The weeds are as important as the clover." She gestured excitedly towards the house.

"All the sown pastures grow the abundance of grass with the proper care, but then you have to balance out the lacking minerals with expensive lick blocks or water blocks. This gives them more of a smorgasbord, too, with all the different flavours in here for them."

Jay cupped the back of his neck and looked with more interest at the mixture of grasses.

"How many paddocks do you have in total?"

"Twenty-five. Twenty seven if you include the bull paddocks. Twenty are in different states of rye pasture, and the other five are like this one."

"So what would happen if you hypothetically ran a fifty-fifty mix?"

Lexi turned to him curiously. Her brown eyes danced with excitement.

"What do you mean? Let half the pastures revert to native grass?"

"Yeah! That's exactly it. I mean, the cost of over-sowing with rye every few years and keeping up with the fertilisers, is it worth the effort if you're likely to get better performance with the native pastures? You could run a comparison, see which method works better for you and the cattle."

Lexi's eyes widened.

"I could run two smaller herds! One on rye with the supplements and the fertilising programme I've been using for years, and one lot on the native grasses, and see which results in sturdier beasts! I think that would be exciting, Jay! It just might work!"

She was breathless in her enthusiasm. Jay delighted in watching the show of hope and challenge play in her expressions. They conversed like a team, discussing the possibilities and concerns until they'd worn a crop circle with their pacing.

"I'll check out the best fertilisers to run on the native grasses after lunch, but right now this sun is cooking me. There's another place you have to see." She grinned and tilted her head. In their stimulating exchange, she'd forgotten herself. She dropped the stiffness from her limbs, and she moved like a carefree feline with unhindered pleasure radiating from her. This is who she was; the Lexi who felt safe, the Lexi who planted her feet firmly in the soil and bloomed for herself. The Lexi with the land in her veins and Jay's heart in her hands. The only time Jay had seen her as relaxed and open as this was the night he met her. The night she took his heart from his chest.

She directed Jay to turn down a narrow track that seemed to drop over the side of a hill. She sat taller as he crested the rise, wiggling her anticipation as they descended towards the tree line.

An old twisted peppercorn tree stood proud and resilient on the banks of the stream that wound through the farm. It was fenced off so the cattle couldn't disturb the waterway with hooves or manure.

"This is where I come to think. My grandfather planted this tree when he was a boy, so he could find the prettiest place on the farm easily. It makes me feel closer to my ancestors here, my father. I talk to him here."

Jay grinned behind her back, following as she led him enthusiastically to the grassy banks. This is where she disappeared to the morning he turned up to fix Old John. Before she returned and accepted his terms to teach him about the farm. This place knew all her secrets, the answers to all her mysteries. And she trusted him enough to share it with him. With a spark in his eye, he gazed into the slow flowing water and pointed.

"So you must have left that here then."

Lexi appeared beside him, searching the water with a frown.

"Wha-" With a grin that showed his teeth, Jay shoved. She gasped as the cool water dived into her jeans and shirt, Jay's laughter drowned out the birds as she sat wide eyed and mouth hanging waist deep in the water.

A thunderstorm of rage and shock built on her face. It was adorable, and Jay couldn't stop laughing. He tried to honour the regret that dangled below the surface of his laughter, knowing her backlash would be formidable based on her expression, but he was still chuckling as he took the hand she shoved silently at him. He saw her eyes flash a heartbeat before she gripped his hand and jerked him down beside her.

He landed face first in the icy stream. Lexi roared. Her head flew back to the sky and her cheeks lifted, the clear ring of her mirth filling the air. She scooped up water and flung it towards him, doubling over as he spluttered.

"You did say you were hot. I thought you could use some cooling down." Jay smirked.

"You're no gentleman, are you?" She shoved his soggy shoulder. Jay pushed a wave of water over her head, soaking her hair.

"That's because you're no lady." He laughed. Lexi released a battle cry and launched herself on him, trying to dunk him as he held her at bay. In the end, he scooped her saturated form up and deposited her on a patch of grass in the shade of the peppercorn.

\* \* \*

"It really is beautiful here. It's this wedge of paradise with every-thing you could want." Jay took in the towering gums leaning over the creek, the rises and dips in the undulating land, the beautiful girl beside him with wet locks plastered against her forehead, and muscles softening in utter tranquillity.

"Mmm" Her lashes rested on her cheeks.

Jay lay down, pulling her length along his as the sunny morning took their worries away.

\* \* \*

Jay cracked his eyes on the midday sun. Their clothes had dried in the warmth. Lexi lay still, her breaths sliding through her parted lips. His heart caught in his throat. She had that ethereal, sprite-like appearance that made her seem vulnerable. But she wasn't. She was fierce strength and stubborn independence wrapped in endurance. He trailed his fingers over the curve of her neck, the angle of her shoulder. He couldn't not touch her.

Opening one eye, she focused on his mouth.

"Ready for another dunking?" She smirked sleepily. He chuckled and grazed his lips against hers.

"What are you thinking?" She asked languidly. His smile spread.

"Would you believe that for years I lived each day with the strict schedule dictating my every move. I thought I'd found comfort in the boundaries of those pages. Not sure what to do? Check the diary, do what it tells me then tick it off. Move to the next item on the agenda. But look at me now. No routine outside of night and day, and I'm…..happy."

With a feline stretch she reflected. "I wouldn't have pegged you for a routine kind of guy. You look at home here, on a farm. In regards to a diary, I used to keep one, too. Appointments, farm stuff. You know, Saturday at 10am - spray for capeweed in bottom paddock. That sort of thing. But having Brandy made keeping to a schedule difficult. I found I pushed her away to tick off a task, and I started missing things. A smile, a laugh. Just because I wrote on a piece of paper that I had to be elsewhere. Then she'd fall sick, and I'd worry about not crossing those tasks off. And one day I simply stopped writing tasks in. And the most wonderful thing happened. I wasn't out on the farm checking fences, or checking water points in empty paddocks. I was in the house, having an extra long lunch. And I was there to see Brandy take her first steps. I could have missed it. And the grass still grew, the cattle didn't drop dead, and I was exactly where I was supposed to be. I realised then that the most incredible opportunities are hidden in the empty pages of a diary. From then on, If the day is sunny, I spray. If its not, I stock take medicines, or simply have a day off. It's liberating."

Her words resonated. He'd met up with her on a spontaneous whim. This time he was investing in her was not in his schedule, either.

"How are you so brave and perfect?"

Lexi snorted. "I'm so far from perfect it's not even a blip on the horizon."

"You're perfect for me."

Lexi shuffled away so she could get a clearer look at him and narrowed her eyes.

"How can you be so sure about us when I'm not even sure what's happening here?"

# CHAPTER 23

## ALEX

*H*e set his loaded stare on her.

"I'm as sure as I'm taking my next breath. Can't you feel it? There's nothing more logical that this right here, where the only people in the world are you and me. I believe life offers but a single chance at absolute happiness. The kind that withstands every obstacle and period of darkness in its path. We've come through the darkness, Lexi. Now it's time to fight past the last of the barriers. But for this battle, I need you to fight with me like the warrior I know you are."

Her lashes hid her fear. She wanted to believe. The things he stirred up inside her screamed their agreement, but her doubts bared their teeth.

"Aren't you afraid? What if the obstructions are bigger than us? What if, by fighting the battle we end up losing pieces of ourselves?"

"I believe in what we could have, Lex. I know we can get through it all and become the us we are supposed to be. I have to try, because I'm more afraid of walking away and missing out on how incredible this feels. Of course I'm afraid of getting hurt, and I know I'm setting myself up for something I'm not sure I can come back from, but I've never felt so strongly about anything in my life. I know that if I let this slip through my fingers without trying I'll regret it until my very last breath. So I'm swallowing my fear and moving towards the possibility."

Alex cupped his strong jaw in her tiny hand.

"You're so intense, Jay. Sometimes when you look at me I swear you're able to penetrate so far inside me that you see my heart beat."

"Is that a bad thing?"

Her brow crinkled. "I guess I think it should be, but it's not. It's such a turn-on that your attention is anchored to me. I feel like I'm everything to you."

"You are."

She sighed.

"There you go again. You're so potently connected to your heart. You just come at me with single-minded determination and I forget what I should be doing. You confuse me."

"Confuse you? Do you not feel this…thing between us? The electric pull that keeps tightening and drawing us closer together? That tells me that I have to hold on tight to what we have. It's what I want more than anything. What is it that you want?" He propped himself on his elbow, resting his handsome face on his hand, his water tousled hair flopping sexily in every direction. She scanned the incredible body stretched out before her and pinched her lips together.

"You know what I want." Exasperation blew out. Jay's hand ran gently down the curve of her waist and rested on her hip. The warmth spread through her blood.

"Do you know what *I* want, Lexi? I want you to trust me. To let me in. I want you to find something inside me that you need as much as I need you. You are the most independent person I know, but if you don't need anybody, then you don't need me. I want you to *need* me. Need us. Then everything else will fall away."

Alex groaned. "It's just not that easy. Some things just don't go away." She thought of Edward with a shudder.

"Look deep inside yourself. What do you need?" His tone was rough.

"I...I need a home for Brandy and Mum. I need security."

"What about happiness?"

"I don't want happiness. I was happy with my family, and I lost Dad. I was happy managing the farm with my brother, and he left me, too. I found happiness with you, Jay. And I woke to empty sheets. Happiness doesn't last. It goes away and leaves debilitating pain. All I want is to not hurt. That's all.' She finished on a whisper.

"Don't you feel happy now, with me?" His velvet voice lit a fire inside her.

"I do. So happy and...protected, like nothing can touch me when you're by my side. That's why I'm so scared. It's like nothing I've ever felt before. But it won't last. I've lived this, and it doesn't end well. It's not just me any more, either. I have Brandy to think about."

"It doesn't have to be like that. Just take a second to consider a reality where we wake in each other's arms every morning. Where we spend the days working the farm. Just you. And Me. And Sass."

Alex shivered at the thought. They were images already floating around in the fear in her head.

"There are too many things in the way. I'm not the carefree girl you met in the pub that night any more, Jay. She was full of family and heart and delusions of happiness. She was innocent and stupid-"

"Bullshit." Jay growled. "The woman I'm holding now is still in possession of that spirit and fire. You were not stupid, you were a vision of sin and desire. Just as you are now. And innocent..?" His eyes darkened and his voice deepened. "There was absolutely *nothing* innocent about you then or now. The way you touched me…you completely owned me. My body is a slave to your touch in a way I never thought possible. No, Lex. You were *never* innocent."

The sound of his voice, rough with desire caused her body to respond. As it always did for him. Her pulse clattered as she caught his sensuous lips in her mouth. He instantly dived in, as hungry as she was. They became a frantic dance of breathless need, clawing at each other with the urgency to connect, to be closer.

"Christ Lex, you bring out the animal in me. I'm insatiable around you. I want to be inside you every moment of every day."

"Yesss." She sighed. "That sounds like a plan. I know what you mean. You don't even have to touch me and I melt. It's as simple as a look, or a tone of voice and my blood just sings for you."

Jay growled his arousal.

"Oh, Jesus, Jay. That sound!" Her eyes were heavy with heat, but she registered the amusement that danced in his silver gaze. Alex pushed his chest.

"You know exactly what you're doing to me, you beast. That's it! Half the day is gone and I want to show you the rest of the farm."

"Are there any more creeks?" His eyebrow twitched.

"No, but if you don't behave I'll toss you into the bull paddock!" His laughter burned her veins and he angled his Akubra over his eyes, the full force of his maleness causing her groin to pulse.

"Stop it!" She laughed. He was deliberately setting her nerves on fire. His victorious smirk was short-lived, though, when she shot him a sultry glance over her shoulder full of sinful promise.

"Lexi!" He growled.

# CHAPTER 24

## JAY

His phone vibrated in his pocket.

*Daniel.* He listened to the shower still running in the bathroom, and accepted the call.

"Jesus, Jay, when you decide to spice up your life a bit, you like to make it count!"

"Hey, Daniel, what did you find out?" He couldn't be sure over the tinny phone line, but his brother sounded agitated.

"This cop you wanted me to check out? There's something really messed up with that. Apparently, this town hasn't had an officer on duty for over five years. They have no idea who he is, but he's been getting away with impersonating an officer for a very long time. He's managed to get access to all the police files, and for all intents and purposes, he's been doing a pretty good job of ensuring the peace. It all sounds peachy, but if you ask me, there's mental issues in a bloke that impersonates a cop like that. I mean, generally they have to do a psych test before they can be accepted. My contacts assume that he's done the training but failed that last step. That could be dangerous, especially when he has access to police issue arsenal. They're looking into anyone who may have displayed a higher than average desire to become a cop that failed their psych. They want to be well armed with the facts before they move in on him. Just... be careful, Jay. Please. This guy has been staking out her place from your farm. Assume he's always watching."

Jay's hand tightened on the back of his neck and rested his forehead on the door frame.

"Jesus" He whistled.

"Yeah." His brother's voice flattened. "As soon as they know something more they'll call me, so we just need to hold tight until then. It's the best I can offer at the moment."

The silence stretched, heavy with trepidation.

"Hey, Dan, while I have you, there's something else I need you to do." Jay spoke at length, issuing instructions.

"Consider it done, man." Daniel said. Jay heard the bathroom door open.

"Oh, and that reminds me. Lexi and I are coming to dinner at Mum and Dads on Monday. Are you two coming?

"Tilly has to work. She won't fly in until Tuesday. I'll be there, though. I'm glad to hear you two are working through some stuff."

\* \* \*

Lexi paced nervously.

"I'm not going anywhere, Lex" Especially not when that creep was out there. Jay snared her around the waist, pulling her tightly against him. Electrical pulses blistered between them. He loved that about her. Her body reacted to his in a way he'd felt with no other. His thoughts strayed to the real reason he left her alone in the bed that morning. No. He would tell her in time. When he had her trust. Right now the heat from her touch demanded his attention. She stood rigid in his arms.

"Quiet the noise in your head, Lexi. If you don't want to tell me, don't let it interfere with this. With us. I want nothing between us... Oh Jesus!"

"What is it?" She flinched at his unexpected outburst.

"I'm so sorry, Lex, I didn't think. Last night...I...we weren't safe..." Lexi's eyes widened and her hand caught her mouth.

"Oh, shit, Jay, that's so unlike me. I'm so sorry, too. I just...couldn't think straight."

A thin chuckle escaped him.

"I admit, I wasn't thinking at all. I'm clean, if that helps?"

"Me too. I got tested when...yeah, I'm clean." Jay held her eyes with his.

"When you found out the condom failed..." He finished for her. She bobbed her head in agreement.

"Why won't you tell me who Brandy's father was? Do I know him?" She looked at him through hooded eyes and Jay unravelled. He knew she was deflecting, but she was his girl, offering herself to him, and there was no way he could hold back. His reaction to her made it impossible for him to entertain logic, the haze of desire dulling all sense and reason.

"I don't have condoms, Lex." She frowned, her stunning pools of brown windows to her thoughts. If only they would tell him more.

"Neither do I." He caught her lips in his teeth, feeling her breathing dip sharply into panting. She was so responsive it made his veins boil.

His breath hissed as she hastily loosened the buckle of his jeans, her warm hand releasing him from the confines of denim.

"I don't care right now." He whispered around his groan. He scraped his teeth along her neck, sinking them gently into the soft curve of her shoulder.

Her gasp shuddered through her as she felt fog penetrate her reason.

"Nor do I" she stuttered.

Jay slid the bathrobe from her shoulders, still damp from bathing. Her mere nakedness challenging his constraint. This woman was far too potent to resist. He was thirst and she was his lake.

"Christ, I need to be inside you. Now."

He lifted her up, pinning her to the wall as the heat of her body seared him. She locked her legs around his waist, drowning in her own passion, her frantic hands all over him. He grabbed his cock, hovering against her slick entrance.

"Lex?" He paused.

"Hell yes" she breathed.

He slammed into her, revelling in the tight heat that was made for him.

"Christ I love you" He growled as he plunged into her, buried to the hilt in his woman. He groaned at the perfect joining of his body and hers, his bones fizzing with the ultimate intimacy. Their heartbeats jumped, reached and beat together, panting their harmony. Their eyes fused together, acknowledging the sacred ritual they were immersed in, timeless as the earth. This wasn't sex. This was the merging of hearts, the amalgamation of souls, the meaning of life, the reason for existence.

She tightened around him as her body adjusted, milking him as she savoured his delicious invasion. Jay pulled back slowly, shivering at the gentle friction that tumbled through his nerve endings. With a languid lick of his hips, she rolled hers to urge him deeper, and he didn't deny her, worshipping her with every stroke. Her mouth formed an O as her eyes rolled back, her body pressing against his in feral urgency. The sounds she made were his drug of choice, sending him into a gasping spiral of exhilaration. He felt his sac tighten.

"I'm coming!" He drove so deep inside her he could feel the end of her stretch as he emptied inside her.

"Jay!" Her scream was guttural. Her inner walls convulsed and gripped as her own orgasm washed over her. Her bruised mouth, fallen wide as she tasted her release, eyes closed over, her nails embedded in his shoulders. He'd never heard a more incredible sound or witnessed a more erotic sight.

He held her as he caught his breath, running the tip of his nose along her jaw.

"How are you so perfect?" He whispered against her neck. When her breath hitched, he pulled back and searched her face, still buried inside her.

"Damn, I didn't hurt you, did I?" She gently shook her head, dislodging a tear. Jay darted out his tongue to taste it.

"What is it, Lex?"

"It's just that...it's all too perfect."

"What's wrong with that?" He grazed his lips across her forehead.

"You said you loved me." She breathed. She searched his face for regret. He didn't mean to say that aloud. Not yet, anyway. He loved her intrinsically. He'd loved her instantly, deeply and desperately. And when he found her again, it was hungrier, more frantic than ever before. But he was still uncertain about how she felt about him. She had baggage. Lots of it. It was packed with fear, responsibility, fight and failure. It bulged at the seams. But Jay knew he wanted it all. He wanted his girl with all her scars, all her tears, all her imperfections. Because he loved all of her.

"I do."

"You have no right to make me fall for you, Jay." Jay lifted her chin with his finger, forcing her to meet his eyes. His lungs froze. He almost feared the answer, but he needed it.

"Are you falling for me?"

Her voice was a tight whisper of fear.

"Yes."

# CHAPTER 25

## ALEX

*H*e loved her. God damn it. And she loved him. Entirely. She wondered what would happen if she were to defy Edward, desperately wanting to hold onto this dream that was playing out before her.

She shook her head. Dreams break. She knew that. Jay had refused to leave that night, still wielding his agreement with Sabrina as a weapon. She submitted with the growling prod of dread pressing harder on her stomach.

\* \* \*

Alex's phone buzzed. The sound of her bellowing cows ringtone filtered from her pocket, and the topless god sipping coffee opposite her raised an eyebrow and quirked his lips.

"Alex" She answered. Her mouth fell open and she caught Jay's puzzled stare.

"Thank-you!" She muttered and ended the call.

"We topped the market, Jay! Oh my God! The calves we put in yesterday? Record high, they said. I mean, they have great blood-lines, but this is more than I hoped for!"

She danced around the kitchen in utter exuberance. She flung her arms around Jay and planted a kiss on his startled lips.

"Do you know what this means?"

"Retirement for Old John?" His eyebrows quirked. She shook her head, giggling

"No. I'd miss the game of roulette every time I go to start him. It means I can afford to pay for Mum to stay in town! Oh, my God!" Her laughter clattered between them. Jay's gorgeous lips widened into a happy grin.

"I'm so happy, Lex. I'm so proud of you."

They spent the day in the paddocks grinning like idiots at each other. Even though her life had passed with her undertaking the majority of work on her own, having Jay working at her side gave her a sense of utter contentment. It was much nicer to have someone to talk to instead of talking to herself, or Horace. Someone to share the burden of hard times, as well as celebrating the achievements. His support, his faultless belief in her, his constructive ideas and fearless way he approached whatever work needed doing; It rounded out her existence until she almost overflowed. It was what had been missing in her life that she never knew was absent.

She slammed to a stop, Horace bumping into her.

"What's wrong?" She looked into the concerned face of the man she loved. Had always loved. She stroked his face with the heat of her eyes lit on his gorgeous face. She shivered in the memory of his touch.

"I don't want you to go."

His rough exhale cut the air. She felt large hands encircle her waist, the heat from his chest against her back, the whisper of his breath on her neck.

"So I won't go." She felt his shoulders lift.

She gripped his arms tightly, her focus on the ancient eucalypts along the creek.

"It's not that simple. It's Edward. He's….a bad person, Jay. He'll hurt you."

"It *is* that simple, Lex. I won't let him hurt anyone."

Her focus blurred. He lifted a finger to her chin, catching her attention with his silvery intensity.

"Lex, there is only one obstacle between us now. You need to learn to trust me. I promise you I won't leave you. I won't hurt you. I've been honest and open with you, but I need that from you, too. You say you have feelings for me, but you still guard yourself from me. Tell me what to do. What do you need from me to be able to let me in? Please. I need your trust."

His stare was potent. She felt him probing her responses, the ones that didn't have words. He knew there was something lurking within her that she refused to reveal.

Her breath shuddered. He needed to be told about Brandy. She opened her mouth and then slammed it closed. He said he wouldn't hurt her, but he already had. He'd given her soul deep wounds that refused to heal. She'd lost count of the tears she'd spilled among the peppercorn roots beneath indifferent stars while she grieved over the husk of a heart he'd left her with. It was almost more than she could endure at times. More salt bearing his name than her own brother and father. She needed time to process his betrayal, to be able to finally decide if being with him was indeed what would fade the hurt to a manageable scar. But the most urgent threat right now was Edward. Alex knew his patience would come to an end. Especially if Jay was still in the picture.

His infatuation with her was dangerous. He'd stepped it up after Ryan died, and she knew he wouldn't give up.

"I don't think you understand just how bad Edward is." Her voice trembled.

"Don't worry about Edward." But she detected an edge in his voice, an uncertainty that fed her doubt.

Alex wanted to trust Jay. He made her feel strong and safe. Strong enough to stand up to Edward. Almost. Jay wasn't the one with everything to lose. She had her mother and daughter to consider.

\* \* \*

They'd wandered up to the house together, his hand slipping over hers as they walked through the long grass. It felt natural to be with Jay like this, but the feeling was shadowed by Daniel's warning. *"That cop's been up at Pete's farm almost every day he tells me, and its not to look in on him, either. He's flattened the grass in the lower paddock. The one that...."*

*"Overlooks my place."* She finished for him.

Alex glanced up at the adjoining farm. She wasn't sure if she'd imagined that glint of sun on metal in that paddock. She stepped away from Jay, sliding her hand from his clasp. His jaw tightened and clouds dimmed the happiness of moments before.

"I think he's watching us." Jay tilted his head, scanning the fields, his Akubra casting his eyes in shadows. Alex's pulse blew out. With a day's growth, his cowboy hat perched like that and his tight jeans, he was a walking, breathing wet dream. He was sex in cowboy clothes, and having him so close dislodged everything else. As terrified of Edward as Alex was, it faded away beneath the overpowering potency of her man. She choked. Her man. She shook the fog away and picked up her pace. Letting her guard down for a moment was plain irresponsible of her. Yet she was finding it more and more difficult to care about anything besides what her body craved. And her heart.

* * *

As Alex stepped into the house, she turned towards Jay to ask if he wanted lunch but froze when she saw his expression.

His face was olive stone, chiselled in fury and lust. His silver eyes were hard and sharp as they bored into her. He was a powerhouse of rage and desire. She felt her lips part and heart falter, unable to move as he stalked towards her. He rested his hand over her throat. It should have frightened her, but she found herself leaning into it. Her heart bucked. His low voice rattled.

"I am sick and tired of this hot and cold business, Lex. You're such a contradiction that it riles me up. I want to shake you out of whatever shit you're keeping from me. Give me your honesty, Lexi. I'm taking away your choice. I *will* be in your life. You will *not* keep me away. Get used to it."

Jay stood over her, filling her view with solid muscle and raw determination.

"Don't you think to tell me what I should or shouldn't do, Jay. You have no idea what's -"

"Well damn well tell me then!" He roared at her, lips twisting in anger. Her bones rumbled under his ire, and heat burst from between her legs. Jay's glare held her as the hand on her throat pushed her slowly backwards. Her legs bumped the edge of the kitchen table. Her pulse fired up and sent flames between her legs.

"Make your choice right now. Give it all to me or tell me to walk away. I *won't* share your thoughts with another man."

He didn't wait for a response. His lips crashed against hers with bruising force, one hand fisting her hair, the one at her throat pushing her onto the kitchen table, pinning her down. She watched his nostrils flare as the animal in him took control. She should have been afraid, but instead, she groaned with arousal, arching her body into him with a need that burned.

# CHAPTER 26

## JAY

*H*e couldn't stop himself. She was his, and she kept behaving like Edward owned her. It took him to the brink of rage, then shoved him over thinking of that crooked cop in her thoughts. He barely knew what he was doing. He was furious, but then he caught a whiff of her arousal and reason fled. If she said anything, he was deaf to it. He lost control of himself, his senses flooded with his need, her desire. He saw her spread out before him on the table, lust glazed eyes locked on him from heavy lids, her shirt open to expose the swell of her breasts lurching frantically under his palm. Her jeans were gone, her panties torn from her body.

"Christ!" He snarled. He was suddenly inside her, pounding into that hot nirvana that made him feel like a god. So silken, so hot, so wet. He rutted between her legs like he was fighting a war, diving and thrusting like he could grind her into forgetting everything but him. Light flashed through his vision, spearing the image of Lexi taking all of him, her head thrown back, her taut neck slender and submissive beneath his hand. Her muscles tightened around his cock, clenching hard around his swollen girth. She felt so damn good it was impossible to hold back. Pressure grew in his balls. His head fell back, hand biting into her hip as he yanked her into his thrusts. He was in a limbo without sight or sound, the only sensations were the feel of her and the smell of her. Buried deep in vanilla and honey. And he was going to explode.

He came with a shattering roar, filling her with jet after jet of his seed, giving her everything he had. He heaved air, head swimming with the force of it. It was the most intense orgasm of his life.

He blinked until his vision returned. He saw Lexi was still pinned beneath him, her mouth open and gasping, her lips red and thick from the urgency of his kisses. Her shirt buttons had popped, her bra torn and hanging to the side, still looped over one creamy arm. Her brown eyes unfocused. He felt her breath move beneath the hand still clutching her neck. He yanked it away.

"Oh christ, Lexi! Are you okay? I'm so sorry!"

Her eyes slowly narrowed on him, arms limp at her side. He pulled out of her, grunting as he left her warmth. Lifting her from the table, crushing her to his chest, he was too afraid to let her go in case it was the last time he was able to hold her. He'd lost control, taking her like the wild animal he was. Did she tell him to stop?

"Lexi! Talk to me, are you okay?" He heard her breath rasp over a thick swallow, an arm slowly snaking around the back of his neck. He turned her slightly to face him, her pupils blown out, her pulse still erratic. Jay pushed her hair from her eyes, fear gripping him harder with every second of silence that passed.

"Jay?" Her husky tone tightened his chest.

"Lexi?" He held his breath. Regret thundered through his veins.

"Angry sex is the best sex I've ever had!"

Blowing out his relief, he crushed her closer to him. He hid the tears that fell. He'd never been so afraid in his life.

After a while, she sat up in his lap, straddling his thighs.

"I'm so sorry, Lex. I just lost control. You didn't deserve that. It won't happen again. I was so angry-"

"Shut up, Jay. And it had better happen again. The focus, your need for me, it's so erotic. I love that you want me so much you can't control it."

"It's dangerous…"

"It's empowering!"

He frowned.

"I'll try to explain," She elaborated, searching inside herself. "It makes me feel like I'm everything to you. It makes me feel powerful that a man with such strength is powerless when it comes to me. I mean, you're all muscle and control and power. You look unshakable, but I can bring you undone."

He nodded. He loved the way she analysed it so honestly.

"What if you didn't want to, Lexi? What if you'd said no?"

"You wouldn't hurt me, Jay. If I said no, you'd stop."

The conviction in her stare made his heart seize.

"I was so far gone in you that I couldn't hear you!"

She shivered. "I know. But if you had to, you'd stop. Your expression was...wow! I almost came just looking at you. It wouldn't matter, Jay. I can't control myself around you either. I always want you. You're like a thirst I just can't quench..."

"I know what you mean. I've never lost it before. It was the most intense orgasm of my life, and I never seem to be sated around you. I could have you again right now." His silver eyes darkened as she giggled.

"Me too," she sighed. "But we've got stuff to do." Jay dipped his head in agreement. She was beginning to trust him! She didn't realise it, and she was still cautious, but she was slowly lowering her guard. His heart hummed. She was his, she just needed to reach that conclusion herself.

Jay floated in delirium. She wanted him, was falling for him, and she loved simply working alongside him. There would always be improvements to be made on the farm. His thoughts turned to Brandy, and he cleared his throat.

"Um, I've had a thought I'd like to run by you, actually." It annoyed him that she instinctively tensed at his suggestion.

"I have a mate who owes me a favour, and he owns a timber yard. If I'm not treading on toes, I'd like to organise timber to start fixing up the verandah."

He watched her pride leap to the surface and she set her jaw.

"You're not going to do this, Jay. This farm is my responsibility, and I'm not letting you put your money into it. I know it needs to be done. Desperately. But I can't owe you." She chewed her lip.

"Is that what happened with Edward? You owe him for something?" As soon as he said it he regretted it. "Why is it imperative that you do everything on your own? It's not weakness to ask for help once in a while. There are times we all need the love, support, strength of another person. It's what makes us human."

"Vulnerability leaves scars. It draws a bullseye around your vital organs. Then there's the underlying discomfort of having to repay that debt, and the price far outweighs the rewards. If you deal with everything yourself, there's nobody to have a claim on you."

She shut down, shook her head and turned away, her head jerking up as she looked over into the neighbour's paddock.

"Oh my god! Pete brought my calves!" Jay studied her carefully, waiting for a reaction. She'd met Daniel, but gave no indication she knew they were related. He sighed inwardly at the thought. He'd placed so much importance in honesty, and he was keeping his own secrets from her. *Oh, what a tangled web we weave,* he thought.

It was a conversation they desperately needed to have, one that should have been aired before they slept together. But she always had her walls up, or Edward showed up.

"Lex, we need to talk." She turned to him in confusion, the sunlight from the window behind her made her hair look like a halo. His angel. It was time they revealed their cards.

He gently patted the cushion beside him. He needed to be able to touch her, hold her, reassure her. She slinked like a suspicious cat beside him.

"Please, Lexi. Tell me about Brandy's father."

# CHAPTER 27

## ALEX

She locked her jaw. Did she want to be telling Jay about his daughter here? She glanced around her home. Her dreams and memories were embedded in the wood panelled walls, the sound of Ryan's laughter still lingering in the furniture. Her Father's blood, sweat and tears lodged in the carpets beneath her feet. What if she told him and he hated her for keeping it from him? What if that was the last time she ever saw Jay, sitting on the couch that remembered her contractions? Those memories were sacred. She couldn't have them lost in the pain of Jay's memory. She stroked the worn cushions. She lifted her eyes to his silver ones and took a deep breath.

"I'll tell you, Jay. But I can't tell you here." Her words were slow, deliberate, gentle. She expected him to be disappointed, or angry, but his expression was patient and understanding. It was a look he wore most, only broken occasionally with impatience and frustration. Then she realised. He was waiting for her. She was the destination he was working towards, the firm, reliable security never faltering from his goal. He delivered on his word with iron will, focused determination and unwavering intention.

"Will you tell me *everything*, Lex?" She shivered, but not in fear. In fact she'd never felt so strong as she did under his support.

She noticed how much he liked to say her name. Her name on his lips sounded like forever.

She nodded.

"Tomorrow we visit your family, so the day after that? Wednesday? I'll ask mum to take Brandy for the night."

Jay pulled her into a soul saving embrace.

"I love you, Jay." She whispered. She felt his breath catch.

"I feel like I've waited forever for you to say that. Christ, I love you so much I ache, Lex."

She leaned up and pressed her lips to his. He instantly deepened the kiss, his breath building. She climbed into his lap, straddling his thighs.

"Well, isn't this fucking touching!" Lexi sprung from Jay at the icy tone in the doorway. They hadn't heard the car pull up, or the door open. Edward leaned against the door frame, tension radiating off him, lip twitching and hand on his holster.

Jay stood, positioning himself between Lexi and Edward, but Alex stepped around him. She squared her shoulders and filled her lungs. She lifted her chin and met Edward's eyes. With Jay by her side her courage held steady and she was able to finally face him. The angles and ridges of his face should have made Edward a handsome man. It was the absence of humanity that turned his beauty into something twisted and unappealing. His vibrant blue eyes that invited horror. They were ice and rage.

"Edward. I think it's time to stop this, don't you think? You have no right to tell me who I can or can't see. Just please, Edward, back off and leave us alone."

Edward's lips twisted in a snarl. His left eye twitched, fist flexing over his weapon.

"Get out." His face tight and wild as he rounded on Jay.

"I think it's you who needs to leave, Edward. Lexi didn't invite you in." His temple pulsed and molars jammed. He craned his neck towards Alex.

"You fucking whore! Not so much as a kiss for years, and this piece of shit floats in and you're on your back with your ankles around your ears for him?"

Alex blanched. Jay stepped up, towering over Edward. "Watch your god damn mouth! You're the piece of shit, Edward. Get the hint. She's not interested in you. Never was; never will be."

To Alex it appeared that both men had grown larger. Muscles on both of them were straining and bulging, like two bulls in their prime sizing each other up. The air was tangible with testosterone and adrenaline.

Edward flicked open his holster and drew his gun. Alex choked on a scream. Excitement shone in the cop's cold blue eyes. A trail of saliva formed on Edward's lip, and his breath hissed around it. Alex's stomach knotted. She knew with sharp certainty Edward wouldn't hesitate to pull the trigger.

Like a streak of lightning, Jay's hand snapped up and snatched the weapon from the cop. Edward's eyes widened and his jaw dropped. Jay was still moving, though, stalking into Edwards chest until the cop staggered backwards. With every step of Jay's, the smaller man retreated, struggling to find a clear path. His shoulder crashed into the door frame, his hip into the kitchen bench top. A chair toppled as Edward scrambled. Jay backed him out into the yard where he stepped back, giving the cop some space.

Jay's body was coiled as he lifted the gun, suspending it in a steady hold, aimed above the bridge of Edward's nose.

"Jay!" Alex's plea shook out.

The metallic click of the safety releasing changed Edward's posture completely. His shoulders lowered in fury. There was no fear, no defeat in his expression. Just madness and contempt.

"Jay?" Time stretched.

Jay swung his arm backwards, unloading the gun into the dirt beside them. Edward jumped at the sound, his hat dropping to the dust beside him as he twisted and dodged the noise.

The gun clicked empty.

"Get the fuck out of here, Edward, and don't ever come back!" Jay growled.

The cop should have been beaten. Without his gun Alex expected him to cower and surrender. Instead he boiled with a rage that tipped into insanity. She shuddered. Edward snarled at them when he reached the car.

"You'll pay for that. I'll find out who you are and destroy you." His hate flashed. Jay snapped up the hat from the grass, his determined strides landing his chest against Edward. Edward flinched. Jay pressed the hat and the gun into the cop's chest, pushing him into the driver's seat with them.

"Try" He snarled. The engine fired and wheels spun, sending the police car flying down Lexi's driveway.

She felt Jay's large warm hands run down her shoulders as he knelt before her.

"You okay, Lex?" She looked down into his furrowed brow, nodding slowly.

"I think so. Jesus Jay, he's crazy! He would have shot you. We shouldn't have done that. He's a cop. Couldn't he have you arrested?"

He smiled weakly at her, shaking his head.

"Lex." He began, uncertainly, brushing a stray tendril of hair from her face. There was an edge to his tone that made Alex narrow her focus on him. His tongue darted out over his lips.

"First of all, I need you to trust me. I need you to tell me you believe that no matter what I promise you I will deliver. If I tell you I'm going to keep you safe, I need you to know that I will."

"Jay, you're scaring me" Alex whispered, dropping her eyes. His fingers dug into her upper arms, and he shook her attention back to him. The warm silver of his attention touched her soul. She saw the intensity of his love for her. They were the eyes of her dreams, her nightmares. They were carved on her heart forever, whether they made it through this or not. In that moment, she swallowed down the last of the doubt she held for Jay. He may have discarded her three years ago, but there was no denying he was here for her now, proving his intentions to her.

"Tell me you trust me, Lex." It was the pain in his voice that unravelled her.

"I...I trust you, Jay." With the words forming, she knew it was true. The hesitation she'd felt before seemed to dissolve into forgiveness. Jay explored her face, searching for doubt. Finding none, he huffed out a relieved breath, loosening his grip to stroke her arms with his thumbs.

"Lex, I didn't trust him. I knew he was holding something over you but you wouldn't tell me. So I probed a bit deeper. Lex....this town hasn't had a cop in five years."

Alex clutched her stomach and curled her body. Her head fogged.

"Who is he, then?" Her body trembled. Jay sighed his frustration, stabbing his fingers through his hair.

"We don't know that yet. But I need you to know I'll protect you, Lex. Be careful, but know I'm here."

Alex sank into the verandah, her entire body shaking. Her head pounded. She caught her face in her hands. She couldn't believe that just happened. Edward had backed away so easily. Too easily. He wouldn't accept the humiliation of being beaten like that. Then Jay would pay. And then he'd make her pay.

# CHAPTER 28

## JAY

*T*he victory was bittersweet. Lexi trusted him. He saw the truth of it shine on her face. But now that she knew Edward was a bigger threat, it overshadowed the deeper level of connection they'd reached.

They spent the afternoon organising Sabrina's enrolment into the Care Facility. Alex had called a removalist in to pack her up ready to go. With Edward a real threat, it needed to happen sooner rather than later. Jay offered to make the call.

"Sabrina, sorry to interrupt your lunch, but I need to talk to you."

"What's up, Jay. You sound tense. Is everything okay with you and Lex?"

"Yeah, actually. It is. We're off to meet my parents tomorrow night, but we were hoping you could have Sass the following night too. She said she'd tell me everything."

"Thank the heavens for small miracles. Yes, Jay. I *am* rolling my eyes. I'm pleased for you both. Did you ask her about her brother?" Jay sighed down the line.

"Yeah, but it only poses more questions. Anyway, things got a bit heavy here, and for your own safety and our peace of mind, you're being packed up as we speak for another year in the facility."

"Are you sure you don't need me?" Jay's lips twitched. He knew she'd do whatever Lexi asked, but the delight in her voice was thick. Lexi was right. Sabrina needed this.

"Absolutely, Sabrina. You know Lex. She is so grateful to you, but she knows you need to be with friends now, instead of looking after a toddler. Now that Sass is old enough to go out to work with Lex, she's looking forward to spending more time with her."

He spent the next few minutes filling Sabrina in on Edward, how he staked the place out using the neighbouring farm, and assuring he'd keep Lexi safe.

"I knew you were a good man, Jay."

He smirked at that. "No you didn't. You told me to leave if I recall correctly."

"You'd be a nice challenge for my daughter if you weren't such a smart-arse!" Jay laughed loudly as he heard Brandy reprimand her Nana for saying "Mart-are".

"Be safe, Sabrina, and tell Sass I said hello. I kind of miss her."

Sabrina's tone changed. He heard her exhale twice.

"I'll take Brandy tomorrow night. You two *have* to talk."

After disconnecting with Sabrina, Jay dialled his brother.

"What's going on, Jay? You still coming to my place tomorrow to see Mum and Dad? They're so excited to meet Alex."

Jay confirmed and brought Daniel up to speed on the altercation with Edward. Daniel whistled low and long.

"Shit, Jay. I spoke to my guys yesterday and they had nothing more to tell me. They have narrowed it down to a handful of possible suspects, but it's still a lengthy process. They're hesitant to move on it before they have all the answers in case he gets a whiff of it and he slips away. The good news is he'll be up for substantial jail time when he is caught. Tilly says in her expert opinion, he's a nut job."

Jay laughed. "That's an understatement. How is Tilly?"

Jay winced as Daniel described the depths of morning sickness, and her cravings for peanut butter and beef jerky.

"She's not even human anymore, man. She's this devil creature straight from the underworld spewing hell-fire and brimstone! I have to carry jerky and a jar of PB with me everywhere I go just in case. If she wants it and I'm not already feeding it to her, she's cursing my penis and sobbing about how adorable puppies are. I'm completely freaked out!"

Jay's body shook with laughter. He imagined Tilly with horns and a tail. The image quickly morphed into a serene picture of Lexi gazing up at him with adoration in her warm eyes, her soft hand holding his against her swollen belly. Jay's laughter cut suddenly and he turned towards the house, watching his woman as she paced the kitchen. He smirked. She couldn't sit, or stand still when she was taking a call. She traversed the halls and bedrooms in her verbal circuit.

"I can hear you thinking about her, Jay. You considering knocking her up?"

Jay sighed. "She'd be stunning with her belly big with our baby."

"Shit, Jay. You got it bad! It's a trap, you know. I'm sure they slip us something so we think it's going to be wonderful, until here we are, submissively accepting the blame for their nausea, broken and bloodied from trying to fulfil their perpetually fleeting demands!"

"And you only have seven months to go!" He grinned at Daniel's dramatic groan.

"I'll never survive it!"

* * *

With Sabrina packed up, the van rolled out the driveway. It swayed as it rolled through the potholes.

"I gotta fix that" she muttered. Jay kissed the top of her head and pulled her close.

Her glance strayed into Jay's farm. Jay's stomach flipped. He'd tell her about that tomorrow night. Jay realised their confessions wouldn't be one sided. She didn't know about the farm, or that he wasn't a mechanic. It could wait. Sabrina was bringing Brandy home and collecting her personals.

* * *

"Jay!" He'd never get tired of that excited squeak. Brandy leaned into her run, her dark hair flying behind her. He snatched her up and held her close, smelling that pure, clean toddler smell.

"Hey Sass, I missed you!"

Lexi laughed at them.

"What about your mummy?" She demanded, feigning hurt, her arms stretching out to her daughter. Brandy squirmed into them and rolled her bright grey eyes.

"But Mummy, I seen you *all* my *life!*" She squished her lips on her mother's cheek, then held open arms to Jay. His heart leapt to his throat. The epitome of purity and innocence, wrapped in a cheeky smile. Jay snatched her to him, smiling. She may not have her mother's eyes, but all her emotions danced on the surface of them just like hers.

"How can you be so adorable, Sass?" She flashed her pearly nubs. Tilting her head to the side, she shrugged her shoulders.

"Just am."

She was a tornado of fresh air, dancing around happily, ducking and weaving through Horace's legs as the mare stood patiently. She'd come to greet the toddler with a whinney Brandy tried to mimic, clearly as delighted to see her home again as Alex and Jay were.

* * *

"Stay safe, Sabrina." Jay commanded as she tucked herself behind the wheel. Brandy was sobbing in the car seat, reluctant to leave home for another night. Jay reflected on how domesticated the scene was, waving off visitors with his girl tucked into his arm, the scent of her perfume inviting and engulfing him. He bent and nibbled on the sweet nape of her neck, revelling in the shivers he caused within her. He laughed and pulled away.

"We need to get ready to go or we'll be late, and this is scary enough for me without worrying about tardiness." But her pupils were blown, and her pulse jumped beneath her heating skin.

"I think you need a shower, Lex" He murmured into her hair, flashing a wolfish grin.

Her laughter was an antidote for the tension between his shoulders. He scooped her up, her fingers locking into his hair.

"I'm not the one with the dirty mind, Jay…" She froze suddenly, horror streaking across her face.

"I don't even know your last name. Isn't that awful!"

He smirked at her.

"I guess that makes you a shameless hussy, then. Bedding a bloke without knowing his name." He tut-tutted as his eyes burned with amusement. He pressed a kiss to her lips, speaking against them as he carried her towards the bathroom.

"Morrison. Joseph Morrison." Her balled fists pushed him away. Humour ebbed from her face.

"Joseph?" Why did you tell me it was Jay?" She frowned suspiciously. He sighed inwardly, willing his raging erection to settle down for a moment. He peppered kisses on her neck as he lowered her to the floor.

"My father is Joseph Jay Morrison Senior. I was named after him, but mine was changed to Jay so Dad would stop assuming Mum was angry at him all the time."

Lexi's laughter bubbled and fizzed, her beautiful eyes dropping to the floor.

"We hardly know each other. No. You know plenty about me. You know my name, where I live, my family." She gestured with arms wide. "But you're virtually a stranger to me."

Jay cupped her face, angling her gaze to him.

"Tomorrow night we can talk. We can rewind us and start from scratch. No secrets, okay?" She pulled her lip between her teeth.

"Why do I know that name? Yeah. Okay. Tomorrow." Her voice was small. She looked so fragile right then. He glanced his mouth over hers.

"Lex, I promise I love you. I keep my promises. Tomorrow night. I made a booking at The Eatery at six. Nothing will stop me, because at 6:01 we can begin again." Nipping the sensitive flesh on her shoulder, he grinned into her shudder, led her gently inside and lost himself in his girl.

# CHAPTER 29

## ALEX

*J*ay pulled up at the accommodation. Jay and his brother shared the house while they were in town. She wondered how Jay could afford his share of the rent while he was taking time off from work. Her brow furrowed. What would happen if Jay wanted to go back to his hometown, wherever that was. There was no certainty that Jay would move to her town, or be able to afford to buy a farm here.

"You look amazing, Lex. Stop worrying. They'll love you." Jay pushed the door open, the smell of roast lamb washed over her like gravy.

"Jay!" The woman squealed, pushing her greying hair from her face and hugging him hard. She turned to Alex, grabbing at her hands with a wide smile.

"You must be Lexi. Oh, dear girl, we've heard so much about you. It's wonderful to finally see you in the flesh! I'm Lydia, and this is my husband, Joseph." She stepped up to the man. He was an older version of Jay, very distinguished and handsome in his own right. He released Jay from his bear hug with a slap, and clutched Alex's hands.

"So this is what all the fuss has been about, son. I see you didn't exaggerate her beauty." He bent down and muttered under his breath.

"We thought he was full of shit and was bringing home a hairy, puppy-eating ogre!"

Alex threw her head back and laughed.

"That's exactly what I am when I'm angry!" She retorted with a nod. His laughter rumbled around the room.

Lydia smirked. "She's way too good for you, Junior. Hope she keeps you in line!"

The woman passed her a glass with ice cubes floating. "I hear you're partial to brandy and coke." they touched their glasses together. The men had drifted off into the den, leaving the two women in the dining room to talk.

"Oh, gosh, Lydia. You didn't need to go to so much trouble, really. I'm actually a whiskey or rum girl. It's been a few years since I had brandy." She smiled gently at the memory. She was suddenly aware that Lydia stiffened beside her wearing a thoughtful expression.

"You have a daughter you named after the drink, don't you?" Alex's mouth suddenly dried. She swallowed with the smile fixed on her face. Jay's mother was sharp as a blade. She'd have to think before mentioning her daughter. Just until tomorrow.

"Yes, there's just something about the word that makes you feel warm and happy, isn't there? Jay tells me his brother and wife are expecting?"

Lydia let the silence stretch. Alex took another sip.

"Yes" the woman allowed Alex to deflect with a thoughtful smile. Alex's breath shuddered. Lydia was as perceptive as Jay.

"She's been a right monster with it, poor dear. She's giving our Daniel a run for his money. We, of course, think it's hilarious. Daniel is doing the best he can, but, well, you know how it is, Lexi. I remember feeling so uncomfortable the entire time with both the boys. Craved prawns, if I remember correctly." She sniggered. "I suppose it stands to reason that Jay loves seafood."

Another piece of trivia Alex didn't know about Jay.

"I know you're still learning about each other. It's part of the fun. You'll have plenty of time now, though, being neighbours and all. And the rest of his life, of course, is in the tabloids."

Alex felt the colour drain from her face.

"Oh, shit. He hasn't told you yet, has he?" Lydia's voice quietly cutting through her panic. Her hand shot out around Alex's.

"Honey, he loves you. It probably slipped his mind. He was so happy he found you…" Alex connected the dots.

"Joseph Morrison! That's where I knew the name from. Joseph's Diesel Repairs. I've seen the name enough at Jimmy's. I should have…Jesus…" Her head swam. Tabloids. Reporters. She remembered them closing around her view of him. Working remotely in her pastures, among her cattle, Lexi occasionally found time to scan the newspapers over her morning coffee, but they were the locally run papers reporting on local events, and she rarely watched television. She was unaware of any stories the national papers ran. She pinched her brow. There were so many things she was yet to uncover about Jay.

"You're a huge deal, aren't you?" She steadied her breath.

"Kinda." She squeezed Alex sheepishly. "I'm so sorry. I know things have been busy lately, but I should've thought before opening my mouth."

Alex offered a weak smile. It faltered as she processed the rest of Lydia's words.

"Neighbours?" Lydia closed her eyes and drained her glass. Guiltily she admitted; "He brought the farm next to yours, Lexi." Alex's heart hammered.

"But I've met my neighbour, his name is-"

"Daniel's here!" Jay's timbre rang through the hallway. Alex made a strangled sound in her throat, shaking her head.

"Jesus, Lydia. All these secrets. I don't even know who he is." Bile rose in Alex's throat. What a disaster. Lydia pinned Alex with her stare.

"Who is he? Lexi, he's the man who loves you with every piece of his heart. That's who he is. Never doubt that. I'm so sorry. He would have told you himself if I kept my mouth shut."

"I'm just in shock, Lydia. It's a lot to process right now. With so many things happening...I just can't handle any more surprises tonight."

"Well, you already know Daniel then, let's go greet him. I'll get you a whiskey. I think you deserve it." She winked and took Alex's empty glass.

They sat around the dinner table, Daniel poking fun at Jay. It was obvious to Alex where Jay's family values originated from. They were so close. After the initial awkwardness of her meeting with Daniel, Alex relaxed into the conversation.

Jay squeezed her thigh reassuringly. He bobbed his head, touching his forehead to hers.

You okay, Lex? You can relax, babe. I knew they'd love you." Alex gulped air and nodded.

"Yeah, Just a bit nervous, still. Angry cows I can deal with. People aren't as predictable."

His low chuckle vibrated the air around her.

"Trust me, Lex. I've got your back. So sorry I didn't tell you about Daniel. I didn't think about it until it was too late. Tomorrow we'll talk it all out. Everything's going to be fine." His wink sent tremors between her shoulders. She met his stunning silver eyes and watched them ignite, her lips quirking in response despite her unease.

"Stop those thoughts, Jay. We can work on those…later." His expression was full of heat and hunger before he blinked it away.

"Oh, Lex, Sabrina sent a message a while ago. She's had to take Corrinne to the doctors, so she's on her way to drop Sass off." He brushed his lips over her temple and returned to the conversation.

Sabrina's words lurched into her head. *The second I saw his eyes I could tell who he was!*

Her pulse punched furiously. Her lungs wouldn't fill. She lifted her wide eyes and met the curious stare of Lydia.

"Yes, I'd love to meet your daughter." The calm and thoughtful words were loaded. Alex gulped around the ball of panic rising in her throat.

The doorbell rang, and before Alex could move, Jay rose from his chair, grinning.

"I'll get it. I can't wait for you to meet her. She's an angel."

Like a horror movie in slow motion, she watched as Jay's broad frame made his way to the front door. Sound emptied, except for the quiet murmur of Jay and Sabrina talking, and the squawk of "Jay!" Alex pictured him picking up his daughter. Alex darted a frantic look at Lydia, who'd placed her cutlery on her plate and was watching Alex with quiet interest.

The door closed, and Jay appeared holding Brandy, her arms tight around his neck and her head buried in his chest. *Don't look up!* Alex wanted to scream.

"Hey Sass, say hi to everyone."

Brandy lifted her head and owned the room. Alex drank in the image before her, clutching her mouth in trepidation. Jay filled the room with his energy, his strength, his beauty. He was perfect. His luminous grey eyes burned brighter than everything else around him, except for the matching pair in his arms. Brandy's complexion merged with Jay's, her features softer, but so obviously Jay's that it left her breathless. There it was. The last beautiful image to scratch into her memory before her world fell apart.

"Hi, everyone!" Brandy grinned.

Everyone around the table echoed the greeting except for Lydia. She stepped up to her son and lifted Brandy from his arms. She held the toddler close, breathing her in and kissing her forehead. Then her cold tone rolled clearly through the room.

"Just how old is the child with eyes like my son's?"

The silence was instant.

Jay snapped his handsome face at his mother wearing an expression of confusion. Alex watched numbly a realisation dawned. Brandy turned two a couple of months back. Nine months for the pregnancy and... He looked hard at Brandy and saw his own eyes staring back at him. He baulked, staggering against the wall as he actually saw her for the first time. His throat bobbed.

Jay's gaze launched at Alex with such betrayal that her heart locked.

"You didn't tell me!" The anguish in his eyes revealed the tornado of devastation deeper down.

"You moved on!" She accused. Her own pain replayed behind her tears.

His breathing grew ragged with emotion.

"I *never* moved on, Lex. I searched for you across the entire state and didn't stop for *three god damn years*!"

Alex snapped. Her own pain grew teeth.

"Rubbish!" She snarled. "You're a liar! You lied about everything, Jay! Your job. You lied about buying a farm! I didn't even know your real name until today! And now you're feeding me bull about searching for me? And do you want to know just *how* I know its bull? Unlike you, I was stupid enough to actually do it, Jay. I searched for *you*, and I found you, the following weekend. You were in the foyer of The White Hawk, and I almost called out to you. Then your *fiancee* appeared, jumping into your arms before you took her into your hotel room, just like you did to me the week before, only she was worth more to you than a cheap pub room!"

He hissed his shock. In the silence that followed, Alex's rage forced her legs to move. In a corner of her soul she'd hoped he'd reveal a twist that would prove her wrong. A twin brother? Mistaken identities? Instead, he'd confirmed it with his guilt. She pushed out of her chair, plucked Brandy from Lydia's stunned arms, watching guilt twist his handsome face before she rushed her daughter out of the house, and into the cool night air.

"Jaaaaay!" Brandy sobbed as she was fastened into her car seat.

For the second time in her life, Alex left the shattered shards of her heart at the feet of the man with captivating eyes and drove home.

# CHAPTER 30

## JAY

*J*ay's knees buckled beneath him. The world disappeared and the air thinned.

"Jesus, *fuck!*" He roared. The image of Brandy's eyes burned into his retinas. Brandy. His *daughter*.

*I found out he was seeing someone else. By the time I discovered I was pregnant three months into it, he had already moved on. I never bothered telling him.* Lexi was talking about *him*.

"Are you okay, darling?" Lydia's hand slid over his cheek. Jay jerked away, scrambling to his feet. His mother's face reflected his shock, her silver eyes an older version of Brandy's. He couldn't look.

"I, uh, I need to go." The din around him faded as he stepped into the street.

A daughter. With Lexi. *We used protection and the condom failed. He never would have considered a baby a possibility. He hurt me, Jay.*

Of the few questions she answered, she answered truthfully. He lamented how different things would have been if she hadn't found him the moment his fiancee met with him. His thoughts flashed back three years. He remembered the reporters closing in around him.

*"Is it true you've finally found someone to tie the knot with?"*

*"Yes. Here she is now."* The blonde beauty launched into his arms, planting a lingering kiss on his lips.

*"Isn't she stunning?"* He'd looked adoringly into her face, her make-up immaculate. Her designer red dress glimmered around her body. A crowd gathered behind the reporters.

*"When's the wedding?"* The snaps of the camera sounded around them.

*"Three months from now, and if you all excuse us, my future wife and I need some alone time."* He winked to the crowd, took her hand and led her to the penthouse.

Lexi witnessed it all.

*"Fuuuuuck!"*

With shaking hands, Jay pulled his phone out. After two rings, the call connected.

"Jay, what's going on? You never call me when I'm away." The woman's husky voice stroked Jay's ear like a gentle sedative.

"I need to see you. When can you get here?"

"Tomorrow evening. Sorry, my flight's been delayed and I'm going to miss the connecting one. Are you okay?"

"Shit. No, I'm not okay. I need you. I'll make sure my parents and Daniel are out, so just come home."

"Okay. And Jay?"

"Yeah?"

"I love you."

"I love you too."

* * *

An hour ago his life was perfect. Lexi finally in his arms. Now he perched in the gutter surrounded by the shredded pieces of his life.

*I'm a father.*

*I have a daughter!*

His hands stabbed and pulled roughly through his hair, scattering the dark brown locks into disarray.

And he'd missed it all. The news, the pregnancy. Watching life form and grow from the seed they'd planted. Shared the roller coaster of pregnancy. Watching Lexi's belly fill out. The birth. The first word. The first steps. Her first smile. All her firsts. He should have been there to share it.

His fists balled. It made sense. Lexi's mistrust was valid. He'd not told her that night that he was engaged. It hadn't seemed important. A dry laugh sprung from his throat. It turned out it was *really* important, but the moment he saw her at the bar, he knew he had to make her his. The sparks that leapt between them when he touched her arm…that was more real than anything else in his entire life. Everything had faded to shadows once he fell into the chocolate warmth of her eyes. It all disappeared. His fame, his expensive car, his responsibilities. His *fiancee*. All erased by the enchanting smile with hair the tone of a top shelf drink. Captivated by her tresses, he'd ordered a brandy. The colour of her hair. Brandy. His daughter Brandy.

*"Her father didn't help name her?"*

*"He kinda did…"*

She must have thought he was an idiot.

He paused when he found himself at the entrance to the pub. He shrugged and ascended the earthen steps. The bar was full and lively; a good place to wallow while the rest of the world shifted around him. He found an empty stool, and crooked his finger at the waitress. Her eyes lit and she hurried towards him.

"What can I do for you, hun?" Her shrill tone grated.

"Whiskey. And keep 'em coming." Jay brandished his credit card as she placed the glass in front of him. The waitress lingered, her watery blue eyes devouring him.

"You look like you need to talk, hun." He narrowed his eyes on her.

"If I slept with you, would you tell me if you got pregnant?" Her eyebrows shot up and her expression ignited. Her fingers with their false tips wrapped around her dark hair, twirling the lock seductively. Jay cringed and gulped down the whiskey.

"Sorry, I didn't mean it to come out like that. Just a hypothetical." Jay shook his head.

The waitress leaned in uncomfortably close.

"Darlin, for a night with you, I'd tell you anything you want to hear."

Jay turned away until he heard her footsteps fade away.

"....Arlington's farm next week." Jay's ears pricked and he tuned into the group of five tradesmen seated around the table beside him.

"You lucky bastard! I'll take leave and help if you like!" A man volunteered, laughing. Jay clenched his hand, swivelling on his seat to face them.

"Who's lucky?" He enquired with forced indifference..

"Eric here. Just found out he's got work at Arlington Farm next week." A well-built man with spiked dark hair and 'Nick's Carpentry' embroidered on his shirt grinned his good fortune.

"And why is that lucky?" Jay asked as he scooped up the full glass the waitress placed before him.

"Jesus, man. You must be living under a rock! Alex Arlington is the holy-freaking-grail! Any time she puts through a call for labour, there's not a man alive with a working dick that doesn't volunteer for the job, But everyone knows she's broke, and hasn't called for subbies for years. She refuses to accept "hand-outs" as she calls them. Does everything she can herself, so nobody gets a shot at her. Heard she topped the market last week, so the whole town's been holding out for the call that opens *that* door."

Jay ground his teeth.

"Doesn't she have a kid?" He feigned innocence.

"Yeah. The kid's the reason she's not in town Friday nights anymore. She used to come out and dance every weekend. We all gave it a shot but she never gave a second look at anyone. Story goes she hooked up with someone a couple of towns over. Her father died of a heart attack in the paddocks a couple of weeks later. She hasn't been in town since. "'Parently word is she's been nursing a broken heart alone on that farm. Making the call to get work done, well, we're hoping that means she's gotten over the hurt and is ready to settle down with one of us."

Jay clenched his teeth.

"If you've all been knocked back, doesn't that mean you're out of luck?"

Eric's eyes narrowed on him. "She's a local, and she'll marry local. An outsider like you won't stand a chance, so don't even try, mate."

Jay turned away as the fist of bitterness tightened in his belly. He couldn't stomach the thought of those men touching her. That golden flesh. The heat in her fingers. He winced at the sound of their cheers and glasses tapping together.

"You look like you just buried your best mate." A cowboy surveyed him from a barstool on his left. The man leaned an elbow on the bar, his worn Akubra dipped low on his face. Jay nodded and drained the third glass. The waitress winked at him as she snatched the empty glasses lined up on the counter.

"He's right you know. You look like shit. The offer stands to help you forget your problems" Jay watched the waitress float away with disinterest. She melted through the saloon doors into the kitchen. As they swung to a close, Jay's focus lit on a figure lurking in the darkness - straight into the glare of Edward. He leaned into the corner, his chair tilted back on two legs. Amusement darkened his cold blue eyes. He raised his beer towards Jay, ejecting a glob of spittle from between clenched teeth in a thin arc to the floor. With courage he didn't quite feel, Jay turned his back on Edward. He'd have to sort that out, too. But right now, the pain burned inside as he tried to wrap his head around his daughter. Lexi didn't even try to tell him. Had he never found her again, he would never have known.

Jay slammed the glass down on the counter with a growl, lifting the next to his lips.

# CHAPTER 31

## ALEX

*A*lex hugged her knees. A chill that had nothing to do with the spring morning was lodged deep inside her bones.

"Mummy, can we see Jay?" Brandy's little face implored. Alex winced at the thought.

"Not today Princess. He's busy." Her monotone sounded heavy to her own ears. She had been unable to entertain the idea of sleep, so she'd stepped outside after Brandy had fallen asleep and cut the fallen tree into firewood. She worked through the night, and as the dawn lit up her farm, Alex fell into the embrace of the couch. Her muscles ached, her body weary and stretched, but she'd still been unable to find sleep.

What had she done? Her vision blurred with the memory of the betrayal on Jay's gorgeous features. She'd attacked him then, rubbing salt into his freshly gaping wound. He didn't attack her. But he tore her heart from her chest with his confirmation that he'd cheated on his fiancee with her. Then gone back to her like Alex meant nothing. She was so hurt and angry. And it never faded. She lived it in the twilight of every summer night. In the honey colour of the bottle of brandy she kept on the top shelf of the kitchen. In the eyes of her daughter.

In reflection, she was hesitant to admit he was right. She should have told him. In Alex's defence, she tried to tell him - had intended to tell him tonight. But he'd lied, too. Perhaps the lies they wove balanced the others out. No. Not that. He'd promised her forever that night, and the following week he'd cheapened everything she felt for him.

She clenched her teeth. He stalked her! Found her, planted himself in her life, made himself at home when she wasn't well enough to send him away. Then he'd upped the ante, buying Pete's farm and...*buying her calves*! She rubbed her face hard. There were ample opportunities for him to come clean. But he didn't.

"Mummy, I'm hungry. Can I have chips?" Alex's gazed warmly at her daughter. Her grounding, her soul. Her only reason for breathing. She managed a half smile as she unfolded from the couch, opened a pack of chips and handed them to Brandy. Her pudgy fist stabbed into the bag, up to her tiny elbows, and it made Alex laugh. The sound was stiff and rough to her own ears. She dropped to her knee before her daughter and pulled her into an embrace.

"You're the best thing that ever happened to me, Princess." More laughter rattled as Brandy shoved her crumbed fist into her mouth and nodded.

* * *

"So you're still going to meet with him?" Sabrina snorted incredulously. "I have to admit, Lex, I'm generally a good judge of character, but I really read it wrong this time."

Alex tried to fill her collapsed lungs.

"No, Mum. I'm going to see him before we are supposed to go to dinner. What we need to discuss has no place in a restaurant. He's an arsehole, and I don't want to see him again, but I couldn't live with my own conscience if I don't tell him why I didn't let him know about Brandy. I need to find out if he wants to see her. Christ, Mum, I need to know if he's going to try and take her away."

"He wouldn't do that!" Sabrina snapped, but the severity was softened with an element of uncertainty.

"I just don't know anymore."

Alex parked a block away from Jay's home, needing the walk in the hum of dusk to prepare herself for battle. She'd piled her hair into a loose bun, taking the time to find a shape hugging top and snug jeans. The resentment in her wanted him to see what he missed out on. As his front yard loomed, she leaned into a fence in the shadows, taking a handful of breaths to slow her heart. Jay saw how she lived. In its dilapidated state, her home could be seen as a dangerous place for a child to live. Now that she knew he had money, the courts would almost certainly rule in favour of a better lifestyle with the child's father. She breathed through a wave of nausea. *She was Alexandria Arlington, a woman of steel with the land in her veins. She was Maxwell Arlington's daughter, and Max wasn't afraid of anything.* She willed her feet forward, but pulled to a halt as a yellow taxi glided to a stop at his letterbox.

Alex furrowed her brow, dropping back into the shadows.

The driver popped the boot as he pulled up and efficiently lifted a suitcase out, opening the passenger door with a practised twist of his wrist.

Black high heels emerged, followed by long, slender stockinged legs.

"I hope the ride wasn't too rough, Mrs Morrison." He offered a hand.

In the darkness, Alex's body turned to stone. Unable to breathe, she watched as the woman emerged gracefully from the car. Her perfect blonde hair, immaculate make up, her style. Alex clutched the fence to hold herself upright.

*The last time she saw that woman she was leaping into Jay's arms!*

And the driver called her *Mrs. Morrison*! He'd gone on to marry her anyway, clearly playing with Alex while his wife was out of town. She couldn't will her feet to move away.

Heels clacked sharply on the concrete as the taxi peeled away from the curb.

The door opened, Jay's frame silhouetted against the light pouring from the house. Alex's throat closed.

"I'm so glad you made it okay. You have no idea how badly I need you right now" Jay's voice was thick with emotion. The woman dropped her suitcase and pulled him into a hug that pressed their bodies together. Jay wrapped his arms around her waist.

Alex fought the urge to empty her stomach. She heaved and choked as her eyes refused to move from the scene before her.

Jay broke away.

"Your folks and Daniel?" She asked with urgency.

"I made sure they're out for a few hours. They don't know you're here. It would be too awkward if they knew."

She leaned in and kissed him on the lips, and he grabbed her hand, pulling her inside.

The door closed with an impatient slam, and Alex's legs gave way as her stomach emptied into the bushes. The porch light snapped off and the silence was broken by her own rasping breaths. Alex stared wide-eyed into the darkness for an eternity, replaying the scene she'd witnessed. She checked her phone. Three hours before they were meant to meet for dinner. She swallowed roughly.

The woman, his *wife*, had flown in. He'd had this night planned, made sure his family were away to give them time together. Scheduled in her visit so they'd finish before Jay was due to meet with her for dinner. She winced. He'd manipulated Alex. He'd manipulated everyone.

Half an hour passed before her body began to function again. Her eyes were dry with shock, but Alex knew the tears would come. She tapped out a message to Sabrina asking her to keep Brandy overnight. She couldn't have her daughter around her through her breakdown. Brandy wouldn't understand, and Alex didn't want her scared.

Alex barely remembered the drive home. She stumbled into her kitchen and sank onto the chair.

With trembling fingers she tapped out

*Fuck you, Jay. Don't you dare ever contact me again.* Alex stared at it for a moment, then hit send. Leaning her head into her arms, the sobs came.

# CHAPTER 32

## JAY

The moment consciousness descended upon him, Jay was aware of the angry throb of his blood raging in his head. He cracked his eyes, and the general discomfort he felt was instantly apparent. Wooden floorboards stretched out before him, and he could see the edge of his phone poking out from beneath the fridge. He pinched his brows together in confusion, but only succeeded in emitting a soft groan as white flashes of tenderness stabbed his skull.

Jay gingerly pulled himself to his knees from the floor of the kitchen. Every millimetre of his flesh ached. Bruises were rupturing over his arms, and judging by the general sensation of tenderness, the rest of his body would tell a similar story.

The room lifted and tilted, and his brain fogged over as he attempted to recall how he ended up on the hardwood floor of Lexi's kitchen.

The events of yesterday slammed into him, filling his chest with Lexi's betrayal.

Why had he come?

*Don't you dare ever contact me again.*

He remembered his decision to talk it out, to get to the crux of the layers of secrecy and deceit. To see how deep their scars were. To discuss Brandy. There was no question he wanted his daughter in his life, but Lexi? Could he even trust her?

Lexi?

He woke battered and sore in her home to an eerie silence that descend quickly into cloudy confusion. With his head still swimming, Jay crawled slowly to his phone and checked the screen. No missed calls. He dialled his brother.

"Hey bro, kiss and make up already?" Daniel's cackle was soothing.

"Wha-" Jay winced as his lip tore open on his words. A split lip to the bargain. The strong flavour of metal filled his mouth as his tongue stung the wound. He breathed deeply and tried again.

"No. Shit. I don't know what's going on here…" He ran his fingers carefully over the swollen contours of his face

"You sound like shit, Jay. What's wrong? Where are you?" The urgency in Daniel's voice sharpened Jay's thoughts.

"I'm at Lexi's. But there's something wrong, Dan. Lexi's not here." His lungs squeezed. He didn't know how he knew that, but the truth of it strengthened his voice.

"Where is she?"

"I...I don't know. I can't remember what happened, but whatever it was, was huge. I woke up on the floor feeling like somebody beat the shit out of me. Jesus, Daniel! Lexi is gone." Jay felt panic rising.

"I'm at the farm checking on your cows. I'm coming over right now!."

*  *  *

By the time Daniel's car crunched up the stone driveway, Jay had managed to climb onto a chair. The world was beginning to steady itself. Daniel climbed the stairs and walked in without knocking.

"Jesus Christ, Jay! You weren't kidding, were you?" Daniel appraised his brother beneath the purple lumps and dried blood. "You need to let me take you to the hospital. There's some stitches in that mess."

Jay shook his head. "Daniel, I don't know what happened, but I've got this awful feeling is was something bad, and I can't fucking remember..." He balled his fists. A stabbing pain brought his attention to them, and he lifted his knuckles to his face. They were split and pulpy, dried blood clinging to the backs of his hands, and down his fingers.

Daniel gasped.

"Fuck, you didn't....Lexi?" He stammered in horror.

"What? No! I wouldn't hurt her..." He trailed off with uncertain dread. He couldn't remember. He didn't know. What if he'd hurt her, and she gave him bruises trying to fight him off?

Daniel's voice demanded. "Where did she go, Jay?"

Jay shot his brother a pleading glance.

"I don't know." He whispered.

Daniel locked eyes with him, seeking truth.

"But her car is in the driveway, Jay. She *has* to be here somewhere."

Jay shook his head. "She's not here, Daniel. I don't know how I know, but I do."

Daniel kept his eyes on Jay as he pulled his phone from his pocket. He dialled a number and held it to his ear.

A ring sounded from outside. Daniel stood and followed it, his footsteps heavy on the verandah.

He reappeared with a phone in each hand, the colour drained from his face. His eyes flicked to Jays.

"It's Lexi's. She dropped it on the path outside..."

She wouldn't drop it. She needed it to keep in contact with Brandy. She carried it everywhere with her in case Sabrina needed her.

*Where the hell did she go?*

Daniel swept his gaze over the room, zeroing in on the strange, faint flicker of a light protruding slightly from beneath layers of unopened mail on a small cabinet opposite the main entrance.

With sudden purpose, Daniel lengthened his strides and knocked a pile of papers to the floor, his hand closing around the device beneath it.

"It's the security camera I gave her. Looks like she tried to get it going and forgot about it. The light's flashing, so it looks like it's been recording. Hopefully the view is clear." Daniel explained. He sank into the chair beside his brother, his eyebrows in a V of concentration.

"There!" He exclaimed, angling the tiny screen towards them.

A greyscale view of the kitchen came to life, showing the two men sitting staring into the camera. Jay filled his lungs slowly, taking in the damage done to his face. His eyebrow was split, crusty blood dried in streaks on his face, fresh blood sluggishly pulsing from the raw wound. His torn lip swollen and dark on the camera screen.

Daniel tapped at the buttons. The image of Jay sprawled out on the floor played back.

"Rewind it." Jay bit out urgently.

The screen returned to darkness. For Jay, the wait was the longest he'd ever experienced. Longer than his search for Lexi.

His breaths cut up the silence. Daniel brought the screen to life with a stab of his finger. Greyscale Horace wandered into the kitchen, sniffing at cupboards above her head. She nosed the fridge gently.

"Too far. Fast forward." Impatience sharpened his tone.

The time stamp rolled forward. Horace shuffled in short strides back out the door in fast motion. Lexi appeared at the door, her greyscale form racing to the table and crashing to the kitchen chair where Daniel now sat. The video showed her snatching her phone in front of her.

"That was the time she texted me." Jay's heart hammered. His lungs hurt. He'd left immediately once he'd read her text. It took just under an hour for him to get here.

Greyscale Lexi rested her head in her arms. Her body shook with emotion for some time.

Shiny metal glinted through the open kitchen door. Jay's stomach bottomed out.

"That's not me. It's too soon to be me."

Daniel slowed the recording. Lexi showed no indication that she was aware of the visitor, her still form suggesting she'd cried herself to sleep.

A shadow descended on the doorway and the figure appeared.

Daniel and Jay moved simultaneously. Jay jerked towards the camera with a snarl that burst his lip, and Daniel yanked his phone to his ear, not shifting his eyes from the security camera.

"Yes, Its Daniel Morrison. We've run out of time. That cop has taken Alexandria Arlington." His words clipped. "According to the footage, he was at her farm just after 8pm last night. Yes, keep me informed."

Jay's throat burned. His chest heaved. Every thought he'd had of leaving her, of giving up on her, splintered and ground into dust in the dark edges of his stomach.

# CHAPTER 33

## JAY

*L*ike a horror movie on mute, Jay and Daniel watched.

Edward's uniform clad frame burst through the door. Alex jerked from her seat, the chair tipping soundlessly to the floor. She held her hands up at him, motioning him to stop. Edward's mouth moved. Greyscale Alex shook her head vehemently, backing into the corner of the kitchen, out of view of the camera. Edward followed her movements, a slow oily grin on his face. He prowled to the edge of the screen, bending and lowering his torso. He strafed to one side, then the other, his arms wide. Alex was clearly attempting to evade him. Edward disappeared from view. The view of the kitchen returned to a picture of serenity.

"No!" Jay rasped, muscles taut.

Edward's back re-entered the frame, his body straining as he fought with something off the edge of vision. He jerked backwards, pulling Alex with him, his fingers digging into her upper arms. Her shirt hung open, her bra slipped off one shoulder. Her jeans were missing, panties pulled down on one side.

"Oh, Jesus" Daniel breathed in horror.

Edward flexed. Greyscale Alex spun across the room and collided with the kitchen table. Edward's fist closed around her neck. Holding her at a hard angle, Alex's arms flew at him. His body jerked with the force of the blows that connected. Alex stopped lashing out, her fingers digging at his grip on her neck. Suddenly she stopped fighting back. Her entire body relaxed and went limp. The white gleam of his grin lit up his face.

Jay growled. *Shit, Lexi. Please be alright.*

Edward manoeuvred greyscale Alex to the table. Her head fell lifelessly to one side. He slowed his movements, almost savouring the moment. He shuffled her around until her bra released her breasts. His fingers dug into them roughly, her flesh bulging around the pressure. He slid his palms over her bare body, stepping backwards as he dragged her panties slowly down her thighs.

Daniel retched. Jay's jaw ground.

As Edward fumbled with his belt buckle, a figure stumbled into the kitchen.

"Jay! Thank Christ!" Daniel rasped.

Jay's shoulders heaved as if he'd been running. The tortured expression on his face locked on Lexi. Greyscale Jay's face twisted in rage, his words screamed silently on the screen. And then he was on top of Edward, his elbows pulling back over and over again as he rained silent punches with all of his strength into the face of the cop. Edward slumped, but Jay continued his punishment. His blows slowed. His frame heaved. His head lifted suddenly and he scrambled to Lexi's side. The camera captured an expression of such torment, an agony deeper than death, on his face.

He bent over greyscale Alex, pulling her to his chest, stroking her face, shaking her gently. Jay watched his mouth form her name.

Greyscale Alex moved. She became a whirlwind of limbs until she recognised Jay, collapsing into his chest. He sat her up, snatching her clothes from the floor. Jay helping her into them, buttoning up her jeans. In the bottom of the screen, Edward's body stirred.

"No!" Daniel whispered. Jay's fists clenched.

Edward found his feet and sprang forward, taking Jay to the ground. Jay's head snapped backwards as he struck the table on the way down. The cop's fists landed on Jay's head, the smile on his bloodied face the mark of insanity. Jay's head lolled limply from side to side. Greyscale Alex attacked Edward's back, nails snaking around to rake his eyes. He shook her off, grabbing her wrist. He pushed her against the wall as she fought to dodge his brutal grabs. Jay shook his head and staggered to his feet, launching himself at Edward.

Edward released Alex, spinning towards Jay. He landed an elbow in Jay's face, and Jay folded to the ground.

"Oh shit." Jay blew out a breath.

The images faded to blurs. Edward returned to Greyscale Alex who was fighting and defending with added vigour.

Suddenly, Edward yanked Alex's hair, ripping her head backwards. Her arms flung out. He swung her around, sending her spinning into the wall. She hit the back of her head and slumped to the floor.

Edward advanced on the still form of Jay. He stopped and stared down at him, hands on hips for a moment before he paused, deliberating. He took a glance back towards Alex, then closed in on her still body. Gripping Alex, he dragged her towards the door by one arm and a fistful of her hair. As he pulled Alex through the door, her head lifted. The camera catching the fear and panic on her face. Her mouth moved. Her chest strained with silent force.

*Jay!*

*Jay!*

*Jay!*

* * *

Daniel barked orders and updates into his phone as his brother paced the kitchen his breathing growing faster, louder as loathing and justice thickened his airways. He had to find her. Needed to gather her into the safety of his arms and never let her go. Daniel's fingers closing around his bicep snagged his attention.

"Jay, cool it. The detectives are on their way. You need to settle down."

Jay rounded on his brother.

"Cool it? *Fuck you*, Daniel. Where is he?"

Daniel's glare bored into Jay's. A glacial darkness crackled from Jay, pulsing and spreading. His nostrils flared around the instinct to annihilate, to wreak catastrophic vengeance on the man who sought to bring harm to Lexi. Jaw twitching and locked, his fury wild, his pain forgotten. Daniel stepped back, intimidated by Jay's intensity. He closed his eyes.

"I'll drive. Tilly thinks he'd take her to the police station. Says with how he flaunts his status, it's the greatest likelihood."

With steely purpose, Jay stalked to the car. Daniel slid behind the wheel, spewing stones from the tyres as he pointed the car towards town.

# CHAPTER 34

## ALEX

*H*er arms clasped her legs to her chest as she forced her darkest glare at Edward. She had squeezed herself in the corner of the tiny room, creating as much distance between herself and her captor as she could. He closed the door behind him, the keys snapping the locking mechanism securely.

"Good morning, darling." The smooth dark voice chilled Alex. Light incinerated the darkness.

"Jay?" Alex whispered around the pain in her jaw.

She heard the scrape of a chair as Edward moved to straddle it.

"Jay! Jay! Jay!" He mimicked in a whiny tone. "He's not coming for you, beautiful. Once I convinced him that you belonged to me, he backed down. You saw how easily he gave up. He's no match for me."

She closed her eyes on the vision of Jay crumpling to the floor, his handsome face broken and slack as his temple struck the corner of the table. His eyes emptied on her as he dropped. Her heart clenched. She needed him to be okay. Bile rose unexpectedly on her realisation. If he was alright, he would have been here by now. The shock of her certainty collided with dread. As sure as the sun rose he would come for her. She felt it without question. He always came for her. He'd chased her for years. He returned to her when she sent him away. She told him last night never to contact her again. And he came for her, then, too. But he lay so still on her floor…

And the night had come and gone in silence.

Edward watched her, his malevolent smirk lodged amongst the cuts and bruises Jay had rained down on his face. His split lip tore open on his grin and blood trickled sluggishly down his chin. Madness swirled behind his eyes.

"Yep, that pretty boy isn't so pretty anymore. In fact, I'd go so far as to say he's pretty much fucked after last night. I would have finished him off if I thought he'd make it." Edward leaned toward Alex, showing teeth. A soft chuckle escaped.

"And now he's out of the way, you can finally relax and start focusing on us. We got ourselves a baby to make, darling. We're going to be a happy family, Alex, you, me and all our babies."

Gravel collected in her throat. Edward might be right. It was like she watched the light burn out of his silver eyes as he fell. His gaze never left hers until that moment. She swallowed around the thought.

*Please be alright, Jay. Even if you're still angry, I need you to be okay.*

"There will never be an us!" She seethed, the rage in her muscles stiffening her spine.

The maniacal grin slid from his face, and Alex pressed harder into the corner as he shuffled his chair closer. His warm breath puffed against her face. She couldn't back up any further. Dark excitement burned in his glare.

"There always was an us, darling. You've just wasted my time fighting it. I've been so very patient with you, but I'm done waiting. I'm going to convince you that we are meant to be." He rose from the chair, his oily expression locking on Alex. She swallowed thickly as he slid the chair aside. The fire in his eyes conveyed his intention.

Edward reached out a pale hand and caught her chin in his pinch. Alex recoiled and snapped her hand out to knock his arm aside.

He scowled at her defiance, his breaths shortening with the dark heat raging within him. His lip twisted.

"Oh, darling. This is going to be better than I imagined" He whispered. "You're so feisty and stunning. I've waited so long to tame you. Fight me all you like, Alexandria; it's my favourite kind of foreplay."

The thought of his hands on her curdled her insides.

In a furious cyclone of fingernails and elbows she sprung into attack, adrenaline powering every swipe and punch. Edward toppled in surprise and Alex landed hard on him, blows angled to damage his already split lip. In the cold anger of her assault, she targeted every bruise, every wound she could find.

Edward grunted below her as he scrambled to stop the pain. She was no match for his testosterone induced strength, but she screamed and snarled until her voice was hoarse.

Edward's hands shot around her wrists and stilled her.

Her eyes widened on his. Beneath the shine of fresh blood, a dark and cruel desire was erupting. His breaths were fast and shallow. He ran his tongue over his lip, tasting the blood as he held her astride him.

Alex whimpered. In her exhaustion she saw his power growing. She was aware of the thick throbbing in his groin nudging her backside. In revulsion she scrambled off him, yanking at her wrists. He tightened his grip as he swung her underneath him.

The cold concrete was unyielding as Edward positioned his large body over hers, crushing her chest. He tilted his hips forward, pushing his erection into her thigh.

"Christ, you're such a turn-on. I knew you'd enjoy this as much as me. I always knew you'd liked it rough."

Panic burst through Alex. She bucked and twisted, succeeding only on inflaming Edward's lust.

"Oh, yes, darling. Fight me, baby. Make me earn it." His heated ardour repulsed her. He manoeuvred both her wrists into one hard grip, and his free hand dug into the flesh of her breast. She cried out in pain. Edward hummed his pleasure. In gut-wrenching terror, she filled her lungs and snapped her head upwards. The impact of her forehead slamming into his face had her seeing stars, but it had the desired result. The heat from his body left hers, and she scrambled against the wall for support.

"You broke my fucking nose, you whore! Fuck!" He roared. Blood flooded from between his hands. Alex regarded him warily. His damaged face glowed red with rage and lust. Every fibre and sinew in his body was coiled tightly ready to attack. And his eyes lit on Alex. He smeared the blood from his upper lip on the back of his hand, raging with an inferno of ambition towards her.

# CHAPTER 35

## ALEX

*E*dward moved with slow and deliberate paces towards her, lust and vindictive excitement dulling his expression. Alex's stomach crashed in, and she pushed back into the wall. Already exhausted and aching, she tightened her core and flicked her hair from her face, preparing for another round. As long as she was breathing she wouldn't stop fighting.

Edward's lips curled, and he prowled the last step towards Alex. She lifted her arms protectively before her, her fists hovering at eye level. Edward bypassed it with ease, his grip snapping the buttons of her shirt, pinning her to the wall with his chest. The scent of sweat and anger filled Alex's nostrils with stifling bitterness. The damp heat radiating from his body was suffocating, her panic causing her arms to stab out and connect with her captor anywhere she could. He ignored her attempts, none of her blows carrying enough force to do anything but erode her energy. Her nails tore at his shirt, seeking to inflict pain on his skin.

Edward hissed his delight. He popped a button off his shirt in his urgency to remove it, then pressed her with his bare chest so hard into the wall that she struggled to fill her lungs. Her arm yanked up and managed to connect with the swelling pulp of his nose. The impact was satisfying.

He shrieked in her face, raining blood over both of them, warm crimson rolling down her neck and soaking into her bra. Alex struggled against him, Edward's blood a slick river between them. She broke away and whirled towards the door, her grasp slipping over the handle.

"It's locked, darlin'. You're mine until I say otherwise."

# CHAPTER 36

## JAY

*J*ay sat frigid in the silence. Daniel kept shooting sideways looks at him as the town loomed. Jay's expression flickered between haunted and icy madness.

"Drive faster!" Snarled the stranger in Jay's skin. Daniel clenched his jaw and did as he was bid.

"Once we get there, get the fuck out of the way and wait for the detectives. Don't follow me." His voice was void of emotion.

At the approach of the police station, Jay growled in his throat. Edward's cop car was parked slightly askew behind the fence at the rear of the building, like it'd been parked with some urgency.

Jay jumped out before they stopped, stalking through the doors with single minded purpose, torn fists flexing and releasing.

*"Edward!"* Jay's thundering roar was a reverberating tornado of rocks, louder than his lungs. Crimson retribution painted his vision

234

with primal destruction, the need for barbaric chaos anchored in his kidneys. He hesitated barely a second before vaulting his length over the front desk, lowered his shoulder and collided with the office door with splintering force.

Desks and chairs clattered as Jay shoved them aside. The thick doors of the two holding cells caused him to hesitate, unsure of his next move.

He heard Lexi's scream. His frantic rage burned through his skull. She was in *that* one. And she was alive. He struggled to calm his mind. Edward was probably armed, and deranged enough to lash out indiscriminately. He could hurt her.

# CHAPTER 37

## ALEX

"*Edward!*" The battle cry rattled the door and widened her eyes. Edward paused in his tracks, empty expression narrowing indecisively.

Alex almost believed she recognised Jay's voice. Her heart pounded with hope. She dived at the wooden chair, brandishing it between them as she caught her breath. With blood staining his lips and teeth, his demented laughter diluted her resolve.

"I love that you're so tenacious, Alex. You were made for me."

He sprung towards her, splintering the chair as he landed on top of her. She felt him shift. Her throat locked as he pulled his belt free. The heavy buckle clanged to the floor at the same time as a violent crash sounded from behind the locked door.

Alex screamed.

Furious at the interruption outside, Edward lifted off Alex, and fed the keys into the lock with an impatient twist. He disappeared through the door, leaving Alex alone with straining lungs that ached with terror, crashing with the erratic explosions in her chest.

She stood slowly on shaking legs. Eyeing the wooden splinters of the chair Edward had broken, she snatched a length with long, jagged points from the pile. Looping Edward's abandoned belt around the other hand, buckle hanging heavily, she splayed her feet apart and squared her shoulders as she lifted her chin with grim determination.

# CHAPTER 38

## JAY

*T*he door opened and Edward materialised, eyes dark blue with a demented desire that stabbed through Jay. He was missing his shirt. His belt gone and his zipper peeled down.

Jay's fury exploded. He grabbed the cop by the neck, lifting him off his feet and throwing him onto a desk.

Fear erased Edward's madness and he held up his hands. Jay advanced slowly.

"Touch me and her farm is gone!"

Jay glared down, his lips twisted at the pitiful man.

"It's true. Her brother didn't have a will and it's in the hands of the state. I can stop the state selling it on her, just let me go and I'll send the email."

Jay faltered, and Edward relaxed a little.

"So that's it. That's why you've been calling the shots. You black-mailed her into dating you." Jay's whisper was cruel resolve. He covered the last two steps between them. Edward was still smiling when Jay reared back his arm and connected with his face. As Edward's cheek split open, realisation flooded his damaged face; Jay intended to kill him.

# CHAPTER 39

## ALEX

*T*he sound of furniture skidding along the wooden floor carried through the door. Every fibre in Alex's frame strained, her knees flexed and ready to move. The crashes sounded closer. She heard plaster punch in, the noise of flesh on flesh, tumbling and colliding; the grunts and groans of conflict. Alex's breathing tightened and shallowed.

Thud.

The wall shook. The door popped open. And there he stood. Jay. A wall of muscle and strength, head and shoulders above Edward, his bloodied fists bursting on flesh. With a savage snarl, he closed his fingers around Edward's throat, even as the smaller man drummed his punches into Jay's stomach.

Alex's world stopped on Jay. His pure power, his flexing, bunching fury was utterly breathtaking. His silver eyes were honed into feral razors, hard and blazing as he unleashed his vengeance upon his enemy. He roared his blood-lust as Edward twisted free from his ruthless grip.

He looked nothing like the languid and sensual lover who had pulled her so gently against him. This was a man with war in his veins and damage in his movements. He was more beast than human, every step, every blow a dance of deadly purpose.

"Jay!" Her voice rasped. He flicked his eyes to her, sweeping her up in his gaze, pausing on the wooden weapon in her grip.

Alex watched as clarity washed over him, and he lowered his shoulder into Edward's chest. His larger and bulkier frame over-powered Edward, and with an animalistic roar, he sent Edward flying against the wall in the cell Alex occupied.

At the last moment, Alex lifted the stake between Edward and the wall, snarling into the thick air with savage adrenaline and desperate exhaustion, her focus never moving from Jay. Beneath her grip, the splitting and slicing of flesh, muscle and vital organs shuddered around the wood.

She turned her attention to Edward's inhuman roar of agony. His mouth hung wide as his eyes searched Alex's. The confusion made him appear soft; a flash of a man he could have been. Air whispered from his lips and the betrayal on his face congealed and dulled as he slid to the ground, the broken chair leg impaled between his ribs. Locking her knees, she fought the desire to sink to the ground in relief. She didn't want to spend another moment in the vicinity of this creep, but she knew if she even took one step, her boneless limbs would crumple.

She ached for Jay, to feel the security of his embrace, but she faltered under the wild stone of his expression.

"Jay?" She gasped.

A strange emotion flittered over his features as he explored her. His lips parted, and desire blazed as his pulse stuttered in his throat. His lips moved around the beginnings of a word. Then his expression clouded and dulled. He thinned his lips and turned away from her.

"Jay?" Her voice cracked around her heart. Without a backwards glance, Jay walked out of the office.

Alex fought to get her legs to chase him but they collapsed uselessly beneath her and she sank to the floor. She sat numbly as paramedics arrived at her side, staring at the door Jay evaporated from.

What had just happened?

# CHAPTER 40

## JAY

The image imprinted in his heart.

She stood, her brandy mane wild with her proud stance and savage vengeance. Her shirt hung open and loose, crimson smeared across her chest to her coiled stomach. Fire and earth entwined through her demeanour like a bloodthirsty angel. Such resilience and grit in the face of the horrors she'd witnessed. The woman would never stop fighting.

And that's when it hit him. She was so full of fight and resistance that she would never allow herself to accept the love she had for him. She would resist opening herself completely to him, too caught up in her own fears. He came to protect her, and she didn't need it. She could do it herself as she'd told him countless times before. He hadn't wanted to believe her, but here they stood in the moment of truth. She didn't need him. She couldn't love him. Jay deserved more than that.

If he didn't walk away now, he knew he wouldn't be capable of it, so strong was his pull to her.

"Jay?" She pleaded. The depth in her eyes in that moment made his heart stop. That look was what he ached for. It shone with light and hope and promises like she finally held her heart out for him to see. But Jay knew different. Like every other time it would be fleeting. He had to protect his own heart. She would survive this with the same determination as she'd endure the fight for her family, her farm. Sabotaging her own heart. With iron will and stubborn denial. He knew in that moment that while this woman owned his whole heart, he held only pieces of hers.

He took her in one last time, steeled himself, and snapping the last threads that held his heart to hers, walked away.

"Jay?" Daniel's face twisted in concern.

"I'm fine. She's fine. Edward's dead. Let's go." His statements fell in monotone from lifeless lips. Daniel threw a dark stare at his brother, and gave a stiff nod.

He met Daniel's questions with silence. He watched the town pass by, his heart hollow and cold. He'd done what he promised. He'd kept her safe. Her jeans, still buttoned, had reassured him. The wild flame in her eyes told him she'd survive this. Alone. She didn't need Jay. Not like he needed her. In another three years she would be working the farm on her own, struggling and managing, and never conceding defeat. No different to what she'd done before. If she finally decided to settle down with a man, he would never have all of her, either. Like Jay he'd live every day in hope that she would free her heart and love him entirely. But in the end she'd inevitably protect herself, locking that most precious piece of herself away from the world.

Lexi was everything to him, but Jay was not quite enough for her.

As they neared their villa, Jay made a call.

"Can you draw up papers for access to my daughter? I need them done by tomorrow midday. I can sign them on my way to the airport."

Calm anaesthesia overtook him.

When Daniel pulled up, Jay ignored his brother's pleas and headed inside to pack.

# CHAPTER 41

## ALEX

*C*overed in bandages and stitches, the only ache that couldn't heal was the emptiness of her heart. After the detectives had finished questioning her at the hospital, they assured her that both she and Jay were officially exonerated as having acted in self defence, and as such, they were free to go. Alex had seen no sign of Jay since then, and any probing of the detectives resulted in a standard, "Joseph was released without charges being laid."

In the days that passed, Alex hollowed out. She didn't leave the bedroom except to eat. Horace nosed her way in to sniff her, as if assuring herself Alex was still alive.

Alex wrestled with her actions with Edward. She'd killed a man. Taken a life that hadn't finished and snuffed it like she was entitled to make that decision. Playing God wasn't new to her. Working a farm required the strength of will to decide which of her cattle would live or die, but this was different. So different that it left bruises on her identity She mourned the person he could have been, the thoughts he'd never get the chance to have, but the underlying relief is what she struggled with the most. She regretted taking a life, but no longer having Edward's threats looming over her lifted the darkness she'd lived under for so long. She fought the guilt of being unable to regret Edward's death. She stole his existence, but within that act of execution, it meant her daughter was safe. Brandy could live a life free from fear that Alex always wanted for her. Her mother could enjoy her retirement without concerning herself with Alex's happiness. Alex's happiness. It was something she'd not given thought to since Edward arrived in her life and uprooted her serenity. She hadn't dared hope for anything greater than security for herself, Sabrina and Brandy. Edward's death had managed to expand her world far beyond the perimeters she'd existed within since that night with Jay. In the dawn of her freedom, she found herself at a loss about how to fill her future. Without the burden of Edward's secret threats, she was free to think and feel as she pleased. She no longer needed to guard against his evil, controlling her thoughts, monitoring her movements.

An image of Jay resting on his side by the peppercorn tree mere days ago made her heart constrict. Her body stilled as the light of hope drained from her. Because he was married. The future she wanted would never be because the man she loved and the father of her child had left the deepest scars with his deceit. She hated that she still loved him. She needed to guard her heart and process her grief.

She'd returned home to the solicitor's notice outlining Jay's demands. He requested fortnightly access, and outlined a more than generous weekly figure to be paid to Alex for Brandy's upkeep. Fury had battled with agony. She didn't want his money. But her rage eventually subsided. Brandy needed her father in her life. She adored him. She would simply have to steel herself with all the reminders of Jay when Brandy returned. He didn't want to take

Brandy away from her. The relief was palpable when she read that paragraph. But relief was all she could summon.

With morbid fascination Alex scrutinised how her body could function, drawing on shards of shattered heart to move through the hours of each day.

* * *

Horace stamping beside her bedroom window pulled her from sleep. She heard the rolling crunch of tyres on her driveway. She wasn't expecting visitors, so she slipped from her bed, and pulled her rifle from the gun safe in the closet. The only people she wanted to see today were Sabrina and Brandy.

Alex's lungs failed as she saw Jay's car through the window.

Her dead heart burst to life, and Alex swallowed a groan as it ripped through her again. She would choose feeling nothing to this pain any day. She opened the door and rested against the frame, cold hatred firmly in place, gun resting on her shoulder.

*Protect your heart, Alex.*

It wasn't Jay who emerged though. Alex watched enraged as his wife stepped awkwardly in stilettos around scatterings of Horace's dung. When she reached the porch she lifted her head, stumbling backwards with a gasp when she registered the weapon. She threw her hands up.

"I'm not here to hurt you." She begged. Alex watched silently as she warily climbed the steps.

The woman managed a frightened grin. It bent the perfect lines of her lipstick.

"You must be Lexi, I'm-"

"I *know* who you are" She growled."What do you want? Are you here to tell me that it was all a mistake he made, needed to sow his wild oats, tell me to keep away from him and rot like that? Because if you are, don't waste your breath. He never wants to see me again. He's all yours, and if I knew he was married….." She trailed off.

"What? Christ! No! It's not what you think, Lexi." She straightened her back and frowned.

Alex almost felt sorry for her. Her husband had cheated on her. At least Alex wasn't married to him. That pain and humiliation belonged to the woman in front of her.

Instead, the blonde fixed her with a hard stare. "Do you have any idea where Jay is right now?" She drilled.

"Look, *Mrs Morrison,* I don't know, nor do I give a damn where he might be. He's *your* husband, you should know. He's probably whoring it up between the sheets with his next victim. Not my problem anymore." Lexi's sneer burned into the blonde.

The woman's eyebrows raised.

"You can't mean that?" She gasped. Alex simply shrugged.

"Lexi. This is important. Can you just put the gun away?. We need to talk *now.*"

The blonde hesitated when Lexi held her ground in silence.

"Please?" She added softly.

Alex sighed heavily. Curiosity burned. Why would Jay's wife want to talk to her? Alex couldn't hurt any more than she was already.

"Why not? It's either talking to you or wrestling my grouchy bull away from his girls, and I'm not quite up to that torture yet."

Alex withdrew the bullets from the chamber of her gun and leaned it against the wall, leading the woman inside.

Alex pulled two mugs from the cupboard. The woman pulled up a seat and made a quick call.

"Daniel, I'm here and I'm okay."

Alex coiled in rage as the woman disconnected. Poison dripped from her tongue.

"Daniel was in on this, too? You need to know, they all welcomed me into their home for a family meal as if everything was normal and peachy. The lot of them must be six kinds of screwed up to do that!"

The blonde lifted her hand and smiled softly. "Lets clear a few things up before we go any further. My name is Mrs. Tilly Morrison, and I have been happily married to my husband of two years, Daniel Morrison."

"Sorry? Daniel? But I saw you that night with Jay…"

"Yes, you did. But it wasn't what you thought-"

"I call bullshit. I've seen you before. Three years ago when you announced your engagement to Jay! Not Daniel"

Tilly sighed heavily.

"Yeah. Yeah you did. Lexi, I want to tell you what Jay should have told you when he first found you again. Will you listen to me? Please?" Alex gripped the counter top. She decided to shut Jay out of her life forever. Not that she had an option in the matter. Jay made it perfectly clear he had no desire to see her. All she wanted to do was curl in a ball in her bed, and shut out the world for a while longer. She looked at Tilly. She was perched elegantly on the edge of the kitchen chair closest to the exit, her gaze darting around the room.

"Tea or coffee?" She relented.

"Tea, please. One sugar. I'd kill for a coffee, but I have to cut back now I'm pregnant. Daniel's baby" She added when Alex stiffened.

* * *

Tilly closed her eyes on the first sip.

"Thank you." She smiled.

Alex wanted to hate her, but found her tone softening as she sunk into the chair opposite.

"You were saying?"

Tilly ran a manicured fingernail over the design on the mug. She fixed her eyes on Alex as she began.

"Jay and I became friends in kindergarten. We were the same age and lived close by so it started as a friendship of convenience. By high school he was screening my boyfriends and helping me study. Jay is highly intelligent. Switched on like the rest of his family. I had a hard time studying. By the time we graduated, I left behind me a string of failed and messed up relationships. Jay, not so much. He was always drop dead gorgeous, but was never interested in a relationship." She paused for another sip.

"When we turned eighteen we made a pact. It was a silly thing, but we thought it was foolproof at the time. If we hadn't found love by his twenty eighth birthday, we would marry each other. We decided that marrying our best friend was preferable to any of the disasters we'd already experienced. We shook on it. When he turned twenty eight he was overseeing his father's empire. He found that the women he attracted once his life spread across the newspapers were all after his money, his fame etcetera. Over drinks one night we decided our silly pact was our only opportunity for a good life, so we agreed, and Joseph and Lydia released it to the press so that Jay would be left alone. He didn't want the bother of empty headed women, or the notoriety of his father."

Tilly sat back and speared Alex with her gaze.

"The thing was, the weekend before the scheduled press release was due to take place, Jay happened to stroll into a certain bar where he saw a woman with brandy coloured hair, and proceeded to fall instantly and hopelessly in love."

Alex's mouth fell. "No." She whispered, her fingertips pressed against her bottom lip. "That's not true! When I woke up, he was gone."

# CHAPTER 42

JAY

*J*n the darkness, Jay shivered. The cold pulled into his bones.

"Lexi?" The effort to form words hurt. He snarled at the thought. Not Lexi. She was gone. Was never his.

A woman's voice purred in his ear.

"I can take you back to my place if you like? It's not far. You can sleep it off there."

He blinked up from the floor of the hotel bar. His mouth thinned in distaste as he focussed on the redhead's face. She was pretty enough, but...she wasn't Lexi. A hole burned in his chest.

"I'm okay" he slurred as the world tilted. He pushed her gently away. "I just need another drink.'

\* \* \*

His stubble thickened into a beard. He lifted level with the bathroom mirror and groaned at the pathetic man in the reflection.

"One week down, one lifetime to go." he muttered. One week of drinking himself under the bar. One week of setting out with the intention of losing himself in a body that wasn't Lexi. He couldn't. The moment he touched them his own flesh recoiled. He couldn't even kiss that girl with the laugh like a parrot and the hair like his Lexi.

One week behind him. Next weekend he was scheduled to see Brandy. His daughter. The first time he'd see her since he'd found out he was a father. A lifetime had passed by in that time. Would she like being with him? Would she miss her mother?

He'd blocked her number. He had to. If she'd called him, he'd never be able to restrain himself from taking the call. To hear her voice. To hear how her breath formed his name.

Jay brought his fist down on the bathroom cabinet. The force smarted, and he relished in the sharpness it brought to him. He couldn't be drunk for his daughter. Brandy. The bruises were fading and the scabs were beginning to drop away. The puckered line splitting his eyebrow would scar. A constant visual reminder of his warrior, and how he arrived to save the day only to find her fully equipped to deal with the situation.

His teeth ground.

Lexi.

Shit.

Manoeuvring the blade around the few scabs remaining, Jay scraped the beard from his face. For his daughter.

# CHAPTER 43

## ALEX

*T*illy held up her hand.

"Can I trouble you for a snack, please? I don't want to be a bother, but I get the feeling if this demon inside me isn't fed two minutes ago, it will start eating my insides."

Alex laughed sympathetically.

"I fail to understand how, with a clear mind, I thought this was going to be a great idea." She rolled her eyes and groaned.

Alex reached the cupboard above the fridge, retrieving a fistful of Brandy's snack sized packet biscuits. "Sorry, I'd whip up a sandwich, but deli meats…"

Tilly chuckled.

"I know. It's incredible the foods I used to live on quite happily are suddenly snacks of doom." She shook her head, then looked imploringly at Alex. "Just tell me it's worth it."

Alex considered. The last six months of her pregnancy were a nightmare, then the night time feeds after she was born, surviving on autopilot and an hour's sleep a night.

"Without question, Brandy is the best thing that's ever happened to me.." Alex watched as Tilly crumpled into tears at her admission.

"You get used to the tears, too. I promise." She laughed. As she leaned over to draw the box of tissues to her, she winced and caught her breath as a sharp pain ignited from the motion.

"What's wrong?" Tilly swiped her eyes dry.

Alex frowned. "I'll be okay. I just need rest. It's been an... exhausting few days." She topped up Tilly's tea and poured herself another coffee.

Tilly continued. "By utter coincidence, I was having second thoughts about this whole marriage farce, and I set out to talk to him about it. He wasn't home of course. He had already been talking to you for five minutes if I remember correctly." Her lip tightened in a nostalgic smile and her eyes glazed.

"Daniel answered the door instead. He'd just stepped out of the shower, and was wearing nothing but a towel. His hair was all messed up from drying it. He...he gave me a look, and it just fired up my pulse..."

Alex snorted. "You don't have to tell me about that look. I think men use it as a weapon. They hear us coming, make sure their muscles are glistening and on display, throw in a pint of raw testosterone, and we're gone."

Tilly nodded fervently. "That's it! Yes! That's what it felt like. And my, I don't know, my body responded to it in a way that I'd never known before."

Alex gave her a knowing grin.

"Well, anyway, he invited me in and changed into jeans, but still no shirt. It messed with my head a lot. Anyway, I figured in that moment if I carried out this fake marriage to Jay, I'd miss out on the very real and exciting feeling that was happening between Daniel and I. And so would Jay. It didn't seem fair to either of us, but the meeting with the press was already scheduled, so..." She shrugged.

"So you talked to Daniel about it?" Alex pushed.

"Yeah. We talked about the marriage for a bit, then we just chatted about ourselves, learned about each other. Daniel was my best friend's younger brother and I'd never really looked twice at him growing up. When we were kids, the 2 year age gap was too big, but as adults we connected in a very different way. In the hours before dawn, Daniel admitted he'd been attracted to me for years. I was shocked, but...well, I'm sure you know that body *zing* when their words just bring you home?"

Alex's body reminded her with a shiver the moment Jay told her he loved her. Tilly nodded.

"Yep, you do. Well, needless to say, I fell in love with Daniel that night. To cut a long story short, Daniel and I agreed on how the whole fiasco would play out. With the press on Jay's back, we would carry on with the charade just long enough for the buzz to die down, then announce a mutual and amicable split."

Alex nodded. It appeared to make sense, but she couldn't shake that niggling itch.

"I saw you kiss him." Tilly laughed with her whole body.

"Yeah, you did. It was for show, and for the record, that's the most intimate Jay and I have been. As soon as we were out of sight, I wiped my mouth at the same time Jay kind of…retched. He tried to be the gentleman and hide it, but I caught him and we laughed all the way to the penthouse."

Alex pulled a breath. Dread settled in her stomach. According to Tilly, she'd misread the entire situation. All the pain, all the heartache could have been avoided.

"Is that why he was gone when I woke up?"

"Yes and no." She moved so quickly away from the question that Alex frowned. "You need to hear this, though. Jay has always lived a meticulously ordered life. He could tell you what time he would polish his shoes three weeks from now. When you disappeared he completely lost his grip on reality. His life was painful chaos. He found every restaurant, bar, club, cafe in the entire state and searched them for you. A darkness crept into him in that first year. He had every venue on speed dial, jumped on every call that came through no matter what time of day or night it was. By the second year he was desperate. Nobody had ever seen or heard of a woman named Lexi."

"People in these parts call me Alex." She whispered.

Tilly nodded. "So that brings me to the other night. I have been a fully qualified trauma psychologist for five years. I sat with Jay through the pain for three years. Last night I was there in the capacity of his psychologist."

Tears ran unnoticed over Alex's cheeks. "Jesus, what have I done?" She huffed.

A warm hand encompassed Lexi's.

"It's nobody's fault. I completely understand that you did what was best for you. If I had witnessed what you did in the White Hawk, I'd reach the same conclusion. He's so hurt and angry, though. So much so he doesn't know what to do with himself. You've been in his every thought, his every breath for so long, that he feels betrayed and overwhelmed. The Morrison boys fall deeply, completely and eternally with their whole hearts. He told me he was coming to speak to you, but obviously he never got to. But he won't talk to anyone now. I think that same despair is eating at him."

"He blocked my number, Tilly. What can I do? I wasted all this time fighting him, protecting myself against a betrayal that was all in my head. He won't take my calls. Damn it, he's even instructed Mum to be there instead of me to drop off Brandy so he can avoid seeing me. He doesn't want me" Misery washed over her. All he'd wanted was her. All misunderstandings aside, his single-minded determination to embed himself in her life and heart never wavered. Across years, miles, heartbeats, he was closing in on her. And she'd pushed him away.

*Alexandria Arlington isn't afraid of anything. Except losing the best thing that ever happened to her.*

She'd lived through heartbreak before. She was barely surviving it now, but she couldn't carry on a moment longer knowing she let him go without fighting.

"Give me his address. I have to find him."

# CHAPTER 44

## JAY

*D*ressed in black suit pants and grey shirt, Jay studied his hands. He turned them over, noticing the fine lines were now scrubbed clear of grease. He was almost disappointed. He missed the feel of steel beneath his hands, knowing his work assisted grateful farmers to create artwork in the fields of their land, enable trucks to keep hauling loads. He shook his head.

Two more days until he saw Brandy. His breath filled his lungs and he held it as he gazed over the rooftops of the city. He released it slowly, leaning forward as he glanced around the plush office. Brandy's father would be a successful businessman. Not a mechanic. He depressed the button.

"Okay, send him in."

He stroked his diary pages gently. His life was reforming in these pages. Running his eyes over the day's appointments, he flipped a week in advance to more filled pages. As if led by impulse, he turned the pages back a week. Two weeks. Blank. Empty. The time before. Nothing there. As if it wasn't real.

The door opened, and a lanky middle aged man appeared. His fingernails were black with grease, and nicks and gouges scattered in various stages of healing. A smile spread over Jay's face, not quite reaching his eyes.

"Your name?"

"Terry Pritchard."

"Terry Pritchard, you're hired." He clasped the hand of the stunned man. Jay explained.

"Your hands. They tell the story of how hard you work, how deeply you care. I admire that. And the references I called sang your praises. It was almost a done deal yesterday, but I needed to see your hands."

Terry nodded his understanding. His shoulders squared. "When do you want me to start?"

Jay knew Jimmy wasn't quite ready, but he needed this man, his heart and his ethics.

"As soon as you can organise to move the family. Jimmy will teach you everything you need to know, but as he's been with us from the beginning, you will learn from him and work alongside him indefinitely until he decides to retire. With full managerial wages, of course."

Terry beamed, standing to pump Jay's hand. "I won't let you down."

* * *

As Terry left to read over the terms of employment, Jay leaned back in his leather chair. The buzzer sounded on the desk beside him.

"Joseph, do you have time for a visitor?" Jay huffed. He wished Audrey would just stick to his schedule. He might as well, it was probably Daniel bringing a replacement phone after he'd lost his last one.

"Okay, Audrey, thank you."

Daniel's head wound around the door.

"How are you doing?" he asked carefully.

"Good. The bruises are almost disappeared and I'm almost back to looking normal."

"I'm not talking about that, Jay, and you know it. How *are* you?"

Jay growled. "Not this shit again, Daniel. I'm perfectly fine. See, I'm back at work, not a drop for four days, and I even remembered my pants today" He glared sarcastically at his brother.

"Oh, and I see your cheery disposition has returned, Mr Sunshine and Light!"

"What the hell else am I supposed to do, Daniel? She told me so many times she didn't need me, and I didn't want to listen. There is nothing I can offer her that she can't manage herself."

"Nobody but you can offer your heart, Jay."

Jay rounded on his brother, stepping around the desk and into his space.

"She didn't want it, remember? I offered it to her and she could only ever give me a sliver of hers in return. I can't live like that, Daniel. I deserve to have somebody love me completely. The way I

262

love her. *Loved* her. Christ!" He shoved his fingers through his hair, his chest heaving in the silence.

"Come out tonight, Jay. Tilly says she has something to tell you. And before you check your diary, Audrey already told me you're free. I'll see you at Sergeants' at seven. Dress to impress." Daniel winked and headed for the door.

"I'm not out to impress anyone, Daniel. Screw that." He snapped.

Jay stepped out into the retreating afternoon light, instructing Audrey to lock up behind her. He searched the concrete paths for grass and found none. The sound of his shoes blended with the clatter of the other folk around him. He scanned the crowd. Not looking for Lexi, he convinced himself, but to search for a friendly face. Blank expressions stared through him as he made his way through the park. Finding an empty bench, he leaned into it, arms resting on its wooden back, ankle pulled up onto his thigh.

He came here often in the last week. The only slice of nature in the city. He remembered.

*Her face softened with laughter, her chocolate eyes sparkling. Her expression morphed into pleasure, her glance hooded and lips slack. The way her breath hitched as she sighed his name. The scent of her flesh his drug.*

Christ he missed her. Her voice floated through the void in his chest. Nothing seemed to alleviate the hollow ache inside. He'd tried to fill it with structure, order, rigid predictability. Anything to distract him from the urge to jump on a plane and beg her to take him back. Accept the parts of her that she would let him see. Take everything she was willing to offer him, even if his heart fractured over the parts hidden from him. His scarred knuckles whitened as he forced the urge away. If he allowed the darkness into his thoughts it would send him mad.

Jay contemplated Daniel's invitation darkly. The furtherest desire from his mind was to spend the night in a pub watching happiness blossom between his brother and Tilly.

Why hadn't he told Lexi about him and Tilly?

It didn't seem important. It wasn't important. Not to him, anyway. There was never anything between them but a simple farce that spiralled out of control in Lexi's world. If only she hadn't been there that day.

Jay jerked rigid, immediately alert and aware.

*She was there that day because she had been looking for him. Before* she knew she was pregnant, *before* she knew who he was. He knew first hand what kind of crazy was required to try and track a one night stand. Someone who invaded every waking thought. Someone who returned with crystal clarity every single night.

If he had discovered she was engaged, would he have continued pursuing her, or like Lexi had, buried himself in heartbreak that wouldn't relent?

But she was still witholding Edward's blackmail details. Still holding back. Jay's spine curved into the bench. He knew he'd never find again what he had with Lexi. The pull, the wonder, the ecstasy, the *saturation* of a woman like her. He just knew he couldn't bring himself to chase her. He would let the past dull, the feelings fade and his heart heal. He would go on alone, back to the man he was before Lexi, before the pages in his diary emptied of appointments and filled with calamity. Tonight, the old Jay would dress up and find a body to lose himself in. He would do it every night until the memory of her burning flesh fell away under the groans of a hundred faceless women.

* * *

The razor slid from his cheekbone to his chin, his movement extending to carve a smooth path down the length of his neck. Jay leaned back and absently surveyed his image. Grateful for his father's kind genetics, Jay knew he cut a striking figure. The wound that separated his eyebrow seemed to enhance his appearance, and he pushed aside the memories that it triggered. *This is not a night to remember.* He dug out his aftershave and applied it like he cared. A meaningless gesture. A means to fill in the space between the days. Slipping his wallet into his pants, he reached for a tiny worn out bag and slid it in his other pocket. His forehead creased and he retrieved it, examining it. The green velvet pouch had rubbed to bare cotton in places, the bright hue faded and abused. He ran a thumb over the outline of its contents slowly. The other reason he'd left Lexi that morning. He should throw it in the bin instead of carrying it with him. Rid himself of the tiny reminder he hadn't been without since he'd first woken beside her. Was he ready to do that yet? In the dim light of his penthouse apartment, he returned it to his pocket and made for the door.

* * *

"Wow!" Tilly's eyebrows arched appreciatively. Jay sauntered towards them with a light scowl.

"If you weren't such a moody prick right now, Jay, I'd say you are up for a good night!" Daniel flashed his teeth.

As they seated themselves, the waitress appeared. A dark haired thing with long, lean legs and flashing green eyes. She paused as she spotted Jay, and his interest piqued a little.

"Would you like to order drinks?" She asked in a slightly shrill voice, her attention focused on Jay.

The woman was too thin. Too…shapeless for his taste, but she was pretty enough.

They placed their orders, two whiskeys and a soda water. As she turned to leave, Jay snapped out a hand and caught her wrist. Her eyes rounded and darkened as they landed on Jay. His thumb stroked her skin and he was immediately disappointed but unsurprised that he felt nothing.

"I forgot to order a bowl of nuts, please." He allowed his drawl to penetrate, and inwardly smiled as her thin lips parted. Suddenly flustered, she nodded and pulled free.

"Well, you're in fine form tonight, big brother." Daniel sniggered. Tilly shifted uncomfortably.

"It won't help you forget, Jay." She warned.

Jays laughter seemed obnoxious, even to his own ears. "No, but maybe the next one. Or the one after that will. Either way…" He lifted his shoulders non-committally.

Tilly firmed her expression and turned away.

The waitress returned with a double order of their drinks, and a large bowl of peanuts. Jay rewarded her with a smile that used to set Lexi on fire. She flushed deeply and slipped a scrap of folded paper with her number on the wooden table in front of him, suddenly awkward, and scurried away.

Daniel laughed and shook his head. "You've just gone from clueless to predator in zero seconds flat. I guess I know what you're doing tonight."

# CHAPTER 45

## ALEX

The taxi pulled up to the curb. The moment the door closed behind her, it merged with the rest of the traffic. Alex clutched her purse close to her stomach. The sheer volume of people pushing through the streets was overwhelming, and she wondered why she even ventured into town at all. She used to, which was why she was here. She'd loved dancing to the live music, the friendly warmth of a crowded bar, enjoying the snippets of conversations around her.

But now? She pulled the stuffy city air into her chest as she looked around. Her lungs jolted at the building before her. This was the place. She studied her reflection in the shop front. Tight green top that emphasised the swell of her breasts, offering a modest glimpse of cleavage, figure hugging black skirt that showed off her legs. She wasn't a fan of make-up, but she'd taken the time to apply a little mascara and a smear of lipstick. Her hair was styled in a fun pile on the crown of her head, a few stray locks framing her face. She swallowed around the dry edges of her mouth, and snapped her heels up the steps.

* * *

It took a moment for her eyes to adjust to the sombre lighting. A man perched on a bar stool in one corner with a guitar, filling the room with his vocals. The room was thick with bodies. Alex scanned the tables for a familiar face, and landed on the shock on Daniel's face, and Tilly's panicked expression. Tilly lifted her chin in the direction of the bar, and Alex followed her direction.

Alex's expression fractured when she found him. Jay had his wide back to her, but there was no mistaking it was him. So handsome and erotic, he stood head and shoulders above most of the patrons, but it was the sheer intensity of his presence that eclipsed everyone else. The crowd faded away as Alex moved towards him. As she neared him, she slowed her gait. Jay hadn't turned. Hadn't moved. He was leaning with one palm flat against the wall, blocking her view of what had his attention. Then something shifted, and it wasn't Jay. Something was hovering in the space between Jay and the wall.

Alex froze as a slim hand appeared over Jay's shoulder, running slowly towards the curve of his neck.

A woman's hand.

A woman's hand that wasn't Alex's.

The world faded away and Alex's stomach bottomed out. Her heartbeat burst.

Unable to move, she watched as Jay's head lowered slowly. The woman's other hand snaked into the thick dark hair on the nape of his neck. Alex's lungs tightened and her breath failed. Jay was *hers*.

Alex saw red.

She closed the distance between them. The trashy waitress was pulling Jay towards a kiss when Alex cleared her throat. Jay paused. The waitress increased her pressure. Almost reluctantly, Jay lifted his eyes and blanched when he recognised her. He pushed away from the wall and the woman, guilt lighting his features before turning to stone.

"What's going on, Jay?" the woman glanced between them. The glacial expression on Jay's face terrified Alex. He wasn't happy to see her. *Of course not*, she thought. *He doesn't want to see me.* Doubt flared inside. *What am I doing?*

Alex drank him in. He appeared even more breathtaking than she recalled. The unyielding lines of his sculptured face were strengthened steel, the lack of humanity in his cold stare, and the jagged line through his eyebrow. He was dangerous. And hard. And utterly magnificent in his scowling detachment. Her heart fluttered to life around the pounding of dread.

His nostrils flared.

"What are you doing here, Alexandria?" She cringed at her full name. His deep, rumbling voice was bitter.

"You know her?" The waitress demanded. Without breaking visual contact, Alex retorted.

"We were seeing each other."

"Well, obviously you're not any longer. You can leave now." the woman snarled possessively. Fire burned in Alex's chest.

"He's still the father of my child." Her venom caused the waitress to start. She fell silent, but didn't leave. She was skulking around like a vulture for Jay to send Alex away.

Jay's lips twisted in a sneer.

"Those words fall from your tongue like a weapon, Alexandria. When I needed those words, you withheld them. I'm not a game, sweetheart. You can't keep me at arms length, then pull me close when it serves you. You forget. I *know* what you're capable of!"

Alex felt those words like a slap. She gasped.

"Is it because I killed Edward?" Jay's shoulders tightened. The waitress squeaked and backed away. Jay turned to face her.

"Shit. No. Lexi." He stabbed his fingers into his hair, then clasped the back of his neck.

Alex's vision blurred.

"Then why, Jay?" She whispered.

His anger turned nuclear.

"Because you guard your heart with such vehemence that it was never available to me. I can't live like that. I deserve more. You turned my world upside down, and I chased you to the ends of it. I gave you my heart and you scarred it with lies and secrets. I hunted you down again and again when you pulled away from me. I came after you with the intent to *kill for you*, and you made it clear. You *can't* love me. You. Don't. Need. Me." His chest heaved with emotion and pain.

Alex opened her mouth but nothing came. He towered over her, dark and commanding.

"You need to leave. Get out of my life and let me learn to live without you."

"No." She whispered.

"What?" He barked. She jumped at his rage.

"I can't Jay. I can't let you go."

"Stop playing me, Lex. I can be cruel if I need to be." His growl rumbled in her bones.

Alex stepped back from the acid in his tone. He was fearsome.

"You're wrong, Jay. I do need you." He scoffed in her face, turning his back on her as he walked away. She swallowed her fear and squared her shoulders, raising her voice above the din in the room.

"I am Alexandria Arlington, sixth generation farmer, a woman of steel with the land in my veins. I am Maxwell Arlington's daughter, and I am not afraid of anything. Except taking another breath without you beside me. I'm terrified of that, Jay. Your breath is my oxygen. I need you more than I need my life."

Her tears were running freely, the pub disappearing behind her grief. She closed her eyes, inhaled the smoky air, and spoke to the fog.

"Someone important to me once said that following your heart can shake everything you once knew to rubble, but not seeing it through is simply not an option. I want to see us through, Jay. I need it on a level I can't fully comprehend yet. I need to hold your heart in my hands, and I need you to hold mine. My *whole* heart, Jay." Her breath hitched. Her chin lifted. The silence spun around her. She tilted her head to seek courage from the dingy rafters. She filled her lungs and scanned the faceless crowd unsuccessfully for him. She continued, hoping he could hear her.

"I'm stubborn, opinionated and wilful. I'm sure I have more faults than that. But I gave you my heart that night, and I'm so, so sorry it's been tangled in fear and misunderstandings. I messed up. I know I did. But you are worth fighting for. This time the tables are turned and I'm telling you *my* intentions. I love you. I need you. Give us a chance to begin again. No lies. No secrets. No holding back. You know where I'll be if you think we're worth another shot."

She blinked away her tears, but Jay was nowhere to be seen. Neither was the waitress. The ocean of patrons faced her in rapt silence. She turned slowly, hoping she'd hear Jay call her name. When the conversations resumed and the singer began plucking the chords on his guitar, Alex stepped from the pub without pausing to acknowledge Daniel or Tilly and hailed a taxi.

Within the deadly sting of Jay's silent rejection, Alex discovered a new level of pain.

*The day I was finally brave enough to give you what was already yours was the moment after you'd given up on me.*

# CHAPTER 46

## JAY

*H*e listened to his heart beating in the silence. He sat hidden behind the bulk of two tradesmen as he watched her, taking in every expression on her face. Christ she was stunning. Her spirit, her fire. Her fight. She stood alone in the centre of the room in her beautiful surrender like a warrior, bravely exposing to the world the wounds that could defeat her. One wound. Jay. Her voice stroked his shattered heart, her admissions the glue sticking it back together again. He swallowed down the desire to sweep her up and kiss her pain away.

She needed him. She didn't need him to protect her. She could do that herself. She didn't need him to labour for her. She could do that, too. But she needed him to be able to breathe… He had seen the truth of it in the tears that fell, in the silken hum of her voice. He stared as she scanned the room for him, watched defeat slump her shoulders when she couldn't spot him, felt the cloud of hope fade around her as the door closed behind her.

Daniel's hand fell on his arm.

"Damn, Jay. She was amazing."

"You're not wrong, there, mate. If her fella doesn't snap her up, I'm first in line!" The suited man whistled long and low. "That woman's everybody's wet dream come to life."

Jay's fists balled and Daniel pulled him away before he could react.

"What are you going to do, Jay?" Tilly impaled Jay with a sharp stare.

"You spoke to her, didn't you, Tilly?" Jay growled.

"Of course I did, Jay." She snapped. "Lexi had come to see you, and caught my arrival. She thought you were married to me." Jay shot her an incredulous sneer.

"Just use your god damn head for a moment, Junior. She backed away from you when she saw us announce our engagement to the universe. Lexi's world doesn't involve tabloids or television. She'd have no idea that we separated soon afterwards. She was coming to speak to you the night I arrived. She'd almost reached your door when I showed up. Now think hard about what happened when you greeted me that night. After the taxi driver wished *Mrs Morrison* a safe trip in his car!"

Jay's glare gradually morphed into shock, then panic.

*The door opened, Jay's frame silhouetted against the light pouring from the house.*

*"I'm so glad you made it okay. You have no idea how badly I need you right now" Jay's voice was thick with emotion. The woman dropped her suitcase and pulled him into a hug that pressed their bodies together. Jay wrapped his arms around her waist.*

*"Your folks and Daniel?" She asked with urgency.*

*"I made sure they're out for a few hours. They don't know you're here. It would be too awkward if they knew."*

*She leaned in and kissed him on the lips, and he grabbed her hand, pulling her inside.*

Tilly nodded as she witnessed realisation finally settle over him.

"You're an utter idiot sometimes, Jay. If I hadn't clarified, there was no way she would know I married your brother. You are not completely innocent in this. In her eyes, you cheated with her in a one night stand, then years later continued to see her behind your wife's back. Frankly, Jay, I'd be pretty disgusted if she pursued anything with you after that. And just so you know, If I were in the same situation Lexi thought she was, I wouldn't be telling you I was carrying your child either, unless I wanted to screw you for every cent you had!" Tilly stood away from the table and threw her napkin down.

"You're not worth shit if you let her go without apologising to her." She spun away and stormed out the door.

Jay's eyebrows jumped at her rage. In all the years he'd known her, she'd always been calm and reasonable. Daniel watched after his wife, adoration plastered on his face.

"So what are you going to do?" Daniel finally returned his attention to Jay.

Jay's mouth spread slowly. "She used our daughter to scare off the waitress."

Wednesday afternoon crashed when a shout and a flurry of activity tore his attention outward.

Audrey's flustered tone carried through the closed office door.

"You can't just walk in there! You need to make an appointment! Stop!"

Jay made to launch himself at whatever threat was heading his way.

"So stop me!"

Jay jerked back into his seat. He knew the voice as well as his own. The courage and strength in her determination.

*Why did she come?* He filled his lungs and steadied himself, emptying his expression before…

"Jay?" Lexi burst into his office, pinning him with her gaze as she arrived at his desk. When she noted the look on his face she faltered. Audrey poked her glasses around the frame.

"I'm sorry, sir, do you want me to call security?"

Without moving his eyes from Lexi, he said "It's fine, thanks Audrey. I'll deal with…*this*." He noted Lexi's cringe with a shiver of delight. She stood before him in figure hugging jeans and an off the shoulder shirt that gave him a tantalising glimpse of the wings of her collarbones and a hint of her full breasts. Her hair was swept from her face in a ponytail that reached her waist. Her bruises had faded away, leaving her skin once again a blank canvas of perfection. But the most stunning view was the way her eyes were puffy and raw. Like she finally found her pain and sat with it. Like she was almost ready to face her fear and find the hidden parts of her heart. She couldn't know that they both stood balanced on the precipice of their future, but he could see she felt it.

They stood in silence, his stony expression hard against her softer, imploring one.

"Jay? I…" She stuttered and her lungs emptied.

"What do you want, Alexandria?" He tossed her name at her like an insult, and Lexi recoiled, gripping his desk for support.

"Jay….I have to talk to you. I need…..I need to tell you…." Jay refused to make this easy for her. She was a fighter, and if she wouldn't fight for him he would know once and for all that they were finished.

"I haven't got all day. I have appointments to keep." He snapped ice at her. He leaned forward, hostility stamped on his features. "Five minutes, Alexandria. I'm a busy man." He steeled himself against her bobbing throat, her submissive inability to meet his glare. She shook her head, and he thought she'd walk away, but instead she filled her lungs and stiffened her spine.

"I don't do one night stands. That night at the bar, the air between us seemed to crackle, and I knew I belonged in your arms. I was beyond destroyed when I woke up to find it was one sided. But I couldn't let it go. I just had this primal need to see you again that I couldn't control. When I witnessed you and Tilly announce your engagement, I broke on a molecular level. When I found out I was carrying Brandy, it was too late to abort. But I wouldn't have even if I'd known in time. I figured if I couldn't have you, then something created from one perfect night would be just as amazing. I was right, but every time I saw her, I looked straight into your eyes. Every. Single. Time. It was like I was reliving the agony of seeing you in another's arms. There are layers and layers and layers of pain, heartbreak and joy mixed up in the scars inside me. I didn't just lose you that morning, Jay. I lose you over and over every time

Brandy looks at me. I never stop reliving that betrayal. When Dad died, Ryan helped me through. Then he left me too. When you showed up I was terrified. I had nobody but Brandy, and you'd already left me. Twice. I knew inside that you'd leave me a third time, but you might also take away Brandy. You saw my house. I know it's not a safe place to bring her up. But it's all I have. The last connection I had with Dad and Ryan."

"And then there was Edward. I didn't realise how sick he was at the time, but he told me the state would sell the farm because Ryan didn't have a will. He told me he could pull some strings and have it legally put in my name. But the catch was that he wanted me as payment."

Jay couldn't help but lean forward. Edward revealed this before he was killed, but it was the last secret he needed to hear. To know she wasn't holding back.

Lexi was pale, her lips twisted in disgust.

"I just couldn't bring myself to allow him to touch me" She whispered, her eyes seeking Jay's understanding. He gave her nothing. His vacant stare lingered between them.

"After I'd managed to delay again and again, he threatened to hurt my family. I couldn't tell Mum that I was going to lose the farm, and I certainly couldn't tell her a policeman was threatening us all. She'd worry and insist I sell up and leave town. I just couldn't. I was trying to find another way. And when he found out you were spending time with me, he threatened your life, too. Too many people were at risk because of me. Anyway, the detectives uncovered the emails where he *was* dealing with the state, but all Edward's correspondence suggested strongly that I was of unsafe mind and that they should sell the farm for my own good. He never intended to help me. They also found a comprehensive schedule of my movements, as well as Mum's." Lexi took a deep breath, her beautiful eyes clouding in pain. Her voice raw and soft.

"I love you with everything I am, Jay. I loved you from the moment I met you and I never once stopped. I loved you through what I believed was your betrayal, and even when I hated you I loved you. The parts of me that I kept from you, Jay? They were yours all along, too. I was just too afraid to show you."

Jay watched as Lexi sought something in his face. A glimpse of anything. Jay stiffened his jaw but forced himself to appear indifferent.

Her lashes rested against her cheeks in exquisite defeat. It twisted his heart to watch her hurt, but he knew he needed space to think. She turned her back slowly, but hesitated at the door.

"I never sought to deceive you. Every mistake that I made was a result of my fear. But I've held on to that fear for so long it became second nature. I'm so regretful that it caused such a rift between us, but I'm making peace with it, now. I'm finally able to move towards a future I want. The only person with the ability to hurt me right now is you, but I know what we have…had…is worth whatever pain you can throw at me now. So go ahead and do it, Jay. My heart is yours to keep or discard, and I have no control over that."

"I've laid it all out on the table for you. I don't know what else I can do to change your mind. But there is one thing I need to know, before I go. The morning I woke to empty sheets, you said you stepped out for two reasons. One was to call Tilly. I know that now, but you never told me the other."

His throat burned as he considered her question. He could see her agony, the effort it cost her to tap into all the scariest parts of her and find the painful truth, but his truth might break her. It might break *him*. A single tear broke free and slid down her cheek but she ignored it. The beauty of it shimmering as her heart broke decimated him.

No more secrets.

He had to honour that. But he knew he wasn't strong enough to watch her break.

Her eyes widened with hope that quickly shattered as he pushed away from his desk, placing the tiny bag he'd carried in his pocket for years on his desk before her. He gave her a hard look before pushing past her, walking out in silence.

# CHAPTER 47

## ALEX

*H*e walked away.

Not a word.

Just heart-wrenching indifference in a tailored suit, dashing the last of her hope. And it hurt so badly she struggled to remain standing. Through the blur, she reached for the tiny cloth bag he'd left on his desk. It was forest green with a gold braided cord woven through the top. It had once been velvet, but was so beaten and worn through it was mostly tufted between lighter sections of cotton. This had obviously travelled in every pocket, against his thigh, every day for a long time. It was a truth she felt as she ran her fingers over it. Feeling something small and heavy tucked in the bottom corner, she tipped it out.

A ring of gold fell into her palm like a knife through her chest. The stone was deep green with a tiny diamond embedded in the band either side of the stone.

*The Morrison boys fall deeply, completely and eternally with their whole hearts.*

The soul-shredding, heart shattering sobs that heaved her body echoed with futility. He knew. He knew that morning that he wanted her forever, just as she felt for him.

Alex impatiently brushed the tears that blurred her vision. That's when she noticed the inscription. In graceful lettering, a date preceded the words: *Lexi & brandy*. The date they met in the bar, his memory engraved in careful script. He was so sure they were supposed to be together, he woke first thing, called off his farce of an engagement and ordered a ring for her.

In the breath of a moment, time slowed enough for a series of misunderstandings to come into play. Now, there were no more misunderstandings. But judging by the cold resolve in his steel grey eyes there was also nothing left to salvage.

# CHAPTER 48

## JAY

*N*o more secrets.

But his chest was hollow and barren. Now she knew what a fool he'd been for her. He'd never thought something that started out so perfect would bring so much pain. When Lexi appeared in his life like a radiant apparition of eternity she gave him a taste of heaven. And he chased after it with a ferocity that sent his entire world spiralling. She made him crave. He was so consumed by her that he'd lost his mind.

With a new heaviness, Jay flipped the pages of his schedule. He turned the pages backwards. Yesterday was thick with appointments, but his night at the pub and seeing Lexi wasn't written in there. And today was clear of meetings to prepare for his weekend with his daughter. The next three pages were blank, too. He scrubbed his face thoughtfully. Lexi had told him that the most wonderful things happened in the spaces that weren't planned. That the most precious moments came from a blank canvas of spontaneity and whim. Jay tapped his pen against the bare page. He didn't collect his daughter until 5pm tomorrow, but the whole day was beckoning. How could he fill it?

* * *

Jay clattered up the driveway, winding around the potholes. His heart pounded furiously. He approached the homestead carefully, searching the periphery for movement. There was none. No Horace coming to greet him, no little girl squealing in delight. No angel to catch him at the door.

At the driveway he deliberated. He felt hesitant to enter the house. It seemed cold and sad without Lexi there.

He'd expected her to be waiting for him, and she wasn't.

In the typical Lexi style, she dragged herself forward and got on with life. The fallen tree had been cut up, split, and stacked neatly in the woodshed. Patches of garden emerged behind the piles of weeds that had been ripped out. The wilted head of a daffodil poked out from one pile. Jay grinned. Brandy had been helping.

He scanned the horizon. Not a sign of Lexi, Brandy or Horace.

His head moved towards a sound coming from behind the house. Low voices. A man's voice. Jay frowned and rounded the side of the house. A tradesman's ute was parked up close to verandah. Nick's Carpentry. She was beginning repairs on the homestead.

Jay recalled the company logo from the one worn by the workmen at the pub in town the other week. The ones discussing their interest in tempting Lexi to settle down.

Jay lightened his footsteps and crept closer. Lexi came into view first. With torn jeans hugging her hips and a stained farm shirt, she was a gorgeous mess. Her brandy locks coiled messily on her head, the usual strands flying free around her face like fragments of a halo. She was dressed to work, but she still took his breath away.

"Come on, show me how to do it and we can get done faster." She muttered impatiently. Jay stifled a chuckle. The carpenter moved behind her, and Jay stiffened with the urge to get him away from her. He leaned into her, his hand gripping hers on the hand saw. Jay flexed his jaw. Lexi shoved an elbow into his stomach, and the young man bent over the jab. Jay gasped as the sun glinted off the ring he'd given her. *She was wearing his ring!*

"You can show me without touching me, you know." She snapped. The poor man rubbed his gut. He tried again as she began sawing angles with the mitre. The man sidled up to her again, and Lexi exaggerated her movement, this time winding him with the force of her blow.

"Oh, oops. Try not to stand too close or I might accidentally get you." Her tone light. Jay doubled over in laughter. With fire and light she refused to take shit from anyone. The saw clattered from her grip as Jay stepped out of the shadows.

"Hey, aren't you the guy from the pub? You've got balls showing up here." The carpenter growled and glared at Jay.

"Looks like the lady still isn't interested." Jay smirked at him then faced the woman he loved. He smiled the smile he knew made his girl's pulse clatter.

"Jay?" She breathed, her eyes misting on hope.

"Lex." All the words he couldn't say were printed in her name. She sought his eyes, found what she needed, and lunged at him, wrapping her legs around his waist and burying her nose into the crook of his neck. Her body shook with euphoric sobs, and Jay held her against him, relishing her heat against his, his heart soaring.

He couldn't help the tears that escaped when a thin voice carried through the warm air.

"Jay!" Lexi dropped to the ground and stepped back as Brandy exploded in giggles of delight, running into her father's arms. Jay felt her thin arms bite into his neck with the force of her hug. His heart threatened to burst from his chest. *His daughter*.

The carpenter grunted in surprise, his posture slumping in defeat.

*Take this back to the boys in the pub.* Jay dared him with a victorious glare.

"Mummy said I'm having a sleepover with you tomorrow!" He saw his own eyes stare back at him, filled with love and adoration and he melted.

"Well, Sass, I was kind of hoping that instead, I could have a sleepover here tonight, if your mummy thinks its a good idea?" He held his breath and turned towards Lexi. Brandy squirmed free, staring up at her mother with hands on hips.

"Can he stay tonight, Mummy?"

With a gentle smile Lexi shook her head.

Brandy frowned and pouted.

Jay froze.

"Why?" Brandy whined. Lexi glanced shyly up at Jay.

"I thought instead, he might want to stay a bit longer."

# CHAPTER 49

## JAY

*J*ay found Lexi in serene contemplation on the verandah. She sat on the cane chair swing, the silken length of her bare legs curled under her from her tiny denim shorts. A soft yellow halter top showed too much skin for Jay's control, but he stood for a moment to feast his eyes on her. She hadn't noticed him there and he wanted to capture forever that far-away look she wore. They'd come a long way, Lexi and Jay. In the months that followed their reconnection they'd relearned each other. They argued often in the beginning, Her spark setting fire to his own determination. But they always found one another at the end of each raised tone with the passion that turned everything else to ashes. In the gasping aftermath of their love, they always found a compromise.

They'd moved into the farmhouse on Jay's farm, but only while the renovations were carried out. Lexi needed to live amongst the memories and ghosts of her ancestors, and Jay didn't care where he lived, as long as Lexi and Brandy were with him. He'd move into the shed if that was the only way to be with them. When Lexi's farmhouse had been brought back to its former glory, they'd moved in, and Joseph and Lydia moved into Jay's house. They wanted to be close to Brandy, and they adored Lexi.

A deep friendship forged between Tilly and Lexi, and a wing was added to their place for Daniel and Tilly to stay whenever they wanted. Tilly's initial reluctance to embrace farm life was melting fast, and the plan was that Daniel's family would eventually settle on Arlington Farm.

Brandy continued to light his world with her bright curiosity and bubbly innocence. Her third birthday was nothing short of perfection. With her entire family gathered around her, they surprised her with Henry, the little filly Horace gave birth to. The spindly-legged baby was already showing signs of becoming a miniature version of crazy like her mother.

Their days were filled as a family with the breeze in their hair, honest sweat on their brows and smiling contentment. Every night saw them tangled in each other. He never had his fill of Lexi. She was a siren, and Jay her willing victim.

The expression she now wore on her face echoed his own happiness. She blinked proudly over the pastures of her home as Jay watched. A smile tugged at her perfect lips, the sun's kiss lending a slightly flushed appearance to cheeks that knew laughter. She sighed gently and the summer breeze shifted her hair. Lifting her hand, she tucked a strand behind her ear, finally catching sight of Jay. She grinned at him and patted the cushion beside her. These days she smiled easily and often.

"It was a wonderful afternoon." Jay smiled back as he sank beside her, gently swinging them.

"Mmm" she agreed, her fingers reaching for his leg. Brandy was still out cold in bed from the afternoon full of family. Lydia and Sabrina had baked the perfect Sunday roast, and Tilly and Daniel had dropped in to join them as part of the surprise. With only two months to go in her pregnancy, Tilly looked radiant with her big belly. They couldn't wait.

"What's on your mind that has you looking so happy?" Jay asked.

"I was just wondering how my life could be any better. The farm's doing great, I have such an incredible support network around me, and I have a best friend in my sister-in-law." She looked up at Jay with blazing adoration.

"And just having you and Brandy in my life; I never thought I could be this happy, Jay." Her wistful sigh tugged at his full heart.

Jay pressed a kiss on her forehead.

"I love you, Lex. I know what you mean. There is nothing more perfect than this moment, right now."

Lexi grinned, and Jay noted the shimmer of mischief in her eyes as she fixed her stare at him.

"We have a problem I need you to help me with, though. It might mean a huge change in plans."

Jay lifted his brow, puzzled. A huge problem that Lexi was smiling about didn't strike him as being a problem at all.

"What is it?" They always faced problems as a team. There was no wall too high for them to conquer.

"We might have to bring our wedding forward a few months."

Jay frowned. His girl was speaking in riddles.

"Why? Everything's organised. Did you decide you wanted the bigger venue after all? If that's the case, I can see if I can pull a few strings-" Something flashed in her eyes that made him falter.

Lexi turned towards him and slid her fingers over his jaw.

"No. It's...its because I'm deeply concerned my wedding dress won't fit over my giant belly in six months time." She smiled her secret smile and his eyes widened.

Jay felt the colour drain from his face. A baby. A brother or sister for Brandy. New life starting in the belly of the woman he loved that he would be responsible for. Another precious creation for him to protect.

"Really? Lex? You're *pregnant*?" He gasped as laughter bubbled from her, her head nodding in delight.

When Jay's breath hissed, her smile hesitated.

"This is good, right? I mean, it wasn't exactly planned, but we weren't being real careful either. I...I thought you'd be happy."

Jay noted the way she gripped the cushion. He loved the way she wore her emotions so close to the surface. He shook his head clear and clutched her hands in his.

"Jesus, Lex. A baby?" He swallowed the lump of emotion. He searched her eyes, seeking the words for what he was feeling. There were none. So instead he yanked her to him and kissed her so hard he felt her teeth. She melted into him before he tore his mouth away.

"Oh my God, Lexi! I can't believe it. A baby?!" He staggered to his feet and dragged Lexi into his arms. Her relieved laughter reached into Jay's soul.

"I'm going to get to watch our baby grow in your belly, and hold my son or daughter at the end of it? Christ, Lex, you've just lifted the bar for perfection. Let's get married today!"

Lexi waggled a finger at him in a mock scowl.

"Joseph Jay Morrison Junior, you will *not* deny this farm girl her one opportunity to be a princess before she turns into a beached whale, and you wouldn't have the courage to face your daughter and tell her she can't be flower girl!"

"Daddy!" Jay's head swivelled towards Brandy and caught her in the middle of a sleep-edged leap. His own eyes glared back at him.

"You shouldn't have let me sleep, Daddy. Naps are for babies, and I'm a big girl."

Jay rained smiling kisses on his daughter's face.

"Because you are such a big girl, Mummy and I have a big secret to tell you."

Her tiny body stilled, her eyes widened at the importance of a secret.

"How do you like the idea of being a big sister?" Lexi's sweet voice stroked the side of Jay's face, and he turned instinctively to kiss her forehead.

Brandy's mouth dropped open. "No way! You're going to have a giant tummy like Aunt Tilly? And a baby's gonna come out?"

Jay and Lexi nodded together. Brandy's gaze darted between her parents and wiggled until she felt the ground under her feet.

At that very moment, Horace brought Henry up onto the verandah and Brandy ran to fling her arms around the soft, springy fur of her filly.

"Henry! Big news. I'm going to be a big sister, so I'm *very* important now."

Jay and Lexi's grins of relief faded away quickly as Brandy continued.

"My little sister will be my responsibility, Henry, so I will have to train her. I can teach her to fetch my dolls from the blackberry patch, she can muck out your stall for me, and I'll teach her to fight, when she grows teeth, of course. She can eat all the vegetables I don't like at dinner time. Oh…" She threw over her shoulder as she led her filly away. "And don't worry, Mummy, I'll teach her that 'shit' is a bad word."

Lexi looked pained, and Jay roared his laughter.

"I hope to Christ its a boy then" muttered Lexi with a shake of her brandy tresses. He wrapped his arms around his girl and sighed his contentment into her neck, smiling at her shudder of pleasure. She was made for him. From the moment he laid his eyes on her in a dingy bar he stumbled upon on a whim their fate was sealed. They may have lost the path along the way, but here they were, finally where they were always destined to be, Jay and the woman who loved him with her whole heart.

"I have one stipulation, though." Jay breathed into her ear. "I get to name this one."

# ACKNOWLEDGMENTS

I am eternally grateful to my closest friends and family who have supported and encouraged my writing journey. It takes some pretty incredible people to understand where my heart lay many years before I did, and a great deal of patience to empathise with my perpetual self-doubt.

So to my lifelong sisters, Sharyn Constantine, Dora Kambouris and Katie Dunn, you three are my world.

To my beta readers, Sue Constantine, Christine Poulter and Emily Slade, how I've valued your imput! Along with your critique you've given me the confidence to show the world my story.

Shaz, my esteemed editor, thanks for your hours of patience and dedication. I didn't realise just how much I needed you until you worked your magic!

To the real life Lexi, who is not a farmer, but a resilient and beautiful person in her own right, thanks for your name. I couldn't think of a more apt name for my leading lady.

For everyone reading this, from the bottom of my heart I thank you, my dear readers. Without you I'm nothing, for if nobody reads a book, is it even a story? I hope you enjoyed the journey, and I hope you will join me for more adventures.

Finally my wonderful husband, Paul. My rock, my soul mate.

My cowboy.

With your unwavering confidence in me, you pulled me out of some pretty negative places. To have the honour of sharing my life with such an incredible human is more than I could wish for.

Thanks for being my greatest inspiration.

## ABOUT THE AUTHOR

Born with an obsession for the written word,
Rowena Spark navigated her youth armed with pen, paper and an
overactive imagination, characters whispering to her from the
shadows.
Rowena weaves romantic tales of flawed heroes who fall hard and
love deeply, and strong, passionate heroines courageous enough to
take a risk.
She lives on her farm with her husband, doing her best writing
against the backdrop of Victoria's breathtaking South Gippsland
hills surrounded by cows, sheep and two dogs.

Please visit me at
www.rowenaspark.com

f facebook.com/RowenaSparkAuthor

# ALSO BY ROWENA SPARK

## OTHER BOOKS

### STAND ALONE ROMANCE

**Stealing Brynn** (Release 2020)

### DARK ROMANCE TRILOGY

**Credence** (Release 2020)

**Prudence** (Release 2020)

**Reticence** (Release late 2020)

www.ingramcontent.com/pod-product-compliance
Lightning Source LLC
Chambersburg PA
CBHW050026120726
47903CB00006B/1931